The Twinning

THE TWINNING

Verse One:
The Silver Coins

Justin R. Cary

The journey is what you make it,

Justin Cary

iUniverse, Inc.
New York Lincoln Shanghai

The Twinning
Verse One: The Silver Coins

iUniverse books may be ordered through booksellers or by contacting:

iUniverse
2021 Pine Lake Road, Suite 100
Lincoln, NE 68512
www.iuniverse.com
1-800-Authors (1-800-288-4677)

ISBN-13: 978-0-595-39395-4 (pbk)
ISBN-13: 978-0-595-83793-9 (ebk)
ISBN-10: 0-595-39395-0 (pbk)
ISBN-10: 0-595-83793-X (ebk)

Printed in the United States of America

For Carol, John, Jared and Jordan; a truly wonderful family and for Erica, my constant reader.

Go then. There are other worlds than these.

—Jake, Stephen King's *The Dark Tower*

PROLOGUE

▼

The woman sitting in the prison cell was, in fact, the Queen of the very kingdom responsible for her condemnation. Murder was her crime. Her husband, the King himself, had sentenced her to execution. After all, she had killed his brother...and in the Forbidden way. The woman in the cell knew the real reason why she was sitting there, soaked and dejected, but that did not matter anymore. She would not be killed by the executioner's blade or the hangman's noose; it would be the thought of leaving her young daughter that would truly kill her. She was consoled, however, because she had another child on the way...and this one would be special. Not that the new could ever replace the old, but this world had emptied for her like water flowing from a shattered pitcher. She could not stay here. She knew she would have to start over again on the other side, and things would be difficult at first...but she would adapt.

Lightning rang out in the sky above the castle as the kingdom was drowned by the torrential rain. The woman's execution was scheduled for the next morning at dawn. She would have to leave tonight, with no goodbyes, no condolences. She was alone now, but on the other side she would be comforted.

She rubbed her belly, still small and unnoticeable, making it easier to keep the baby a secret for quite a while. That didn't even matter now. There was nothing she could do. Soon the child would be home. No amount of pleading could save her for her husband's heart had been hardened and decayed. Not even he could see her innocence, not even he could see the web of lies and decent that had been spun around her, entangling her and choking her very life. She had no alternative but to flee from this place and never come back. She had gone back and forth so many times before...the thought that this would be her last time tore at her heart. Sadly, the choice was already made.

She waited for the proper moment, with the guard out of earshot and sight, she bid farewell to her beautiful world, and closed her eyes. She thought for a moment, concentrated, and then seemed to grow thin and opaque. Her body faded out, like a dying flame, and she was gone. The prison cell was empty. When the guard returned and saw she was missing, he raised the alarm. The search would go on for days, the entire kingdom in an uproar, everyone from the highest official to the smallest peasant would search for her, but the Queen would not be found.

CHAPTER 1

▼

CHANGES

Michael Smith was in the eighth grade at Levi Middle School and he hated it. He had never had so much work in his short life. He felt like the whole world was on top of his shoulders. After his parents' divorce, everything changed. Nothing was the same for Michael. The kids treated him differently; his friends thought he was weird now and they didn't want to be friends anymore. Even the teachers treated him differently, like he had some kind of disease or mental condition and they had to always treat him a certain way. Michael felt like he was some piece of gossip that could only be whispered about and he didn't like it.

Michael wore jeans and a t-shirt. He always dressed simply. His book bag was a Ranger, bought with the hopes that somehow the stitched together fabric and metal zippers would make him cool. He felt like writing to the Ranger Company and telling them just how cool its stupid book bag made you. He had scruffy dark hair and several pimples on his face, but nothing too serious, not enough to worry about. Michael went through the same routine everyday; wake up, eat breakfast, ride the bus, go to class, get laughed at, go home, not necessarily in that exact order, but he was really getting tired of it. Soon, however, everything would change. Of course, Michael did not know that. It happened one day in, of all places, the boys' bathroom.

As he so often went to the bathroom to escape the looks and lurid comments of his peers, Michael found himself even more deeply troubled today as he sat in his favorite stall, thinking. He was thinking of his mother. He had not seen her since the divorce trial. Michael's father had informed his son that Michael would not be able to see his mother on a regular basis and that full custody would rest with Mr. Smith. Michael remembered that day well. He had been so angry because he was not allowed to be at the trial, to see his mother one last time; he had to wait in some hotel room with a babysitter and watch morning television. After that, he never saw his mother again and she seemed to fade out of his life like a ghost; there one minute and gone the next. The only information about her that he received was from his father. Michael sorely missed his mother. He sat there, in the dark pea green toilet stall, inside the small blue tiled bathroom, and felt like weeping. No, not felt like; Michael was on the verge of weeping like a cliff diver taking that last breath before plummeting down, and he did. Michael wept for his family, his mother whom he loved deeply but also hated for leaving, for his father, now alone, for himself, and all his problems. Then it happened.

The air seemed to become thicker, heavier somehow. Michael began to sweat from his brow, droplets running down the length of his nose and falling off the end, *plink-plink-plink.* He could feel his head spinning, the stall seemed to grow hazy and out of focus. He didn't know what was happening. He thought he was dying, and this is what death must be like, everything spinning and getting fuzzy. Just when Michael thought the end was upon him, it stopped, and instead of the porcelain toilet seat he had been sitting on moments before, he found himself seated on a large tree stump in a field of what looked like roses of the deepest red.

Michael looked around and wondered exactly where he was and what had happened to the bathroom. His mind tried to make some sense of the situation, like someone putting together a large and intricate puzzle. One moment he was in his stall in the boys' room of Levi. The next, he was sitting on a tree stump in a field of roses, and was that a little girl playing in the flowers? He did not know what to think. Was he dreaming? Was he hallucinating? Did he die in that stall at Levi, and was this some sort of after life? All these thoughts and more flew around inside Michael's head as he surveyed the deep blue sky, the grass a green so brilliant it nearly hurt the eyes to look at, a green so rich it was as if this green was not the color green, but the perfect idea of the color green culled straight from the imagination of a child. The air held a certain sweet and cool essence, unmistakable to Michael. Even the clouds in the sky looked unrestrained, free of labels and words, roaming the blue expanse like wild animals on an open plain. In fact, everything here seemed to be too colorful, too bright. He couldn't understand it. Before he could think about anything else and before he ever noticed it, the figure he thought was a little girl had walked over to him and now stood a few feet away, examining him with a disapproving eye.

"Pardon me, but who are you? This is my field, and you are not permitted to be here. Furthermore, from where do you hail? I have never seen garments such as those. Are you from across the sea? Did you arrive here in a ship? If you did, my father should be informed at once."

Michael was puzzled by the way this girl, young, but nearly the same age as Michael, used the type of language he had heard his father use; commanding and authoritative, confident and bold. And what did she mean by Kingdom? Michael was very confused, and all he could muster to say was his name.

He said, "Michael."

"Michael. I have a servant named Michael. Are you of the Van-Dorenstein family perhaps? Or the Oliviansters? Maybe the Sar-Dorchesters? Well, are you going to say anything?"

"Um, well, my last name is um…er…Smith?"

"Smith; you are a blacksmith, then? Yes, a simple name such as that, you must be a commoner. Well, you had better leave my field before my father returns. Go now."

Michael made to get up from the stump, but before he could stand, he felt his head swimming again, the same sensation as before.

"Michael the Smith, what is the matter?"

Michael barely heard the girl. He began to sweat again, and the colorful world spun, swayed, and got fuzzy all at once, just like what had happened in the bathroom stall before. He could see the bright blue sky fading to dark blue ceiling. He could see the girl disappear, and be replaced by the dark green stall door. Slowly the green grass and the blue sky faded completely until only the faintest trace of that sweet air lingered in Michael's nose, and soon that vanished as well. Michael was back in his stall at Levi. He sat there on the toilet, which seconds before had been a stump, and tried to figure out what had just happened. He sat there for another ten minutes, calming down, trying to understand, to make sense of whatever had just happened to him. He shook his head, trying to remember everything; just to be sure it was real. He remembered the girl, and the roses, and the colors and smells and concluded it must have been real. He also concluded the girl in the rose field was very pretty, a perfect match for that strange place.

Michael's thoughts were disrupted by a group of boys entering the bathroom. Michael promptly got up and left, checked his face in the mirror, pulled his bag onto his shoulders, and went to math class.

CHAPTER 2

▼

DREAMS

After the incident in the bathroom, the rest of the school day dragged on for Michael like a bad movie. He wanted nothing more than to go home and ponder the strange place he visited while feeling sorry for himself in the bathroom. When the bell finally did ring at three o'clock, Michael Smith ran to his bus without even stopping to get his books.

That night, as Mr. Smith stood over the stovetop stirring the sizzling hamburger and noodles with a long wooden spoon, Michael sat at the kitchen table, his mind fixed entirely on what had happened earlier at school. Michael sat scratching the side of his plate with his knife when Mr. Smith spoke.

"Michael is something the matter? You seem, I don't know, sad, depressed. What's up?" Mr. Smith looked back over his shoulder where he had draped a white and blue striped cloth as he asked, "What's up?"

Michael knew he wasn't about to tell his dad about the episode in the bathroom that afternoon, so he just made up a response, the usual get-the-parent-off-your-back type of thing.

"Oh, nothing, just a long day at school. We are doing this really hard stuff in math right now, that's all."

"Okay," said Mr. Smith turning back to the noodles and meat. After dinner Mr. Smith retired to his study to work on the case he was handling. Michael went up to his room under the premise of studying, but what he really wanted to do was find a way to go back to that colorful place. Although he had been confused and a little afraid, he had been in awe of that new place. Now, being back in this mundane, normal world, he felt like he couldn't take it. Everything was so dull compared to there. The sky was like an old sock here. There, in that strange place, the sky shone brighter than a thousand vagrant constellations. Everything was so full of life and color. The boy could not deny the impulse that throbbed inside his mind; Michael knew he had to go back, no matter what.

He lay back on his bed and thought about what had happened earlier. He was sitting in the stall in the boys' bathroom, thinking about his mother, and he felt as if he was going to cry. It must have been around twelve thirty, he guessed. He had eaten a turkey sandwich for lunch, washed down with some soda and had enjoyed a brownie for desert-the soft kind without nuts in it, he hated nuts. He was wearing his red t-shirt with his dark blue jeans. He couldn't think of anything else specific to that exact time and place. He fell asleep as he thought about what happened to him that afternoon and he had a dream. It was about the girl.

She was standing in the same field as the one he had seen that day. Only this time, instead of roses as far as the eye could see, there was only one, single rose. It sprung up from the ground exactly next to where the girl was standing. It was white. He was again sitting on the tree stump as before. It was night now in this place, but everything was still alive with color. Even the black velvet of the nighttime sky seemed to shine and gleam. Michael looked from the rose, to the girl, and back to the rose. He noticed the girl was wearing the same odd clothes as before except this time her dirty blonde hair was let down to dangle just above her shoulders. Before it had been tied up into a tight bun. Michael now noticed for the first time how blue the girl's eyes were. Her eyes shone ten times more brilliant than the daytime sky of this place, beacons lighting the world. They were full of such life and energy as Michael had never seen before. Those eyes seemed to shine as if casting their own light into Michael's personal darkness. Then something strange happened.

The girl's blonde hair turned red. At first Michael didn't realize what was happening, but then he suddenly saw it: her hair was bleeding, the blood pouring down from the middle of her skull. Only, it wasn't blood, was it? It certainly looked red like blood. But Michael was not appalled by it like he was when he saw blood on television or in a movie. This red liquid seemed gentler, and the girl clearly was in no pain. It seemed almost as though the red was flowing out of her like a small creek in the forest, as though the girl wanted it to flow. Even stranger was the way the blood (redness) was falling. Instead of simply splattering upon the ground, it seemed as though the blood was being sucked into the rose, like a vacuum cleaner. After a few moments, the flow of red stopped abruptly and the white rose faded to deep, deep red in color. Realizing something was different, Michael looked more closely at the ground and now saw that there was another rose, identical to the first, sprouting next to his foot. This one was red, and it seemed to match the first rose exactly, as though they were twins, one for Michael and one for the young girl.

Michael again looked from rose to rose to girl, and suddenly the girl was no longer standing next to the rose, but right in front of him. Something else had happened too. The girl's face had changed and grown different somehow. Michael felt a great sense of recognition looking at this new face and he was certain he knew the woman who stared back at him. In dreams, however, things are odd. He could not determine who the woman was, but her eyes were the same deep blue as the girl's who had been there moments before. He stared into those deep, brilliant, blue eyes and wanted to simply stare into them forever. Then the woman grabbed Michael's shoulders, her expression changing to a look of desperation, as if she wanted to say something, but couldn't. She shook him and shook him, until he awoke breathing hard and sweating. His first waking thought screamed inside his head to find a way back to that strange place.

Thoughts of getting to the boys' bathroom occupied Michael's mind all morning and he barely heard his teacher telling him about the Civil War. At lunch Michael made his way to the boys' restroom, full of hope and anticipation. He had been unable to concentrate on his classes prior to this because of the hope of seeing the mysterious girl from his dreams (or maybe reality) again. He reached the big green door with the white figure of a man plastered against the black panel in the center. He pushed the door open and entered.

Jacob Niles was standing by the mirror, combing his jet-black hair down against his scalp until it was as flat as a pancake and shone with profuse amounts of hair gel. Jacobs's eyes met Michael's in the mirror; they stood for only a moment, locked in each other's stares, until Jacob looked away and back to his hair. Michael opened the door to the same stall he was in yesterday, stepped in, turned, closed it behind him, put his bag on the floor, and sat down. He waited until he heard Jacob leave. Once he was sure Niles had gone, Michael tried to recreate the circumstances of the day before.

The boy looked at his watch, 12:23. When he was in the bathroom yesterday, it had been 12:45, so he had probably shifted (that's what Michael was beginning to call what had happened to him) around 12:30. He sat down and cleared his mind. Five minutes, nothing. He thought about the girl. Eight minutes, nothing.

He thought about Jacob. Ten minutes, nothing. He thought about his father. He was about to get up and go back to the cafeteria and finish his tuna sandwich when he suddenly remembered (as if out of nowhere) that his mother had made the most unbelievably good tuna fish sandwiches. He began to feel dizzy, lightheaded. He knew at once it was happening again. He was shifting. The green stall door became hazy, the slow and steady drip, drip of the sink faded away. The colors of his world slowly became darker, grayer, until they were gone completely. Then…

Thwip! The air snapped for a moment and Michael was somewhere new.

Michael's senses were bombarded with stimuli. Colors, so bright he had to squint for a moment, sounds of birds and bugs, chirping carelessly. The smell of roses, so strong he felt he was drowning in them. The wind blowing through his hair, lifting it ever so gently off his forehead, made all of Michael's senses come alive. His eyes adjusted. He looked up at the deep blue sky, spotless of clouds. He gazed down at the stump, and indeed it seemed he was in the same place as yesterday. Then he looked out at the rose field, and his heart sank: the girl was no where in sight. He had now been to this extraordinary place twice, and Michael felt the need to test his boundaries. He slowly began to stand up, and as he did so he felt the world begin to sway and swoon. He held onto the colors and sounds and smells of the place and the feeling shortly passed. Michael stood there, a large tree stump at his feet, the sky a blue no Earthly human had ever seen above, and an endless field of roses of the deepest red before him. He began to walk.

Jacob Niles was waiting outside the boys' room door for Michael. He was going to send the kid flying face first when he tripped him coming out of the bathroom. It would be great. Jacob waited five, then ten minutes. He was getting bored. He decided to take the direct approach and just go into the bathroom and punch

Michael while he was talking a dump. Jacob went back inside, quietly. He tiptoed over to the stall he had seen Michael enter. Jacob could see Michael's bag on the floor in the stall. He reached for the handle, and swung open the door, ready to spring. But there was nothing there. Just an empty toilet; Michael was gone. Jacob was baffled. He had been standing by the door ever since he came out of the bathroom. Surely Michael could not have slipped by, and besides, the loser's bag was still sitting in the stall. Jacob scanned the rest of the bathroom, under every stall, but found no trace of his victim. Instead of wasting anymore time on this silly matter, Jacob put Michael's bag in the toilet and flushed. Then he left, content that he had still been able to bring some misfortune upon the life of Michael Smith.

CHAPTER 3

▼

BARTLEBUG

The roses seemed to go on forever. Michael must have been walking for twenty minutes, and still the field of red velvet stretched out in all directions before him as far as he could see. Looking behind him, the stump on which he had been sitting when he first arrived was no longer in sight. Just a sea of red and he was in the middle of it, although he had observed something odd while he was walking. In some places, random patches of the red roses were faded and dull. In others, the roses seem to have disappeared all together and at times, Michael swore he had observed bunches of the roses fading in and out, like the reception on his television when the weather kicked up. But he didn't care. It was utter bliss. He loved every moment he was in this strange new place. He loved the too bright colors. The smell of the roses seemed to attack him in waves, drifting carelessly through the air until it found him, then bombarding his senses with that sweet smell. As he walked he noticed a bee, only it was ten times larger than any bee he had ever seen. Michael thought it was about the size of a small dog, maybe a bull dog. It had the same yellow and black stripes, but no stinger on its bottom, at least none that Michael could see. It had a pair of large antenna, and a face that resembled something human. In fact, Michael thought it was watching him with the same wonderment and awe with which Michael looked back at the bee. He did not notice the bee start to follow him.

So on he walked, stopping every once and a while to rest, simply enjoying the world around and take in every sensation. Thoughts of school or his real life quickly faded. After an hour's worth of walking through the red rose sea, the field abruptly stopped. Michael had been so enthralled with the place, he didn't even notice when one moment he was ankle deep in roses, the next he was on plain old ground with patches of brownish grass here and there. Perhaps, if Michael could have turned around quickly enough while he was walking, he would have noticed the roses appeared only where his eyes were looking, as though putting on a special show for his eyes only. Now, however, the show ended and Michael was left with not a single rose, just dust and hardpan. He stopped and turned around.

"What?" he was completely dumbfounded. The field of roses was completely gone. It had simply vanished. All that stretched out before him now was barren, a massive expanse of hardpan. Crab grass and cracked desert spread in every direction. Sparse vegetation and dead things littered this landscape, this antithesis of what had been here before, this opposite. The sky was now duller than before. It was as if this place had died. The boy noticed several strange animals skitter by. One looked like a cross between a rat and a kangaroo while another, clearly capable of flying, was hopping along the dusty hardpan shooting its tongue at anything that moved. Michael didn't know what to think, but he was suddenly very afraid. He had been wandering carelessly for the past hour, completely content with life, no worries floating around his head. In fact, nothing had been floating around his head. It was as if he had been in a blissful daydream. But now all he wanted was to get as far away from this place as possible.

"Don't look so shocked, boy. I don't know how you were able to hold the Fabrication as long as you did…Mya is the only one in this Kingdom who can use the Fabricant…what are you doing here anyway?"

Michael spun around looking for the source of the voice, looking for another person in this now desolate waste. He didn't see anyone. Then he glanced down at the ground. A few feet away, standing on its hind legs with its other pair of appendages crossed on its chest, was the bee Michael had seen in the rose field. Michael just stared at this strange creature with mixed feelings of fright and amazement. Suddenly, the bee shot into the air, buzzing furiously, and came toward the boy with blinding speed, hovering a few inches away from Michael's face, examining him. He could see this creature was actually quite large and menacing, and the cuteness Michael had seen in it vanished at once. Michael could now see quite a bit more of this creature than he had been able to in the rose field. He did, in fact, have a human face, except it was pitch black, save for his eyes which were white pinpricks, tiny points of piercing white among a sooty backdrop. His nose was long and straight. Michael could not help but notice a small green marking of some kind on the creature's hind quarters in the shape of a circle. The bee-creature looked very menacing.

"I will not repeat myself again boy. Why are you here? Are you a citizen of BlanchField?"

Michael wasn't sure what to do. He could tell this creature meant business, and although Michael was scared of the desert that had taken the place of the lovely rose field, he felt he needed to stay in this world a bit longer, as if he was supposed to do something. So he lied.

"Of course I am," he said.

"Well then explain your clothes?" Snipped the bee.

"I…well…I made them myself," he said. Thinking back to what the pretty girl in the rose field had said, Michael added, "My family is poor, like commoners. We can't afford good clothes. We have to make our own."

"Humph, sounds like lies to me," muttered the bee. Then looking up at Michael, he said, "What is your name, boy?" The bee furrowed his eyebrows.

Michael thought again to the conversation with the girl. "Michael the Smith."

"Michael the Smith? A blacksmith then are you? Fine, come with me. I think the King would like to speak with you…" The bee examined Michael, looking him up and down with untrusting, sinister eyes. "You seem…odd and I still can't work out how you were able to hold onto Mya's Fabrication like that…come with me boy." The bee turned, gesturing for Michael to follow him.

Michael had heard this creature mention something quite a few times now in their brief conversation; something Michael thought he heard the bee call Fabricant, or Fabrication. Whatever that was, Michael had no idea. He would simply stay alert, keep his story warm in his head, and see what happened.

"By the way," said the bee, turning back in mid-air and glancing at Michael, "I am Bartlebug." The bee turned back and continued his flight.

Michael had no idea where they were going. It seemed the desert stretched out before them endlessly. He could see mountains far off in the distance, and crab grass growing on the caked hardpan ahead of them, but nothing else. The place was quite empty.

Bartlebug suddenly stopped, and hovered. Michael heard him mutter a few words to the air, but he couldn't make them out. Then, the sky seemed to shimmer, and wave; like the air above a gas grill or the road on a hot day. This phenomenon stretched across the expanse of the desert, as far as Michael could see left and right. It was an amazing sight. Michael watched open-mouthed as a city took shape before his eyes. He could see huge spires rising from the tops of buildings. He saw streets begin to snake their way into view. He began to see people moving about, walking here and there. He saw birds flutter out of nothing. He heard noises: horses, children playing, people selling wares, dogs barking. An enormous city now stood before Michael, except he had only seen a city such as this in a history book. Michael realized this was some sort of medieval village; not a bustling metropolis like New York. There were no cars, no skyscrapers, and no street vendors selling hot dogs. Michael liked what he saw.

Bartlebug watched Michael in silence as he stared at the beautiful Kingdom, as if he had never seen the place before, and his suspicions grew even greater.

"Come Michael the Smith. I am taking you to see King Van-Vargot. Follow me," said Bartlebug sternly.

Michael wanted to wander about for a little while and explore this new place, so he made up an excuse to be rid of Bartlebug.

"May I return to my…shop…and speak with my…parents before we go?" asked Michael.

"No," said Bartlebug and that was all.

"But please, I will only be like five minutes."

"Five what?" asked Bartlebug. "It matters not. The answer is no. And if you don't like it…" Now Michael saw what was missing from Bartlebug's bee body. As Bartlebug hovered there in the crowded street, he extended a gleaming black stinger from his bottom, a hard onyx carapace that gleamed with moisture. It was as long as Michael's arm, and just as thick. After it was fully extended, tiny spurs like fishhooks popped out all over the stinger. Michael was instantly intimidated, and resolved then and there to never cross Bartlebug.

"I will use this, and you do not want that. Now, silence until we reach the castle."

Michael did as he was told and followed Bartlebug along the burrows and alleys. Michael noticed a street sign very similar to the one which designated his street back home, and he assumed this Blanch-Field used the same kind of naming system. The sign read Merchant's Row. Indeed, the street's name certainly did it justice. Michael was overwhelmed by the sheer number of people selling things on this long thoroughfare, things Michael had never heard of before, and some he had. The noise was uproarious and deafening. Michael noticed one woman standing in front of a small tent. It was obvious to Michael that she had put the tent up herself.

"What would you like young man? I've got everything your heart could desire," said the woman in front of the tent as Michael and Bartlebug passed by. Michael noticed she was missing several teeth and a yellow liquid of some kind seeped from her sore-covered mouth.

"Duccats? Pearls? Maybe something for a lady?" The woman continued in this manner until Michael could no longer hear her. The boy said nothing and Bartlebug hovered on in silence.

Further down the street, Michael noticed a creature similar to Bartlebug running another tent. There was a sign in front of this blue and green tent which Michael could read. The spidery letters spelled *fruit*.

"Yam-peppers? Sugarberries?" The bee shot wildly through the air, buzzing and shouting. "Silvermollies? We have it all! Cheap prices, no better deals in all the kingdom!"

Michael watched as Bartlebug shot this fellow a nasty glance as they walked by his stall, and the fruit selling bee-creature seemed to quiet down, although only a little. It was clear to Michael that Bartlebug was well known here. At last, they reached the end of Merchant's Row and Bartlebug led the boy onto another wide street.

Michael looked for a sign, but did not see one. This new street was not as crowded as Merchant's Row, but people were coming and going regularly. Michael observed their strange clothing. Many of them wore cloaks and capes of various colors with odd-shaped hats. Some, mostly the children Michael saw, wore outfits resembling overalls except they seemed to be made out of a very soft and colorful fabric.

Several times on this journey through town, Michael thought about running, just taking off as fast as he could and trying to escape Bartlebug and each time he thought otherwise. For one thing, Bartlebug could clearly fly, and it would not take the creature long to stop Michael from the air. Second, Michael's clothes were a dead giveaway and he would not have time to find a disguise. He decided he would just have to find the right moment to shift back to Earth.

As the pair continued down this long road, a loud noise from one of the homes on the side of the street caught Michael's attention. Before he even had time to react, a woman burst through a large door onto the street. She brandished a large rolling pin and was yelling at a child, who tried miserably to get away from her, but she was too big and the child was not crafty enough.

"You rascal! I don't want to find you stealing my pies again!" She brought the rolling pin down with a loud thump. "Come near that window one more time, and I will turn you over to the King himself!"

"What is the trouble here?" asked Bartlebug, lowering himself behind the large woman with the rolling pin. Michael stood close by and watched.

"And who's askin'!" said the woman, turning around. When she saw who it was asking, she dropped the rolling pin and let go of the boy. Instead of running, the boy stood motionless, terrified of the bee creature and too frightened to move.

"Bartlebug is asking wench, the King's Hand!" said the bee. Michael did not know what the term King's Hand meant, but it sounded official.

"A thousand apologies sire. I am in a bit of a rage at the moment. But now I'm fine, a thousand apologizes," said the woman, bowing.

"Ye'sir, I'm sorry too," said the boy. At last his fear melted and the boy bolted, retreating down a nearby alleyway.

"I do not like ruckus, especially when I am escorting someone to the King," said Bartlebug, motioning to Michael.

"Aye," said the woman, eyes turned down.

"So go back to your dwelling, and continue baking your pies. Filth," said Bartlebug.

Michael's anger grew with every word that escaped Bartlebug's soot-colored mouth. He had seen people act this way before, at school. Sometimes teachers would treat the students poorly simply because they could. Michael knew the word for it, *power-trip*. Michael hated people who acted high and mighty, and in that moment, as Bartlebug shunned the poor woman, who wanted only to have her pies left in peace, Michael knew this creature would be his enemy. Michael knew the same way he knew that Jacob Niles was his enemy, the same way he knew that everyone who ever made fun of him and caused him pain became his enemy in some way. Bartlebug brought pain to peoples' lives simply because he could, and Michael hated him.

At last, the woman retreated back to her home and slammed the door. Michael thought he could actually smell the infamous pies baking in her oven.

"Let's go boy," said Bartlebug with disdain. "I don't have all day to waste on the likes of you."

The pair continued down the street until the road ended abruptly. Michael looked up and nearly lost his breath. There was a murky moat running in a circle around the largest and most magnificent edifice Michael had ever laid eyes on. There were spires and pulpits, and windows and steeples at nearly every junction of this building. It was constructed haphazardly, but upon closer inspection one would find it to have perfect design and symmetry. Directly ahead of Michael and Bartlebug, a massive wooden door with large metal buckles stretched from the ground to the top of the castle wall. This palace was so large, Michael was convinced he would be able to fit his entire neighborhood inside and still have room. The castle's design amazed Michael in its uncanny resemblance to castles he had read about in books and seen in movies. It looked like something straight out of *Robin Hood*. Next to the wooden door was a small opening, and inside Michael could see the hovering form of another large bee creature. It called to Bartlebug and Michael's escort told the gatekeeper to open the door. The gatekeeper made a sound of compliance. Michael listened as the massive gears controlling the drawbridge churned and screeched then the wooden door began to lower slowly.

"Step back," demanded Bartlebug. Michael did so. The wooden door crossed the entire moat and landed with a loud thump a few feet ahead of Michael and Bartlebug.

"This way, Michael the Smith," said Bartlebug, taking no measures to hide his sarcasm. Michael followed the bee creature, unsure of where he was going and afraid.

As Michael and Bartlebug traversed the moat surrounding the castle of BlanchField, Michael's history teacher, Mrs. Paige, had just noticed Michael Smith's seat was empty.

"Where is Michael Smith?" asked Mrs. Paige, the eighth-grade history teacher at Levi Middle School. Jacob Niles raised his hand.

"I saw him in the bathroom 'round lunch, but he never came out. Maybe he fell in." This remark was followed by a series of laughs from Jacobs's cronies.

"Alright, that's enough. Jacob, go to Mr. Andrews and tell him Michael is skipping my class. Go now please," said Mrs. Paige.

"Okay Mrs. Paige," replied Jacob.

"Now, who can tell me who defeated General Lee at Appomattox courthouse?"

Chapter 4

▼

Escape

The castle's interior proved more amazing and magnificent than the outside as Michael gazed at the grandiose entrance hall. He saw stone floors, beautifully aged, with cracks here and there. Carpets ran like wild snakes atop these floors, woven of colorful fabric. Huge paintings hung from the walls of the entrance hall, Michael saw one of a man with blonde hair dressed in armor. Another painting depicted a man with long white hair dressed in a robe. The second man did not look as regal and mighty as the first. Directly in front of Michael and Bartlebug a massive marble staircase, looming closer as the two traveled the distance of the entrance hall, led up and then split, one path to the left, and one to the right.

Before he reached the staircase, Michael heard a noise coming from somewhere. He looked around, unsure of what the noise was or where it was coming from. As he got closer to the staircase, the noise grew louder. At last, Bartlebug instructed Michael to climb the steps. Now the noise was very loud. Michael was curious as to why Bartlebug seemed to not hear it, or perhaps he did hear it and simply chose to ignore it. Still, Michael could not figure out what it was. Then it hit him. The noise was music. Michael continued to listen and the more he did, the more the sound began to seem less like noise and more like music. At first, it had sounded like a jumble of different noises, all strewn together carelessly. Now, Michael could hear individual notes, melodies and harmonies, even a refrain. The boy did not understand why the music had sounded so foreign at first, until he and Bartlebug reached the top of the staircase and turned right.

In a small room near the landing at the top of the staircase, a group of men and women sat playing instruments. They all wore the same clothes, and there were perhaps twelve of them in all. The instruments caught Michael's eye immediately. One man played something that resembled a guitar, only it was much longer and the neck curved around the back of the man's head. Michael saw a woman playing a piano; only the keys were all different sizes and colors. Michael noticed two people playing the same instrument together. This particular device consisted of a long metal rod which ran from one player's mouth to the floor. Sprouting from this rod were six other metal rods which player number two seemed to be tapping.

All of this amazed Michael and now he knew why the music sounded so odd at first; he had never heard music played on these instruments before and it had taken a little time for his mind to understand it.

"Do not linger! A liar such as yourself has no right listening to the BlanchField Choir! Now keep moving," said Bartlebug after noticing Michael had stopped to listen to the music. Bartlebug disliked the Choir anyway; he thought the sounds they produced on their disgusting instruments were worse than torture. Michael took one last look at the choir and one last listen to the music, which he now thought was absolutely beautiful, and continued following Bartlebug further into the castle.

As they walked, it became all too clear to Michael what was happening, and he knew he needed to get out. Bartlebug was taking Michael to see this King because Bartlebug knew that Michael did not belong here. Michael also thought Bartlebug simply enjoyed bringing pain to people such as himself. The two had walked down several other hallways and as they did Michael noticed the decorations becoming much more elegant. Instead of a single burning candle for light, now the walls were adorned with a multitude of candles. Instead of a single tapestry hung from the ceiling, now there were three. The carpet in the main entrance hall became a faded memory compared to the lush blue one on which Michael now walked. All of these clues led Michael to the conclusion that they were getting closer to the King, and that meant trouble for Michael. He knew he needed to escape, and he knew of only one way for him to escape Bartlebug. He needed to shift. He did not know how he was going to manage it, but he knew he had to try.

Michael thought about the bathroom at Levi, tried to concentrate on the smells and sights the same way he did when he almost shifted getting up from the stump in the rose field. Nothing happened. He tried harder, made himself smell the disinfectant of the bathroom, the pungent odor of the toilets, but nothing. Now Bartlebug and the boy neared the end of the ornate hallway. At the end of the hall a huge double door loomed before them, painted red, with a large crest plastered on each door, but Michael was too far away to see them in detail. He had a feeling, however, that the King waited for him just beyond those doors. A thought occurred to him as they approached, and Michael cursed himself for not realizing it before. He had been thinking about the bathroom at Levi, trying to shift *back to the bathroom*. His mind now told him that he was no longer in the bathroom at Levi, that he must have walked several miles since shifting here. Michael assumed that by traveling in this place, he also traveled on Earth and when he shifted back he would not be in the same place. It seemed like an obvious conclusion.

Michael tried to imagine where he could be, but he simply could not. With all the twists and turns they had taken in the village and now in this castle, it would have been impossible to predict where, in his world, he was. Michael now stood in front of the double doors, desperation setting in, a sickening sense of helplessness and fear because he knew he would not be able to shift. He knew he would have to go in the red door and face the King. Then the boy looked up, and saw the face of his mother.

The woman's face shone down upon Michael like the North Star, a beautiful replica of the boy's mother chiseled in the large crest, a silver plate upon which his mother's face had been engraved. Michael looked at the door and saw two plaques; the woman's plate adorned the left door while a similar one was fixed on the right, only Michael didn't recognize the face on the right one. He could hardly believe what he was seeing. How was this possible? He wanted so badly to be home with his mother now. His mind flooded with thoughts of her, feelings for her. It had been so long since he last saw her, but her memory would never leave him, the way she smelled, the way she laughed, the way she tucked him into bed at night. Suddenly, he felt the world sway. He started to sweat, and the colors that surrounded him began to fade. He looked at Bartlebug, who hovered a few feet ahead of him. He began to open the door. The bee-creature's body grew transparent and Michael could see through him, into the throne room. Just before the world fully faded, Michael thought he saw a massive and mighty man sitting upon a throne in that room. A feeling of relief at last settled in his nervous mind. He was shifting. He had done it! He would be saved yet! He closed his eyes, trying to steady himself, but before he could open them he felt the floor under his feet disappear and felt that sickening feeling like he was falling overtake his stomach. He did fall, but not far.

"Ahhh!" he yelled. He opened his eyes. He was in a super market he thought he recognized. He looked around and saw jelly and peanut butter on shelves to his left, and crackers on shelves to his right. Luckily, no one else was in the aisle. Michael realized he was in the Thrift Save and an expression of shock filled his face. He knew the Thrift Save was several miles away from the school, much further than he had walked in the other world. He did not know why, but somehow he had ended up traveling much further than he expected. Instead of wasting time trying to figure it out, he decided to get moving and try to make it back to school before it was too late. He stood up, and thought the next time he shifted, he would have to be more careful. He left the store and headed back to school.

Bartlebug opened the red doors and spied the throne room. He envied this room so; its warm fires and animal rugs, the long tables upon which only the most important people feasted, and most of all, the King's throne. He turned to fetch the boy.

"Through here, Michael the…" Bartlebug's small mouth fell open. Michael was gone. A voice bellowed from the beyond the now open door.

"What is it, Bartlebug?"

"Nothing Sire, I am terribly sorry to disrupt you," said Bartlebug, his voice shaking.

"Then be off with you!" shouted the voice.

"Yes your majesty!" called back Bartlebug. He closed the red door, his face twisted in a knot of hate. His sting shot out, not slowly like when Michael had watched it, but almost too fast to see. Bartlebug buzzed down the hallway, scrapping his stinger along the stone wall, the sound drowning out the melodious notes of the BlanchField Choir, now only a distant sound barely heard.

"Michael the Smith," scowled Bartlebug, his face a mural of hate, twisted and cringing in the flickering candlelight.

CHAPTER 5

▼

CONSEQUENCE

Michael occupied his mind on the walk back to Levi with thoughts about what had happened to him this second time in that strange, new world. He thought about how beautiful it all had been while walking through the field of roses, almost too beautiful, then nothing as the field suddenly vanished. How all that beauty just went away in the blink of an eye, and turned to dust, puzzled Michael. He thought about the strange bee creature, Bartlebug. Michael knew he had made an enemy in that little creature, and he was not happy about it. He could picture Bartlebug extending that deadly stinger, a look of rage in his tiny white eyes, and coming at him with intent to kill. Michael thought about the melodious new music he had heard, and now found himself humming the melody, a melody from another world. Most of all, he thought about the crest on the left of the two huge red doors; his mother's face. Michael knew it was her. He was certain. Who else could it have been? He knew his mother's face; he could recall every feature of it in a heartbeat. He didn't understand why, but his mother's face adorned a crest on a door leading to a royal chamber in another world. He didn't know what to think. Who was the man on the other crest, the one on the other red door? Michael did not have any answers to these questions, but he thought about someone who might.

He finally arrived at school, and quietly entered the building through the gym entrance, trying not to draw too much attention to himself. He knew he would be in trouble. It was now five o'clock. He had shifted at noon and spent nearly five hours in the other world. He hoped the school had not called his dad yet. The first thing Michael intended to do was return to the boys' bathroom and reclaim his book bag, but he was intercepted by Mrs. Paige in the hallway.

"Well, Michael, where have you been all day?" said Mrs. Paige, putting her hands on her hips.

"Sorry, Mrs. Paige, I was…um…er…"

"Enough Michael; report to Mr. Andrews office immediately," she said, looking at Michael over the rim of her glasses.

Michael was caught and he knew it so he put up no more defenses and simply accepted the fact that his time in the other world, of course, had consequences. But next time, he thought, it would be easier, and there would most definitely be a next time. Since shifting back, that place was all he could think about. It consumed his mind. He decided he would shift over the weekend and no one would know he was gone.

"Yes, Mrs. Paige," said Michael, head down. He walked sullenly to the principal's office and the secretary ushered him in as soon as he got there. Mr. Andrews sat menacingly behind his large wooden desk peering at a file folder through his large glasses. He was balding and he always wore the same type of suit to school; dark colored, old, and bland; just like him, bland.

"Mr. Smith, what have you been up to this afternoon?" said Mr. Andrews as Michael sat down. Of course, Michael had no intention of telling the truth about his whereabouts that afternoon.

"I…well…Mr. Andrews…I was just going to go down to the market, buy some food. I just got bored in class this afternoon, I'm really sorry. I won't do it again, I promise." His aunts always said he was a very good actor, and this display supported their claim. Mr. Andrews listened with detached attention; obviously his mind had been made up before Michael had even come in the office.

"Two days suspension mister; we will not tolerate skipping class here. You are dismissed. A letter will be sent home with you today. If this happens again, you will be expelled."

Michael had never in his life been suspended from school and now he wondered if his excursion had been worth tarnishing his perfect record; of course it was. He took the letter from Mr. Andrews and left. He needed his book bag. He made his way back to the boys' bathroom. He went in and opened the stall where he had shifted in earlier. He looked down, but no book bag. Then he looked in the toilet and there it was. His bag, soaking wet, in the bowl. He carefully fished it out, and dried it as best he could with the shabby paper towels in the bathroom. He decided that wrinkles were better than wetness, so he put his suspension letter in his pocket, carefully folded. He slung his back pack over his shoulder, ignoring the wetness, and went outside to wait for his dad. As he stood there waiting, his wet book bag on the ground next to him, he thought about what to do next, and he knew exactly what he needed to do next. He needed to see his mother.

CHAPTER 6

▼

VISIT

"What's this?" asked Mr. Smith as Michael handed him the envelope. "From school?" he added, looking at the heading. Mr. Smith had just arrived home from work and Michael had been waiting for him. Now he put down his brief case and before taking off his jacket, stepped into the kitchen and sat down at the table. Michael followed.

Mr. Smith slipped his finger under the seal and tore the envelope open. He read the letter inside casually, like someone would read a Christmas card. Instead of the sudden fit of rage Michael expected, Mr. Smith simply dropped the letter on the table and began massaging his forehead with his thumb and forefinger. After a few moments, Mr. Smith looked up at Michael.

"Where were you?" he asked calmly. Michael had been thinking about the answer to this very question all afternoon as he waited for his father. On the one hand, he could make up a lie that his father would *not* believe and get into even more trouble. On the other hand, he could simply tell the truth. Tell his father he somehow traveled to another world. He had decided earlier to tell the truth.

"Dad, I will tell you, but promise you will listen, and try to believe me, okay?" said Michael. Mr. Smith looked angry and cautious, but he nodded his head. So Michael told him the whole story, from the first time in the bathroom when he shifted, to the dream about the two roses, all the way to this very afternoon. During the course of his story, Michael had looked down at the table and did not look once at his father. Now he did, and what he saw shocked him. His father had gone completely white; he looked as though all the blood in his body had flooded out. His mouth hung fully open, his eyes glazed, staring at his son. Michael had not been expecting this kind of reaction and he was shocked.

"Dad, what's wrong? Dad, please, answer me!" Mr. Smith just kept staring into nothing. "Dad, Dad, Dad!" Michael yelled at his Father and Mr. Smith jumped, coming out of his daze. Mr. Smith looked at Michael like he was a stranger, like he had a horrible disease, then got up and walked to the phone.

"Dad, please, what's the matter?" Michael was getting emotional now. He was worried; he had never in his life seen his father like this, so crazed.

Turning from the phone, Mr. Smith took on a look of authority his son had never seen before. Michael also noticed his father's eyes, which seemed very cold and far away.

"Go to your room. You are coming with me tomorrow, not going to school. I will call and let them know. I don't want to see you for the rest of the night."

Michael's fear would not let him argue with his father. Mr. Smith had never been so strict and cold with Michael, and he was very afraid. He did as he was told and crept upstairs while Mr. Smith concentrated on the phone. As Michael reached the top of the steps and his father's voice faded, the last thing he heard was a name; Dr. Taft.

Exhausted, Michael pulled down his sheets and crept into bed, not even bothering to change his clothes. He looked around at his room. On one wall Mr. Smith had mounted shelves. On these shelves several trophies stood magnificently, proof that Michael was a good athlete, although he suspected that nearly everyone got a trophy at some point for something. The boy's favorite sport was baseball and his room was proof of that. He had posters of famous baseball players hanging from his walls, a well oiled and broken in glove in the corner, and a very special autographed baseball in a small glass case on his desk. Michael looked at this baseball now and sighed. He could feel his eyes getting heavy and he knew very soon he would be asleep. Before he melted into slumber, however, Michael grabbed the baseball from his desk. He read the autograph: *To a Very Special Boy,* Your *#1 Fan, Tom Schilling.* Michael smiled. He held the ball for a little while, and then placed it back on his desk. Within moments sleep came.

It seemed he was only asleep for ten minutes when Mr. Smith woke him. Michael opened his eyes and saw it was still dark out.

"Dad, what time…" said Michael groggily.

"Early, let's go. We have to go now. Get dressed," said Mr. Smith.

Michael did as he was told, threw on some jeans and a sweater, and was ready to go in five minutes. He still had no idea where they were going. Skipping breakfast and proceeding straight to the garage, Michael followed his father.

"Where are we going dad?" asked Michael. No response came. Michael got in the car. As his father started the Volvo, Michael asked, "Dad, where are we going?" The boy's eyes were still crusty with sleep, and there was no urgency in his voice. Michael rubbed his eyes, and yawned.

"I remember you did this once before…" Michael thought back to a similar morning when he was little, maybe five years ago, he was uncertain.

"We went the circus that day, remember dad?" Michael asked his father. Mr. Smith remained silent, eyes focused on the road ahead. "Are we going to the circus today?" Michael knew the answer to his question before the words were even out of his mouth. Of course they weren't. After last night's episode, Michael did not think his father had any intention of taking him anywhere as enjoyable as the circus. Michael no longer felt sleepy.

Mr. Smith remained quiet and Michael's mind drifted back to that day when his father had roused him out of bed early, a huge grin on his face.

"Michael, Michael wake up. We have to go," his father had said, rousing the boy from sleep. Michael had nodded and gotten dressed. In the car, Michael had asked his father where they were going, and his father had told him it was a surprise. Michael could remember how excited he had gotten about that, wondering what it could possibly be.

Father and son had driven through the city and made their way to the country roads. The memory of open fields and immense blue skies was what Michael held onto. He loved those images, the vastness of the land. Even at such a young age Michael had enjoyed open spaces, the breeze, the sky. The longer they drove, the greater Michael's anticipation became to find out where they were going. It seemed like he had been in the car for ages. At last, Mr. Smith pulled the call into a huge field filled with other cars and parked in an unmarked parking spot.

"This is it," he had said. Michael excitedly hopped out of the car, and gazed around. All he could see from his low vantage points was a sea of cars. "This way."

Mr. Smith had taken Michael's hand and led them through the maze of cars. Finally, they came to the last row, and as the boy emerged and saw the spectacle before him, his mouth dropped wide open.

There in front of him, stretching endlessly to the sky in red and yellow sunbursts of color, was an enormous tent; to Michael, it seemed larger than anything he had ever seen. The colors of it were magnificent, dazzling under the bright blue sky. Huge ropes ran from it and pummeled into the Earth to keep the tent grounded. People were coming and going through the huge draped open flaps which led into the tent. From its center rose an enormous flag flapping briskly in the wind. The flag featured a huge lion rearing up on its hind legs. Other tents speckled the landscape like colorful paint splotches. Michael could hear music being carried from the scene, and he could smell popcorn.

"Welcome to the circus Michael," said Mr. Smith grinning. Michael's father hoisted the boy onto his shoulders. Father and son made their way to the main tent, and Michael remembered his father handing the man several silver coins, and they proceeded in.

That day had been extraordinary for Michael. He had watched with awe the lion tamer, acrobats, clowns, and all the other amazing sights. The smell of the popcorn his dad had bought him had been intoxicating and Michael thought he could smell that delicious red and white stripped box of popcorn now. Michael remembered laughing when the clowns all came flowing out of that tiny car, and the way the elephants had reared up on their hind legs towering over the crowd. At one point, Michael's heart had pounded so fast, he thought it would burst when the trapeze artist nearly missed his grab. But they were quite nimble and were able to complete the stunt.

The memory Michael cherished most about that was, without a doubt, the carousel. Mr. Smith had led Michael to an open area behind the tents where a gorgeous old fashioned carousel had been set up, at least Michael remembered his dad calling it old fashioned. Michael clearly remembered standing beneath the crystalline blue sky, gazing up at the hand painted horses as they circled and bobbed before him. The playful and childlike music which emanated from the apparatus like visible gossamer strands had compelled and captivated the young boy.

"I think you like that, huh Michael?" Mr. Smith had asked.

Michael had been too in awe to answer, he just stood there grinning from ear to ear, lost in the fantasy of that carousel. Michael spent the rest of the day riding the carousel, trying out each different horse, laughing with his dad. The magic of that day had been undeniable; something about the circus always seemed magical. When the circus finished, Michael and his dad left the magical grounds but before they did Mr. Smith bought Michael a huge, puffy tuft of cotton candy. It was blue and Michael enjoyed it the whole way home. Michael smiled.

Looking out the window now, he did not see the far open country spaces he remembered from his day at the circus; instead he saw a dreary city morning. He looked at his father.

"Will you please tell me where we are going?" Michael's voice was stern this time, impatient. His father finally looked over at him.

"Alright, since we're already on our way I'll tell you. Michael, I'm sorry about last night. Don't think I was angry with you about skipping school; believe me, that is the least of my worries right now. It was your story that got me scared. You remember your mother, don't you Michael?"

Of course he remembered his mother. He loved her dearly, but he also hated her for leaving the family two years ago. Michael had not been allowed to attend the divorce trial so he never really found out why she went away. His father told him his mother had become an alcoholic. Mr. Smith told Michael that his mother would be gone for a long time, trying to make herself right. Michael had believed him. Of course, Michael had known something was wrong well before the actual divorce. His mother would be gone for weeks at a time with no explanation, she simply disappeared. Sometimes she would make excuses. Other times she would simply go upstairs and close the door. On more than one occasion, she had come home late at night and Michael had heard his parents arguing while he sat helpless in his room, crying. He could still hear his mother making up excuses; nearly incoherent babble that Mr. Smith never believed. Michael thought back to one such night when he had been roused from sleep by his parents' fight.

"Peter, I can't tell you where I have been. It would be catastrophic, detrimental, VanVargot, he would…"

"Who is this VanVargot? Are you having an affair, Judith? Tell me, if you are cheating on me!"

"No, Peter, of course not, I love you. My situation is very complicated. I simply can't explain…"

"So you think you can just leave whenever you want and then show up like this? Do you have any idea what this is doing to Michael? Not to mention the fact that you seem to be having a hard time telling me the plain truth!"

"I know Michael is all I care about. That is why…He is too important…Don't you understand…"

"No, Judith, I don't understand. In fact, I'm done trying to understand. I want a divorce."

That particular night stuck in Michael's mind like a leech. After that conversation, those words, his life had turned upside down. His mother was gone more often after that, and when she did come home, she was delirious. Drunk, Michael thought after his dad had told him about her alcoholism. But now, after the experience Michael had with the new world, he wasn't so sure about his mother anymore, or about some of the reasons his father had given him for her condition. Michael could now understand why his mother might have been gone for those long periods of time, and where she might have been.

"Michael, I know I told you your mother was an alcoholic, but that was a lie."

Michael looked at his father, not shocked by this revelation because he half suspected she did not drink.

"She never touched the stuff, not once in her whole life. I know she and I had some pretty grand fights, and I am sorry to have put you through that. But, well, Michael...I don't know how to tell you this. I didn't then and I still don't."

"Dad, what is it? Please, just tell me. I want to know about mom."

"Michael, your mother is...well...she is mentally unwell." Mr. Smith said, making a right hand turn. Now Michael was surprised. He thought the alcoholism thing was bogus, but insane? He had a hard time believing that.

"What are you saying dad? Mom's crazy? Where are we going?" Michael demanded.

"We are going to see your mother, son. We are going to Pineridge."

Pineridge home for the Mentally Ill was located twenty miles from Michael's middle school. His class had to go there once last year for service work, and Mr. Smith had insisted Michael stay home that day. Of course Michael didn't resist, but now he knew why his father wanted to keep him away from Pineridge.

"Mom...is at...Pineridge?" Michael said, his voice shaking.

"Yes, Michael, I'm so sorry I didn't tell you. Please forgive me."

"I do dad, it's okay. I understand." Although in his heart he was angry. For the last two years his mother had been so close Michael could almost walk to her. All the times he had been bullied and made fun of and his mother had been twenty miles away. All the times over the last two years Michael had wished he could see her and tell her how his day had been and she was only a quick car ride away. Michael did not feel angry, he felt enraged, but he also knew more important things were going on now so he decided not to waste time yelling at his dad.

"But why tell me now, after two years?" Michael had an idea about that, but he wanted to hear it from his father first.

"Well, it's your story. From last night. It's the same type of thing your mother was talking about towards the end. She spoke of other worlds, strange creatures. She was mostly incoherent, but some things were clear. I thought they were just signs of a breakdown. But…" He trailed off.

Now Michael understood. The face on the crest of the red door, a red door a world away in a castle, and on that crest the image of his mother. Now he was certain; the face on the crest did belong to his mother, but why was it there? Michael knew only his mother could answer that. Father and son sat in silence until they arrived at Pineridge.

CHAPTER 7

▼

JUDITH

The building stood large and white upon a hill overlooking a small lake. The wrought iron fence Mr. Smith and Michael now waited at bore the name "Pineridge" spelled in gold letters across it. A long road wound up the hill to the front of the building, then back down the other way to the street. It seemed quaint on the outside, but Michael had a deep feeling of dread mixed with excitement as they drove slowly through the iron gate and up the road to Pineridge.

They drove around to the back of the building and parked in the designated visitor's parking lot. As they walked around to the front door of Pineridge, Mr. Smith put his arm around his son's shoulders and looked at him sadly. Michael knew it was hard for his father to bring him here, as if it shamed Mr. Smith for his son to see his mother in such a condition.

The automatic door leading to the front hall of Pineridge opened lethargically, and Michael and his father went in. Mr. Smith approached the small glass window on the left wall leaving Michael to look at the different paintings adorning the walls of the entrance hall of Pineridge. He saw one painting of two men in a small fishing boat, silhouetted upon a bright orange sunset. He saw another one of a flock of geese soaring over a lake. Another depicted a small boy holding a teddy bear with an innocent look on his face. He also noticed the smell. Even here, in the lobby, the hospital carried the stink of disinfectant and gauze bandages, like something slowly going rotten. Michael was examining another painting which looked vaguely familiar when his father approached him.

"Her room is on the second floor, Michael. I think you should have fair warning…" He paused, and looked anxiously at his son.

"She is not the same woman you remember. She is very different now. Don't be scared." said Mr. Smith.

"I'll be fine dad," said Michael, not sure if he really believed himself. Mr. Smith nodded and again put his arm around Michael's shoulder, leading him to the elevator. A doctor approached them. Michael noticed the man had very fine white hair and walked with a limp.

"Hello, Mr. Smith," said the doctor.

"Hi, Dr. Taft. How is Judith?" said Mr. Smith. Michael remembered hearing the doctor's name last night. He now realized that his father must have called the hospital to set up an appointment.

"Same as always, just fine," said the Doctor with a yellow toothed smile. "Please, this way," he said, motioning for father and son to follow him to the elevator.

They waited perhaps one minute when the door clunked open and they stepped inside. After a quick ride, the doors opened again. Michael gazed down a hallway that was like all the others he had seen in his life. It stretched straight ahead until it stopped at a window on the far end. The sunlight cast a ray through the window and onto the floor, giving the empty hallway a very warm feeling. Spaced along the hallway were crayon drawings hung on the walls, which Michael assumed had been done by the residents. He saw one of a blue bird surrounded by puffy clouds. As they slowly continued down the hall, Michael surveyed another picture of what looked like a large elephant (although it was really nothing more than a grey blotch) with an egg on its back. As the pair neared the last door on the left, Michael saw a drawing that startled him very much. It was a crayon drawing of a bee, only much larger than a normal bee, and it had a huge black shaft protruding from its bottom. The face of the bee in the drawling was pitch-black and seemed to have been colored very roughly. In the middle of the black face tiny white eyes peered out like snow flakes on blacktop. Michael knew it was a drawing of Bartlebug. He said nothing to his father.

They now stood in front of the last door on the left and Michael could feel the sun from the window falling on his shoulders. Mr. Smith looked down at his son, an exchange of preparation passed between them briefly, and then Mr. Smith rapped on the door gently. Doctor Taft waited patiently at the other end of the hallway.

"Enter," said a woman's voice from the other side; it sounded weak. Although he had not seen or heard his mother in over two years, Michael knew the voice belonged to her. Mr. Smith turned the door handle and pushed the door open carefully.

The room was not what Michael had expected. When he thought of a mental hospital, images of white walls and padded rooms crept into his mind. Now, standing in the doorway of his mother's room, all those images washed away. The room was not large, but very quaint. Its single occupant was his mother, now seated facing away from the visitors on the small bed in the corner. A little wooden table with two chairs stood comically in the center of the room. Another chair rested in the corner opposite the bed. The bed itself sat against the wall to Michael's right. Instead of stark white, the walls were papered with blue wallpaper featuring hot air balloons. Michael was reminded of a child's room, seeing the small desk and wallpaper. He noticed an adjacent door on the left wall, which he assumed was the bathroom. Oddly, Michael noticed there was nothing else in the room besides the table, chairs, and bed. No television, no radio, no books, no paper. He again assumed that someone brought everything his mother needed to her.

After scanning the room, Michael's eyes rested on his mother. She had not, in spite of his father's warnings, changed much in two years. Looking at her back from the doorway, Michael saw her long blonde hair, tattered and wavy instead of straight as she always kept it. She wore blue pants and a shirt, but not a hospital gown, Michael noticed. Her outfit appeared to be made of some other, much more comfortable material than a hospital gown. With her legs crossed, hands folded neatly in her lap; Judith stared out of the small window on the far wall of the room.

"Judith…" managed Mr. Smith. "Judith, Michael is here to see you," he finished.

At the sound of her son's name, Judith slowly turned from the window and looked directly at Michael. Now Michael knew what his father was talking about. Her face was much, much older as if instead of aging two years it had been ten. She had deep dark rings under her eyes. To Michael, it looked like she had been given two black eyes. When she realized it was her son standing before her, she managed a small smile revealing a set of perfectly straight, although dirty, teeth. Michael always remembered his mother as having beautiful white teeth, and he couldn't help but reveal his shock at seeing her smile. Now, in Pineridge sitting on her little bed, she looked nothing like the exquisite woman Michael had gazed upon on the crest of that huge red door. But still, he knew that woman and his mother were one in the same.

"Hallo Michael," said Judith softly. Her eyes seemed to look through Michael instead of at him, and they were filled with a far away gaze. And what was that word she had used? Michael was unsure, but he thought it sounded like "Hallo." He pondered this word for a moment and assumed his mother meant "hello."

"Come here, Michael." Michael glanced up at his father, who nodded his approval, and Michael slowly approached the bed on which his mother sat. She seemed very calm. In fact, she seemed almost too calm. Still she looked at Michael with those far away eyes, as if she could see something magnificent on the horizon. As Michael rounded the bed, Judith slowly reached up with her hand and took Michael's in hers. The feel of his mother's skin was exactly as Michael remembered it. He felt a spring of joy rising in his heart to be back with her. He sat down quietly next to his mother.

"Michael, the sky was blue, was it not?" said Judith.

Michael didn't understand the question, but nodded, to his mother's approval. "And the roses? I remember my first time using it…" she said dreamily. "That's why she does it, because I showed her." Michael wasn't sure what to think, or what Judith was talking about, but he was surprised. His mother had just mentioned a rose field and a blue sky. Now Michael thought she could be referring to the other world, which certainly was not out of the question.

"Mom, I…I've seen the roses…" said Michael, unsure of himself. Judith furrowed her eyebrows slowly, eyeing her son. She looked very puzzled. She began to rub the back of Michael's hand.

"Oh, have you then? Pretty aren't they? I always loved them so…" she said, continuing to rub Michael's hand.

"And that's not all. Mom. I…saw lots of things…A pretty girl was in the roses…she talked to me. And I saw a castle, and a thing I think was a bumblebee, and he talked to me too, Mom." At the mention of the bee Judith's look changed from dazed and far away to very concerned.

"A bee you say? Was it large? Black face and white eyes? Did it have a sting? What did his voice sound like? What about the marking?" The questions came very quickly, Michael nodding yes to some and looking confused about others while Mr. Smith waited at the doorway, wishing he had not brought Michael to this god-awful place.

"Yes, Mom. He brought me to the castle and I knew I was in trouble. I didn't like him, Mom. Right from the start I knew I didn't like him. He took me to a huge village and in the middle was a giant castle and we went inside and up a huge staircase. But I knew what was going to happen, so I escaped Mom, before he could bring me through the red doors."

Judith listened intently to this tale with focus Michael had not yet seen during this visit.

"And Mom, I saw…on the door…Mom…it was you I saw…your face…on the door…" Michael looked up at his mother. Judith's face relaxed as did her grip on Michael's hand, then her face melted into a soft smile.

"Royal chambers…I remember." she said. "Wonderful days, yes, yes." She let out a sigh, and looked again at Michael.

"Michael, my son, the bee. Awful creature. Stay away from him. Don't trust him," said Judith.

"No, never. I knew he was bad," replied Michael. Now Judith furrowed her eyebrows again, as if she wanted to ask a question.

"Michael, how did you go?" at first Michael didn't understand. After a few seconds he realized she wanted to know about shifting. He told her. He told her about the bathroom the first time, on the verge of tears because he missed his mother, and about in the bathroom the second time, about to give up and eat tuna; but not as good as his mother had made, and finally about the third time outside the red doors, looking at his mother's face. And finally Michael knew. He knew what he should have known all along, the reason why he was shifting, and the key to controlling it; each shift had been catalyzed by thoughts of his mother. Why had he not seen it before?

Judith smiled, understanding spreading across her face like sunlight illuminating a shadow.

"Peter," said Judith, glancing back at her ex-husband. "Could you possibly give us a moment?" she said dreamily.

"Alright Judith, but please…don't do anything…"

"You have nothing to fear. The time has finally come. Please," she said to Peter. Michael could hear a change in his mother's voice. It no longer had that far away quality but instead a sort of rejoicing, as if Christmas had finally come. Peter looked sternly at Michael, then backed out of the room and quietly closed the door. Once Peter left, Judith continued, but Michael was certain something about her had changed. She did not seem dreamy and distant any longer. Her eyes, which moments ago had been glazed and droopy, now intently focused.

"Michael, they put me in this place two years ago because of that creature you met, Bartlebug." Michael blinked at the blunt mention of the thing's name.

"I knew no one would believe me. I tried to make them believe me but eventually I had to give up…You see, I swore never to go back after I fled my home, never to return to BlanchField, but I did, and I discovered something terrible…" Michael was unsure what his mother was talking about and she was talking so fast. He just continued to listen.

"I knew I couldn't convince anyone there so I came here and tried…then they locked me away," said Judith, looking around the room miserably, "But it has been for the best." Then she looked directly into her son's eyes.

"Michael, do you understand, my son? You have been to Serafina, Michael," she said, the happiness spilling into her words. "The world I once fled from, the world I swore never to go back to…but still did, despite my resolve. I will never forgive myself for my absence in your life, Michael, but you must believe me, I truly had no choice."

"Mom, wait," said Michael abruptly. "Please, can you start from the beginning? I told you what happened to me. Please tell me what happened to you," he said seriously.

Judith paused, and took a deep breath. "Very well, my son. You deserve to know the story in its entirety, having been to Serafina. Michael, listen and listen well, for now that you know, the wheels of fate have begun to spin and time is growing short. The beginning then," said Judith, her voice wavering, preparing herself to tell her son the true nature of the woman he called mother and of the extraordinary responsibility he must now bear.

CHAPTER 8

▼

THE COMING STORM

Bartlebug scoured BlanchField in search of the treacherous Smith. He looked in every Blacksmith shop he knew, interrogated the owners and workers alike, threatened some with his sting, but to no avail. No blacksmith in the Kingdom had seen the boy. Day by day Bartlebug grew more impatient. Not since the mysterious disappearance of the Queen had someone been able to elude his wrath. He expanded his search, disregarding his duties in the palace. He searched the streets, the pubs, the shops. He searched the slums, the hospital, the tailors, any shop or hospice he could find. He searched outside of the village as well, where he had first seen the boy in Mya's Fabrication, but nothing. Bartlebug had even questioned Princess Mya herself on one of these desperate excursions, but she could not remember meeting a boy named Michael, although Bartlebug thought she was lying; too much of her mother in her.

These tedious excursions did nothing to quell the rage building in Bartlebug. The last thing he needed now was a hindrance, a thorn in his side, while the final preparations were made.

Now, sitting in his cold and drafty quarters, Bartlebug amused himself with thoughts about the coming storm. He thought about what had happened years ago and his face grew sour. He had been ready then, all the pieces in place but then they had fallen…

He pushed these thoughts away; they did not matter. Instead, he thought about the future and disregarded the past. Soon, everything would be right again. After meticulous plotting and planning, he had found a way to…return. This thought made him smile and the fire burning in the hearth cast shadows on his sooty face. He liked that word. It was appropriate. Indeed he would return. Earlier than he would have liked-time was not his ally anymore-but that did not matter.

Bartlebug sighed, exhausted. The entire day had been spent searching for the Smith, and he had found nothing. He cursed himself for allowing the child to escape. Bartlebug knew Michael Smith was odd somehow. Something about the boy made Bartlebug's skin crawl, some inkling of dread and wonderment. These feelings led Bartlebug to the conclusion that the Smith was dangerous. He knew these feelings did not come often, and when they did, he knew to trust them. Bartlebug furrowed his brow, deep in thought, trying to decide what to do once he found the boy, and the answer seemed more than obvious. He had to find him, and kill him; it was as simple as that. He had searched all of BlanchField and found nothing, but he would not give up. He would wait; the boy was sure to turn up somewhere. Until then, he would continue with everything as it was, eagerly awaiting the coming storm.

CHAPTER 9

▼

LILLIAN

As Bartlebug began his search for Michael, Judith began a story. A story that would forever change her son's life, for better or worse, she did not know. She began where she promised she would, at the beginning.

"Michael, I am not from this world, from Earth. I was born in Serafina. That is the name of the world you have seen with your own eyes and the world I truly call home. Ever since I was a young girl, I was special; different. I am of the Line of the Fabricantress. As a child, a member of the order discovered me and told me I had…abilities. In Serafina, there is a very powerful force known as the Fabricant, a force used when The Word is spoken. Throughout history, few have been able to use it, and those that could rose in power and prestige in the blink of an eye; half because they were revered, and half because they were feared. Those born with these abilities all came from a single lineage, the Line of Fabricantress."

Judith paused and looked at her son. He seemed perfectly fine, listening to her story as any child would listen to any story before bed. She continued.

"You see Michael, the Fabricant allows the Fabricationer to create *anything* she can imagine, the power to make something from nothing. All it takes is a little concentration and a single utterance of The Word and anything imagined becomes real."

"The Word?" interjected Michael.

"Yes Michael. The Word is what gives the Fabricant substance. Simply thinking is not enough, the desire must be voiced, must be spoken. It is a power which flows through and out of those who can use it, given wing when The Word is spoken."

"Can you show me?" asked Michael.

Judith shook her head and half smiled.

"I am sorry Michael, The Fabricant has no place here on Earth and therefore I cannot use my powers in this realm."

Michael nodded, the story made sense to him thus far.

"The Fabricant is a very powerful gift Michael, as I am sure you can understand. Ever since I was a child, I was trained to use this power. For years my teachers instructed me on how to use my gift, the Cardinal Rules, The Word, and many other things; it was they who reared me and trained me as a Fabricantress. In fact, I learned later that no one as young as I had ever been able to use the Fabricant. Indeed, I was special. As a child, I used to create toys to play with, dolls, and horses, things like that. As I grew older, I was educated in the ways of the Fabricant and realized what a potent and awesome power I possessed," she paused and looked at Michael. He seemed to be taking all this very well, remaining calm, and hearing what she had to say.

"My Fabrication abilities grew so powerful, I was able to create anything I imagined; I simply spoke and it became real, from the smallest Kel to an entire army."

"Kel?" asked Michael.

"Kel is currency in Serafina, like dollars here," said Judith. Michael nodded and she continued.

"You can see what kind of power I had to live with, Michael. I was revered by my people almost as a god, feared and worshiped. My power was so great, I soon began to experiment Fabricating things even more ambitious than armies and cities. I began to think of other worlds, Michael. As I soon discovered, not even the Fabricant is powerful enough to create an entire world...." She stared off, looking solemn and uncertain about this last statement.

Judith paused and looked briefly to the window. Concern splashed across her face then was gone in an instant. Michael barely noticed it.

"However, I did discover a hidden facet of the Fabricant, something none before me had discovered."

Now Michael was exceptionally intrigued.

"What was it Mom? What did you find out?" he asked.

"I discovered the Fabricant could be used to travel between worlds."

Michael had been half expecting this answer. Now he understood. He looked at his mother with awe and understanding.

"I believe that is what you experienced in the bathroom, Michael...although you are male, perhaps it was..." She trailed off, her eyes seeming to search for an answer to a question only she could hear. Michael thought she looked like someone trying to work out a difficult puzzle. After a few seconds, she shook her head and looked again at Michael.

"You see, although the Fabricant cannot be used on Earth, it seems there are places where the fabric between the two worlds grows thin and some of the power from Serafina seeps through. Perhaps you have the power to diminish the barrier between this world and Serafina and this is why you are able to travel back and forth, but I cannot be certain." She paused.

"I suppose it doesn't matter. What matters is that you found your way to Serafina. My prayers to the Seraphim have been answered."

"Wow Mom, I had no idea there was a name for it, Fabricant you said? This power only girls can use. Is that what I used?"

"Not exactly. Although I used the Fabricant to travel between worlds, I believe you have been able to cross over because, like I said, you have thinned the wall between worlds."

"Wow, so I can't use the Fabricant, but I can shift."

Judith nodded.

"An interesting word to use Michael," she added.

"I called it shifting because that's what it felt like. I just had no idea " he said, staring out the window.

"Shifting...that is a good word, Michael, you are very smart," she said. "Anyway, when I was twenty years old and at the peek of my Fabrication power, I shifted, as you call it, for the first time. I shifted here Michael, to this world. And I fell in love. This place seemed so different from Serafina; this Earth. I made many journeys between this world and mine, always making sure no one suspected anything. It was extremely difficult to keep my ability a secret, but I knew I had to. You can see the implications of a power such as this, can't you Michael?

You see, in Serafina, there are five Kingdoms, the OverPowers; BlanchField; my home, Cliffendale, Bouresque, HapMarcom, and LochBarren. If any one of them had found out what I could do, they could have used me to come here and then...I don't know what they may have done. So I kept it secret, shifting whenever I was supposed to be out of town, or if I was alone in my chambers. I began to understand how to travel in this world so I would always end up where I wanted in my world. I found certain landmarks that corresponded to places in Serafina. I became consumed with Earth."

She paused. Michael thought about the last time he shifted. He had arrived in the Thrift Save, not the boys' bathroom, because he had traveled in Serafina. One thing, however, still troubled him.

"Mom, when I shifted back to Earth, it was like I traveled further than I really did…" Michael wasn't sure if he got his message across, but he saw his mother smile and nod and assumed she understood what he meant.

"Yes, that sounds about right. When I fist started shifting, as you call it, I soon discovered that distance was not the same here as on Serafina. If you travel a mile while in Serafina, you travel five on Earth. Do you understand?"

Michael thought he did.

"Go on, Mom," said Michael. Judith nodded and continued her tale.

"When I was twenty-five, I was married to Charles Silverworth VanVargot in my world. He was a prince then. I loved him so, Michael, and I still do, with all my heart."

Michael had been listening intently, accepting everything his mother said, but suddenly he felt angry. His mom was married to some Prince in a different world? What about his father? Did she not love him? Was it all a game to her, Michael's world simply a play thing for her to use as she pleased, his life nothing but an enjoyable distraction from her precious Serafina? Judith saw the anger in Michael's face and patted his hand, smiling softly.

"Michael, don't misunderstand. I love Peter. I do, dearly. He is my life; my life here. Charles is my life there; in Serafina. I know it is difficult to understand, Michael, but it is as if I am two different people. Here, on Earth, I am Judith Smith, loving wife and mother. In Serafina, I am Queen Lillian VanVargot."

Michael blinked and looked at his mother, surprised. His mom, a queen? It sounded crazy. Then again, Michael thought about the face on the red door in that castle and how it had been his mother.

Her story made sense. The face on the other red door must have been her husband, Charles VanVargot, King of BlanchField.

"You're a queen, Mom?" asked Michael.

"Yes, my son, yes. I ruled along side my beloved Charles and there was peace in my kingdom. Until the day I was betrayed, and forced to hide here forever, on Earth. I had to Michael. I had to make everyone believe I was insane, but I think you now know, in your heart, I am not."

"Then why do it Mom? Why leave us and allow yourself to be locked away in here for two years?" asked Michael.

"To protect my family, to protect you and your father. I knew that if Bartlebug ever found me, he would not only hurt me but the ones I love as well. You see, I discovered a sinister plot," Judith trailed off, brow furrowing, worry flooding her eyes. She shrugged

"After I caught wind of what Bartlebug was planning in Serafina, he cooked up another plan to be rid of me, to betray me and in essence sign my death sentence. At this, he succeeded but I was able to escape in the end. I knew he would not stop searching for me. So I came here for good, one last journey across the worlds. The only way to protect you was for me to be here, at Pineridge…he is always searching," she said, her eyes taking on that dejected, far away look.

Michael could see the sadness of this harsh reality in those eyes. He felt his heart twist, and it filled with sadness and love for his mother. He loved her now more than ever. He loved that she was confiding in him, her only son. He loved her for being honest with him, even if she could not be honest with anyone else. He was able to see past the initial anger he felt at her saying she was married in Serafina. Michael knew his mother loved him. He could see that now as he stared into her magnificent blue eyes and that was all that mattered.

"What happened Mom?" said Michael, now voicing a question he had wanted to ask since her mother mentioned being betrayed.

"With Bartlebug, what did he do?" Judith bit her lower lip, as if debating whether or not to tell Michael the answer to his question. She decided he needed to know.

"He tricked me into using the Fabricant in the Forbidden Way. When using the Fabricant, there are Cardinal Rules which must always be obeyed. I was taught these rules by the Line of the Fabricantress' women as a young girl and will never forget them," she trailed off. Michael waited for her to continue. She closed her eyes and began speaking.

> *"To act with greed shows not the course; one's humble life must be enforced.*
>
> *To act with hate shows not the way; one's life of love must rule the day.*
>
> *To act with pride shows not the path; humility will achieve the task.*
>
> *To act with fury shows not the road; patience only will carry the load.*
>
> *Above all these, one truest rule; Protect all life, all innocence, all souls.*
>
> *For power in the Fabricant lies; to help, not hurt; not forsake, but guide."*

Judith slowly opened her eyes and looked at her son.

"The Forbidden Way is murder, Michael. You see, Serafina's history is filled with the abuse of power…" Judith paused and decided not to go into it. "Using the Fabricant for murder is grounds not only for death, but eternal strife. Bartlebug tricked me into killing someone Michael, killing someone with the Fabricant. I am a murderer Michael. I've killed a man," she said, tears now welling in her blue eyes.

"But Mom, if it was a trick, you aren't really a murderer, right?" asked Michael.

"I'm afraid it's not that simple my son. There are no lawyers like your father in Serafina. There is no judicial system. There is only the King's decree. His brother's life weighed more heavily upon his heart than my life, and so he sentenced me to death and damnation…although I'm sure Bartlebug's voice rang in his ears more than once. I spent three days locked in the cold dungeon of Castle BlanchField, trying to decide what to do, trying to decide if I could ever really leave Serafina behind. In the end, I knew I had to. I used my powers and came here the night before my execution; that was four years ago, when you were just a boy. I planned to never return to Serafina, but I did….and perhaps that was a mistake. Before your father and I split up, I often crossed over to Serafina…to see what Bartlebug was up to and to see Mya…" A small smile crept across Judith's face. Michael noticed a strong sadness in that smile, like his mother had just remembered something joyous and sad at the same time.

"Anyway, I felt Bartlebug was planning something big and I think I got too close…That was two years ago. In fact, I shifted, as you call it, the day before the divorce trial and I have been here since, hiding from Bartlebug's wrath. All this time, Michael, I prayed you might somehow discover Serafina and be able to help me. It seems my prayers have been answered," Judith concluded, with a great deal of relief in her voice.

Michael had millions of questions he needed answers to, but one in particular floated at the top of his mind.

"Mom, you killed your husband's brother?" asked Michael gravely.

"Yes. I Fabricated a sword inside his heart. It appeared already in his body, and he died. Of course, I didn't know all of this was really happening. Bartlebug used his poison to deceit me. I thought I was dreaming…only a dream. I often had dreams of using the Fabricant in strange ways. I was sure as soon as the sword materialized I would awake in a cold sweat, but my awakening never came. Only the urgent screams of the King's Ambassador, Bartlebug, yelling that the Queen had murdered King Charles' brother, William, with the Fabricant. I will never forget his tiny white eyes staring at me as I was brought before my husband for judgment. Bartlebug had hovered there, just above the King's shoulder, and I knew he was smiling. I just knew."

Michael didn't know what to say. He simply stared at his mother and they both knew what the other was feeling. Words were unnecessary.

"Michael, there is one more thing I must tell you, something very important, but I want your father to hear it as well. Please fetch him, will you?" she asked suddenly.

"Sure Mom, sure," said Michael rising from the bed. He walked to the door, looking back at his mother over his shoulder. Their eyes met, and a connection was made in their gazes, something substantial and warm; a great love of mother for son and son for mother. Michael wanted to go back to the bed and sit with his mother, but he pushed away the feeling and went to the hall to get his dad. Peter sat in a small chair on the opposite wall from Judith's room, Dr. Taft speaking to him softly. Michael asked him to come in and Peter Smith looked at Dr. Taft, who nodded his head. Father and son went back into the room.

"Is everything alright Judith? Michael?" asked Mr. Smith. He removed his glasses and rubbed them with his shirt. He looked haggard, tired and worn out. This visit had taken a lot out of him. He looked at his son and Judith.

"Peter, Michael, I am not insane. Peter, everything I have ever said to you is true." Peter rolled his eyes. He had had just about enough of this visit and wished his wife would stop spitting these lies. Judith motioned for Michael to come to her, and she placed her

hands on his shoulders, her eyes boring into his with urgent serious-
ness.

"There is something you both must hear. I was married in Serafina. To a man named Charles Silverworth VanVargot," Judith
could already see the anger building in Peter, but she continued,
"and a few years prior to my escape from Serafina, we had a daughter. Her name is Mya."

Michael's eyes lit up at the sound of the name and he remembered the girl he had met in the rose field. She had said her name
was Mya…was it the same girl? If so, then she was his sister. He had
always wanted a sister. Judith continued, "It was while she was
growing up I first began visiting Earth, and I met you Peter, and fell
in love again. It was strange, from the moment I saw you something
told me you were unique…" she paused, hoping Peter would not be
angry. She looked at him and his face told her everything. He didn't
believe her. She decided to prove it to him. "Michael, I want you to
shift right now. I want your father to see that everything is true."

"What Judith? What are you talking about? This is my
son….our son and I will not have him participating in your insane
delusions," said Peter, crossing his arms over his chest in typical
fatherly fashion.

"Peter, please, I'm not…"

"Mom, stop. Dad, sit down over there. Please, trust me Dad.
Just sit," said Michael.

"Michael, this is ridiculous. I don't want you believing these fan-
tasies. You're out of line," said Peter.

"Fine, stay there then," said Michael.

He took his mother's hand. Already he could feel how much easier it was for him to shift with his mother. Almost immediately the
world began to shimmer and sway. Peter Smith became blurry. The
door behind him lost all definition; the figure of Dr. Taft became
only a shadow in the hallway. He could feel himself losing contact

with his mother's hand. He squeezed it, wishing not to leave her side, but he knew he had to. As Earth fully faded away, he could still see the look of shock in his father's eyes.

CHAPTER 10

▼

A History Lesson

He was standing somewhere cold and dark. He could feel water soaking into his jeans, and a slight chill breeze touched his cheek. He could see nothing; the room was pitch black, so Michael groped around in the dark. His hand landed on something large to his right. The object felt like rough wood and it felt and cold. He took a deep breath and tried to decide what to do. Of course, shift back and be with his parents. He had been here long enough to convince his father of his ability and besides, his fear of this black void of a place was growing. He closed his eyes and thoughts of his mother filled his head along with fond memories of certain senses and smells. He tried but nothing happened. Perhaps because of his fear, or the darkness, he simply could not shift. Michael tried once more, just to be certain, and again, nothing happened. He decided he needed to be somewhere more open in order to shift. He looked blindly around, and then felt his hair rustle. Follow the wind, he thought. It will lead to something. He did and sure enough, after nearly tripping on something hard on the floor, he found the source of the wind and a small sliver of light, barely noticeable. He thought maybe this was a door, so he pushed on the wall and it swung, slowly and loudly, open. Candlelight flooded the room. Looking back, Michael saw what he had tripped on, a large crowbar left in the middle of what appeared to be a wine cellar. All along the walls were stacked neat rows of glass wine bottles just like the ones his father kept on the wine rack in their kitchen. In the corner was a large wooden barrel with an emblem of a snake dancing with a lion and the initials L.B. Michael walked through the door.

He now found himself in a large kitchen. Spreading out in front of him like sentinels stood one row of three huge wooden tables neatly cleaned and stacked with plates. On either side of the tables large stoves lumbered bulkily, but they more resembled open pits of charcoal than the stove in Michael's own kitchen. Above each, opened a hole in the ceiling. Only one was open, the rest were closed with a small square piece of wood. Michael looked, but saw no refrigeration unit of any kind. Large chandeliers hung above each of the three long, wooden tables but they were not lit. The kitchen rested quietly, deserted. Michael was not sure where he was, but he had an idea; the castle. He thought about the geography of it for moment and came to the conclusion that it made sense. Pineridge was not far from his school and he remembered passing the Thrift Save on the way so he figured it made sense that shifting in his mother's room would take him here, which was not a good place to be. Bartlebug was probably buzzing around here someplace. He tried again to shift, and again failed. He did not understand why it had been so easy in his mother's room, and now so difficult. He still felt anxious, and he thought maybe that was the reason. If he could find a way out of the castle, into the open air, maybe he would feel safer and be able to shift.

He looked to his right and saw a large doorway, so he decided to try that. The adjacent room was enormous; the largest room Michael had ever seen. There were at least seventy tables, just as large as the three in the kitchen, sitting in the room. On each one dinnerware was set with incredible attention to detail. Plates, bowls, napkins, silverware, (and some gold-ware), candelabras, various dishes and ornate jugs, and an amazing array of many other things Michael had never seen before. Then the thought occurred to him that there was most likely a reason for all this preparation; dinner time. He thought the best course of action now would be to get out of this kitchen before the entire castle arrived for their nightly meal. Just as he was looking for a way out, the large wooden double doors on the other side of the room opened with a loud creak. Michael looked left and right, and then dived under the table closest to him just as ten chefs were entering the room.

"Rabbit tonight then?" asked one voice.

"Right, right. And string peas. They can never get enough of 'em," replied a different voice.

"Which wine did the King request Malcolm?" asked a third voice.

"LaChatlier Four," said yet a fourth.

From under the table Michael could just barely see the tops of the men's heads and they appeared to be wearing the same kind of chef hats Michael had seen the guys on television wearing sometimes.

"Good then. The maids 'ave already set the tables. Right," said one of the men, Michael was having difficulty telling one voice from another. Now the men were closer to Michael, making their way to the kitchen he presumed.

"And dessert, Roy?"

"Cream and Cake 'o course, the King's favorite; I suppose it's everyone's favorite really."

A few seconds later and the chefs walked past Michael's table and into the kitchen. He noticed they all wore the same kind of shoes, brown leather boots with tuffs of fur in scattered places They also wore long white gowns.

Once the men were in the kitchen, Michael, crawling from under one table to another, made his way to the door through which the cooks had entered. He listened for any sound, but could only hear the dull lull of voices from the kitchen and the occasional bang of a pot. He stood up and quietly crept out the door, which the chefs had neglected to close.

The door led to a rather plain looking hallway. A blue, thin carpet ran down the center and the walls were lined with candles and a few paintings. Slowly, Michael made his way down the hall. So far so good, he thought. He had not heard anything since leaving the dining hall. There was a right hand turn up ahead and Michael crept along the wall to peer around.

He poked his head around the corner and found his face pressed into the belly of a very large man. Michael nearly fell over.

"Well, sorry 'bout that mate. Here, you alright then?" said the man.

"Yes, um, fine thank you," said Michael. He thought he was toast.

"Didn't mean to bump you like that, I was just on me way to the dining room. Like to get there early, get the good stuff while it's still hot, you know?" said the man. His face stretched as he cracked a large and jovial smile. "Name's Dunmire, but folk 'round here call me Dunny." Dunny thrust out his large hand and Michael, standing at stomach height against this giant, took it. Michael's entire palm was concealed in Dunny's.

"Michael Smith," said Michael.

"A blacksmith's son then? Very good, very good. You'd best be careful young lad. The whole kingdom is looking for a blacksmith now. That little bugger Bartlebug's been sayin' a blacksmith's son tried to kill the princess! Ha! What nonsense. But no use in goin' against that little flyin' buzzer," said Dunny, crossing his massive arms over chest.

"Why not?" said Michael. He was a little scared now, but not because of Dunny. Obviously this man was not very bright, or he would have discovered Michael was the one they were looking for. But then again, maybe he did know.

"Well, because, Michael. He is the King's-hand, his Ambassador." Dunny took special care to pronounce the word *ambassador* very clearly. "And, they say he knows some…magic." Dunny whispered this last word as if it was something forbidden, and looked around cautiously.

"Magic?" asked Michael.

"Shhhh! Don't be tellin no one I even mentioned it. No one has seen or used *It* since the Days of Wonders. Don't they teach you nothin' in yer history class?"

"Well, I don't think we have gotten to the   Days of Wonders yet."

"Oh, well then let me tell you, work up me appetite. Long ago, *It*, you know, the *M* word, was commonplace. Everybody could use it a little. The folks who were more powerful would get high places, like being an ambassador or an advisor. In fact, me great-great-great-grand dad could do some things, like make the fire so hot it could forge a sword in minutes. There was a name for this power…what was it…oh well, can't remember. Anyway, folks who were really powerful could not keep all their spells and such things by themselves. They needed help and assistance. But they did not trust normal folk. Quite a fix they were in. It was right around that time, like an answer to their prayers that the Bargouls showed up." Dunny paused, as if in thought.

"The Bargouls? What are they?" asked Michael. This was all fascinating to him, this new world, with things like magic and forges, and huge dining rooms. He was beginning to enjoy himself, and forgetting that he was a wanted boy, if only for a few scarce moments.

Finally Dunny looked up. "Well, the Bargouls are the bee-creatures. Bartlebug is a Bargoul. The powerful folk now had an answer to their problem. They soon found these Bargouls were really bright and could remember anything. So the people who were good at using *It* made a pact with the Bargouls. Each person would get a Bargoul as an assistant, to remember spells, help make new ones and such, and in return, the Bargouls would be given what ever they wanted. A life 'o luxury, as some say. In fact, some believe those who could use the power…what was it called…actually created the Bargouls to serve them. No one knows where they come from, but it seems they have taken to LochBarren as their home these days. A great many over there." Dunny shook his head.

"Okay, so what happened, are there still magicans today, because I would….."

"Shhhh! Don'a say that out loud!! Such things are not uttered so freely!" said Dunny, looking around nervously.

"Why?" asked Michael.

"I'm about to tell ya. Anyway, the Bargouls were told all the…M's secrets, you know, spells, incantations, secret words, so the M's wouldn't have to remember everything. Lazy buggers. Well there was one M, I dare not speak his name, who felt he was so powerful that 'e deserved to rule all of Serafina. So he began hurting people and using his powers in Forbidden Ways. Many Bargouls and many M's followed him. There was a great war, but the M's were stopped. A few of the Bargouls who sided with the bad M's are still around today, and I mean a real few. Bartlebug is one of them."

"But if this happened so long ago, how can the Bargouls still be alive?"

"Don't know. Maybe some of the M's glammer rubbed off on 'em. Just can't be sure."

"Okay, then why is Bartlebug the….Kings-Hand?"

"Oh, he was found innocent of all charges, as were all the other Bargouls who survived. The rest are scattered about the place, most went to LochBarren. Yeah, King VanVargot says he sees no harm in old Bartlebug now. Humph. I should not be one to question the King's judgment, but I don't think Bartlebug is innocent at all. He was probably the ring leader, if you catch my meaning. I seen him lad, buzzin' about the castle, lookin' mighty grim and gone, if you ask me. Anyway, as I said I hoped to do, I have conjured a good appetite, so if you'll be excusing me, Michael, I want a good seat!" Dunny turned away from Michael and continued down the blue carpeted hall to the dining room, whistling, with his massive hands behind is back.

Michael was intrigued by Dunny's story; so full of magic and betrayal, and Kings; it occupied his thoughts as he quietly crept down the hall. He imagined himself in a time like the one Dunny had spoken of, performing fabulous magical tricks, casting spells, becoming a King. Then he realized he was in that time right now. The only part Michael left out of his imaginings was the Bargouls; he hadn't liked Bartlebug from the moment he first laid eyes on him in the rose field. Now that he had heard Dunny's story, Michael agreed with the big man. He thought Bartlebug was not as good as the King thought. In fact, Michael was sure of it.

Now he came to another junction and observed two paths, one going right, the other left, and a large stone wall in front. Michael was right handed so he went that way. This new hall had the same blue carpet, except now instead of paintings there were large windows imbedded in the stone walls. Looking out, Michael saw that it was almost dark. Michael remembered it was currently morning on Earth, so he assumed a time difference existed in Serafina as well as a travel distance; or perhaps one was the cause of the other. He would have to ask his mother about that when he got back. Billowing out in front of each window like large boat sails fluttered light blue curtains in the open windows. The night breeze was pushing them out into the hall. Michael considered trying to climb out one of the windows, but they were too high. Regardless, it was a pretty sight, something Michael was sure had come straight out of his Medieval history chapter in school. He continued down this hallway quietly and still saw no one, save Dunny. At the end of the hall stood a large green door. He noticed a symbol like the one he had seen in the wine cellar, except this one featured a snake dancing with a lion and the initials B.F. Seeing no other alternative, Michael decided to try the door. Perhaps he would get lucky and this door would take him outside. Michael grasped the handle and pushed.

As soon as he opened the door, he wished he had gone left. There in front of him stretched a long wooden table, elaborately decorated with candles, instruments, maps, and in the center, a globe. There were men sitting around the table, all very large and important looking, wearing various robes and armor, and at the head at the far end of the room sat King VanVargot. Buzzing above his right shoulder was Bartlebug.

Michael looked around confused, hoping the men would mistake him for a lost servant or something.

"You there, get out at once. You have no business here!!" shouted one of the men around the table. He had long blonde hair, almost golden, and his eyes were sunken in deep.

"Yes sir," muttered Michael. His heart soared. He would be alright; they didn't know who he was. They just wanted to get back to their meeting. Just as he was turning to leave, he noticed Bartlebug whisper something in the King's ear. Michael knew the game was up. He was found out. Why couldn't he shift in the wine cellar?

"Wait boy," bellowed the King. Michael froze; he didn't know what to do. "Come hither," demanded the King. Michael had no choice but to obey so he walked down the right hand side of the room until he was standing next to King Charles. His large, regal chair was three times as tall as Michael, and the King seemed like a giant, all the while Bartlebug hovered there, watching. Michael saw his black, sooty face and his pin-pricks of white eyes and in those eyes he saw vengeance and fury.

"Tell me truthfully now boy or be condemned. Is your name Michael, the Smith?" asked the King. His face was hidden behind a bushy white beard, sprouting down from his head of snow white hair which flowed back down his neck. Atop his head sat a beautiful crown, adorned with rubies and garnets, diamonds and sapphires. His eyes were a keen, brilliant blue. Michael saw the power and authority there, and although he tried not to, his fear overpowered him and he spoke.

"Yes ...," He croaked.

Bartlebug smiled.

"You, then, are the one who attempted to harm my daughter. For this, you are condemned to death. Three days, and you will be no more. Guard!" yelled the King.

The next few moments were a blur for Michael. First, he was standing with the King, and then he was surrounded by huge, muscular men with swords.

"Hey, what…" was all he could manage. They grabbed him, scratched him, and pulled at him. Michael could feel himself becoming enraged. He struggled, trying to get away, but the guards were too big and the more he tried to struggle, the rougher they got with him. He didn't want this. He wanted to be back with his mother. He clenched his fists and gritted his teeth. He could almost feel the fire in his chest flickering, then roaring to life. Michael did not know where this feeling was coming from, this rage, this fiery anger. One of the guards grabbed Michael by the neck, and he tried to twist away but the guard's strength overcame him. Another guard grabbed Michael's legs, and held him suspended in the air. Michael clenched his fists harder. He could feel the fire consuming his whole body now, could feel it rising up with his anger. The boy's face became a contorted image of rage, and longing to be away from these people and back with his mother.

Suddenly, one of the guards dropped to the floor screaming. The men at the table let out gasps of shock. The man on the floor had been the one holding Michael's arm, the man who had been directly in front of Michael's fist when a large ball of fire shot from it. The guard, now rolling on the floor, clutched his chest, trying to put out the fire that was consuming him. Another ball shot from Michael's other fist, and went flying across the room and hit the wall. Michael was just as surprised as the people in the room, but his surprise only lasted a few moments until the world began to get fuzzy.

"Sire, this is not possible!!" exclaimed one of the men at the table, jumping from his seat to get a better look at the boy.

"Guards, restrain that boy!" shouted the King, rising from his throne.

"Did you see that Blake? Could this boy have the...I dare not even say the word."

"Oh for Seraphim's sake Lionel, simply say it. Magicant? It looks like it, indeed," said Blake. While the others jumped and shouted about the fire shooter, Blake just sat there and watched, calmly.

Michael had no idea how he had shot fire from his hands, but suddenly he felt more tired than ever in his life. He gave up the struggle. His eyelids were like bricks, and he swayed to and fro until collapsing on the floor in sheer exhaustion.

Everyone in the room was astounded. No one had seen anything like this display in their lifetimes, except Bartlebug. The same thought was on everyone's mind, but no one wanted to say anything. Finally, King Charles spoke.

"Lieges, no one is to spout a single utterance of the goings on in this chamber today. If word of this...episode got out, it could mean disaster for BlanchField. Are we in agreement?"

One by one, each man drew blood with the tip of his dagger, and signed their names on a parchment the King passed around. Sir Blake Geneon was the last.

"Well done. Guards, take this…boy to the dungeon," said King Charles. The guards that were left cautiously picked up the limp body of Michael Smith; afraid they would be burned by his touch, and carried him to a dark, dank, foul smelling cell. They dropped him on a small pile of hay in the corner, slammed the cold cell doors, and marched down the hallway; their footsteps echoing along the empty corridors.

▼

CHAPTER 11

UNEXPECTED
FEELINGS

Peter Smith had passed out. When he saw his only son Michael disappear before his eyes, as if becoming invisible, he simply could not bear it. The mental stress was too much, and he fainted. Judith called to Dr. Taft in the hallway, who took Peter to a spare bed in one of the rooms. Judith followed. They tried to wake him up, and about five minutes later he came to. By now Judith was wondering why Michael had not shifted back.

"Michael, I can't believe…" Peter sat up groggily, looked around, did not see his son, and that panicked look sprang back into his eyes. "Where is Michael? Michael! Michael!" he shouted, looking around the hospital room.

"Yes, Mrs. Smith, where is your son?" asked Dr. Taft, looking concerned.

"Oh, he just went down to the car. He will be back soon," said Judith, not wanting to receive too many questions from the doctor about the whereabouts of Michael. Peter said nothing.

"Alright, Judith. I will be back soon to check on you. Feel free to go back to your room," said Dr. Taft.

"Thank you doctor," said Judith. Peter just sat there on the bed, looking confused and annoyed.

"Judith. Where is Michael?" he whispered, after Dr. Taft was out of earshot.

"Michael is gone. He went to my world, to Serafina. You believe me now, don't you?" said Judith, taking her husband's hand in hers. The touch of her skin made Peter calm down, as though something about her touch soothed him, and made him understand. She looked at him with her large beautiful eyes, and he saw her hope. Those eyes had always told Peter exactly what he needed to know about his former wife. Right now, sitting here with her in this hospital room, the warm sun rays falling through the window, the soft skin of her hands on his, Peter felt like crying for the time she spent in this place. Right now, he knew she wasn't crazy, something told him to believe her. He wasn't sure if it was just the stress of seeing his son vanish in front of him, but what Judith was saying suddenly felt right. He couldn't explain it. Right now, he knew where Michael was. Right now, he believed everything that had ever come out of her mouth.

"Michael…went to your world? Well, is he alright?" asked Mr. Smith.

"Yes, I believe so. Though I am a little curious why he hasn't come back yet," said Judith, looking down.

"He went to…what did you say….Cherafina?"

"No, Serafina…it is where I…come from."

"Oh."

"And what about your other husband?" he asked sternly. She knew this would be difficult for him to understand, but she tried anyway.

"Peter, understand that in Serafina I am a different person. I don't even have the same name; I am called Lillian in Serafina. Anyway, it doesn't matter. I have always loved you, Peter."

"And what about your daughter, did you say her name was Mya?"

"Yes. She has the same blood in her veins as I…she is of the Line of the Fabricantress…that is why I believe Michael…"

Peter cut her off. "Alright, that's enough. I just don't know what to think." Then he gazed into Judith's eyes.

Everything seemed to clarify for him. He put aside he feelings of anger and jealously and he looked at Judith with new sight. He loved Michael. He wanted him back now, to be here, to share this moment. He also felt something else, something he had not felt in a long time; love. The feeling seemed to spring from nowhere and he simply had no explanation for it. He just looked at Judith and remembered the first time they had met, how beautiful she had looked, he blonde hair flowing all around her, the summer sun casting warmth upon her perfect features. Looking at her now, he knew he loved her still, at this moment, more than ever. He began to cry, and laugh at the same time. Judith moved beside him on the bed, and put her arm around his shoulders like she used to, kissed his head the way she used to, the same way she kissed King Charles's head as well, and wrapped her arms around Peter. "Everything will be alright, Peter," she whispered. Peter and Judith held each other for a long time.

▼

CHAPTER 12

ESCAPE ONCE MORE

Mya VanVargot was playing with Charlie as her mother and a man named Peter were crying together in a hospital in another world. Charlie was her horse. He was a real horse. He moved about by himself, neighed, and brushed his tail, only he was the size of a doll horse. Mya had made it, using the Fabricant. It was her favorite toy, but she found that lately she was growing tired of it, and quickly. She made it disappear and tried to think of something new to play with. The image of a white bunny rabbit popped into her mind, it was cute with long floppy ears and whiskers. She remembered her lessons about The Word, about the precise way in which it must be voiced, in order to fully control the Fabricant. She concentrated.

"Rabbit."

This was all it took, a single word, and the image Mya had fostered in her mind faded into existence before her, every detail accurate to what she had been imagining. Mya watched the bunny hop around, found it dull, and made it disappear. She always wondered why the disappearing part never required The Word. Next she Fabricated a little stuffed doll. She imagined a velvet little girl, dressed like she was, large eyes and dirty blonde hair.

"Doll." Her voice took on a different tone when she used The Word, authoritative and deep, commanding and delicate at the same time; a voice to be obeyed. The doll appeared before her exactly as she had imagined it. There was no question Mya was exceptional in her use of the Fabricant. Others-although few existed now-had the most trouble with speaking The Word. They simply could not Fabricate what they imagined because they could not speak The Word properly and often their creations would come out deformed and frightening. Mya, however, was a true prodigy.

Mya spent the next few minutes sitting crossed-legged on the floor of her large chambers, Fabricating little toys, and then watching them vanish. She was bored, mostly with life in the castle. Her father didn't let her go very far outside. The rose field was about it, and only because it had been her mother's and it was safe. But Mya longed for more. Although young-and only just beginning her studies at the Cerulean School-she already felt poised and ready for bigger things. Her thoughts were interrupted by a loud bang on the door.

"Enter," she called. Her Father, King VanVargot, entered the room.

"Hallo father," said Mya politely. "What brings you here?" she inquired.

"Mya, we captured the boy who tried to harm you. He walked right into my meeting chamber, in the middle of a counsel of Sires. Can you believe that, my dear daughter?" said Charles, laughing, holding his large hands against his stomach.

"But father, I…he…" said Mya, searching for what to say. She wasn't sure what he was talking about, but she had some idea. She guessed the boy her father was talking about was the same boy she had met in the rose field yesterday. He had done nothing wrong. He was just…odd. Mya looked confused.

"He is in the dungeon, will be dead within three days," said Charles, stooping down and holding his hand under Mya's chin. He kissed her lightly on the head and left.

"But Father!" said Mya as the King was leaving.

"Yes?" he asked, turning around.

"The boy did not harm me…" she said.

"Don't be silly Mya. No need to try and protect the rouge. He will be dealt with properly." With that, King Charles left.

Mya decided she would have to go see the boy for herself and find out why he had been in the rose field and what all this business was about harming her. She suspected Bartlebug had something to do with it.

She made her way to the dungeon, stopping only once to enjoy the smell of dinner as she passed the dining hall. She sometimes wished she could eat in there, rather than having her meal brought to her room.

"Oi, Princess Mya, what 'r you doin' 'ere?" asked the dungeon keeper as Mya came around the corner leading to the dungeon.

"I am here to visit one of the prisoners at my Father's request;" she lied "Now let me in."

"Right then Princess. No use me question'in a Princess like ya'sef then," said the man, moving to one side and allowing Mya to enter the long corridor of holding cells.

"Michael is his name, I believe. Which cell is he in?" asked Mya.

"Yes, the boy was brought'en earlier t'day. Last one on the left, Princess."

"Thank you," said Mya.

She walked down the row of cells, looking into some, looking away from others. The smell was putrid down here. She did not like it one bit, but sometimes she had to come down here. Her Father often brought her here, telling her that a good Princess must rule over all, including the criminals. They all knew who she was here, and they were sure not to taunt her, or they would be dead within the hour. Mya was not afraid.

When she finally came to the cell, she looked in and saw a small crumpled figure lying on the hay, the only thing in the cell. The cell itself was tiny, no more than a small square. The walls were purposefully constructed of hard stone and brick, and the cell was always cold. The bars were an ugly rusted brown color.

"Boy," said Mya, placing her hands on her small hips. "Boy," she said again, more loudly. Michael roused, and rolled over to the other side so as to face Mya. His face was scratched and bloody in some places, and Mya could see large welts springing up in some places on his exposed arms. She considered something, and then decided. She concentrated, closed her eyes, and in seconds she was holding a white silk handkerchief. Michael thought that he was so groggy he simply didn't see the girl remove the handkerchief from her pocket.

"Here," she said, dropping the handkerchief between the bars and into the cell.

Michael stretched out a hand, grabbed the hanky, and began to wipe his face with it.

"Thank you," he said. "Hey, you look familiar; we've met before haven't we?" asked Michael.

"Yes, we have, in my field of roses just the other day. You appeared out of thin air on my tree stump," said Mya.

"That's right, the first time I shifted. I remember now."

"The first time you what?" asked Mya.

"Oh, nothing, sorry. My name is Michael Smith."

"My name is Mya VanVargot, Princess of BlanchField and hence you will refer to me as Princess," said Mya sternly.

At last Michael's head cleared and he realized exactly who he was talking to. This was Mya, the girl his mother had told him about, the girl he had met in the field of roses. This was his half-sister.

"VanVargot," whispered Michael, looking up and into the eyes of Mya. For a split second, he saw his mother, Judith standing before him, only thirty years younger. "Mya…VanVargot. You are…we…" Michael was cut off before he could finish.

"Do you have something to say boy or are you just going to stand there stuttering like the village idiot."

"Yes, I have so much to say, so much to tell you!" said Michael, smiling, but before he could continue, a loud voice rang out in the dirty prison.

"Mya!" shouted a voice that could only have been King Charles, which drowned out what Michael was trying to say.

"Mya, please, tell him I did nothing to harm you. Please Mya! They're gonna to kill me!" pleaded Michael as King Charles charged down the corridor. Mya looked around, stunned and bewildered.

"Mya, what are you doing here? Trying to be attacked again? Return to your chambers at once!" shouted King Charles.

"Yes father," said Mya, with a side-long glance at Michael. Michael saw her eyes. They said I'm sorry.

"And as for you," said the King, turning to Michael. "You will be dead by dawn!" he stormed away.

Michael fell down on the hay pile. This whole excursion had only been to prove to Peter that what Judith had said was true, and now it seemed that Michael was going to die. He could not let that happen. He had to shift, and he had to shift now.

He closed his eyes, and concentrated with all his being. He thought of his parents, and nothing. He imagined the smell of his mother's hand soap, her perfume, the way the sun would shine on her face. Still, nothing. He thought of his father, his smell, and his bright eyes. Michael was becoming frustrated and angry. This had been so easy before. Why couldn't he do it now? He tried, harder and harder. Nothing happened, and he grew more and more angry. He was not sure where all of this sudden rage was coming from.

Finally, he slammed his hand down onto the pile of hay, in a gesture of rage and conceit. He furrowed his brow and clenched his teeth. Eyes closed, he smelled something burning. Slowly, he opened his eyes, and looked down. The patch of hay under his hand was on fire. He pulled his hand away, and saw that his palm was on fire too. At first he thought that his hand was going to burn, but upon closer inspection he found that the small flame was hovering above his palm, as if being cradled in his hand, but still he felt no heat or pain. Then he remembered what had happened in the King's room. He had somehow shot fire balls out of his hands. He looked at the tongue hovering silently above his hand, amazed and a little scared. Michael was certain he had made this fire appear and he assumed it happened when he got angry. It made sense. He continued staring at the fire until at last he came to the conclusion that indeed he could control it. He didn't know why, or how, but he could control fire. It came from his anger, his raw emotion. He thought that now he knew a way out of this cell. He would simply melt the lock.

Slowly Michael crept to the bars. He tried to look down the narrow hallway outside of his cell, but he could not see very far down the corridor. He would have to assume the guard had his back to him. He looked at the row of bars in front of him, trying to find the lock. He found it. It was a small, old fashioned lock with a large keyhole like the ones Michael had seen cartoon characters looking through on Saturday morning cartoons. He poked his hand through the bars and grabbed the lock. He held it in his right hand, and closed his eyes. He started to get angry. He thought about those guards who had hit and cut him. He thought about Bartlebug, and how much he hated that little bee. He thought about Jacob Niles. He thought about whoever had put his book bag in the toilet. He thought about all the times when people had treated him badly at school, made fun of him, called him names, thrown things at him, tripped him in the hallway, taken his food at lunch. Suddenly, he felt something hot and oily hit his hand. He opened his eyes, and found the lock was melting. A small ball of fire engulfed it, hovering around the lock in mid air. Michael quickly removed his hands, and the fire stayed around the lock. He watched the lock melt away into nothing, and when it was completely gone the fire disappeared to. Michael glanced around the cell and noticed the handkerchief Mya had given him was gone as well. He quietly grasped the bars, and opened the cell.

His assumption proved to be true when he glanced down the corridor to find the guard sitting on a small stool facing away from Michael. He looked to the other end of the corridor and saw only a huge stone wall. He didn't think he would be able to burn through the wall so that left him with only one option. He crept slowly down the row of cells, hoping none of the other prisoners would shout anything to the guard. Luckily they didn't. When he got within a few feet of the guard, he heard snoring. Michael couldn't help but smile. He thought this was just like in a movie, the convict escapes while the inept guard is asleep. He thought that was just fine.

He tiptoed past the guard and was soon ascending the spiral staircase leading back to the castle.

CHAPTER 13

▼

SOMETHING'S HAPPENED

Judith and Peter were very worried. After dealing with Dr. Taft, the two had gone back to Judith's room in hopes Michael would appear, would shift back to Earth. However, their hopes began to wane when Peter's watch told them Michael had been gone for nearly two hours. Judith knew something was wrong. She paced back and forth in her small room while Peter massaged his forehead.

"Judith, he still isn't back," said Peter, running his hands through his thick black hair.

"I know Pete. Something must have happened." Peter just looked down at the floor, scared for his son and wondering where he could be.

CHAPTER 14

▼

EXIT

Indeed, something had happened, something awful, but now Michael Smith began to understand that it was only awful to begin with. Now, what he began to realize as he silently crept through the quiet stone corridors, was that he had some kind of special power. Not only could he shift back and forth between Serafina and Earth, but he could somehow control fire; and he liked it. He liked knowing that he was different, that he could do something no one else could do, assuming no one else could. As he turned another corner, he couldn't help but remember what that man Dunny had told him about magic. The word had seemed so foreign to Michael the first time Dunny had used it, like something out of a fairy tale, something imaginary and insubstantial. Now, the word magic seemed extremely appropriate and extremely real. Making fire appear in the palm of his hand sure seemed like magic to Michael. The castle was a myriad of corridors and staircases, winding hallways and cold, empty rooms. Michael felt as though he had been creeping through the castle for hours. Several people had passed him by without giving him a second glance, for which he was very thankful. He also saw several Bargouls on his trek, his heart instantly racing each time he saw one in fear it would be Bartlebug, but it never was. At last Michael reached a much larger hallway and followed it until it ended into a very large hall, very much like the entrance hall, but not quite as big.

Michael looked up and there, standing before him, was a large wooden door. It was massive; nearly forty feet tall. Michael looked around the edges of the door and noticed another, regular sized, adjacent to the large one. He made his way over to this smaller door, making sure to remain quiet and unseen. Thankfully, the hall appeared empty. When he got there, he placed his ear to the door and heard nothing. He slowly opened it.

The door opened inward and the small room beyond surprised Michael. The only thing in the room was a huge wooden handle and a massive gear set in the stone floor. There was a slit in the wall on the opposite side of the room. Michael walked over to it and peered through. What he saw was the country side. It was vast. The rolling hills seemed to stretch for miles, the blue sky was like an ocean, and the clouds were sail boats. A few sparse cottages and homes were scattered here and there along a windy dirt road which led straight to the massive wooden door. Michael soon realized this was the back end of BlanchField, the opposite side. Michael was curious why no one guarded this end of the castle. In fact, it appeared there was no one here at all, but that didn't matter. Michael had to get out of the castle and this was his best chance. He knew as soon as he made it outside in the open air he would be able to shift, and then find his way back to his mother's hospital room. He reached for the wooden handle and pulled.

CHAPTER 15

▼

TO SERAFINA

"I'm going back, Peter. That's it. I have to find our son," Judith told her husband, placing her hands on her hips. Peter looked distraught.

"Judith, I have kept you in here against your will long enough. If all you have said is true, and I believe it is, then go right ahead. You have to do what you have to do. But remember, I will be here, and I will always be in love with you," said Peter looking up at her from the bed. Judith shook her head.

"Peter, no. I mean I want you to come with me." Peter's eyes widened.

"Judith, I don't know. I'm a lawyer, not a knight in shining armor…." Peter said, looking to the floor.

"You don't need to be…just trust me," said Judith, moving across the room to him, laying her hands on his shoulders. He raised his head, and looked into her beautiful face. He could see trust and understanding in those eyes. He wasn't sure about this, but if they could find Michael, he was willing to do what Judith wanted.

"Let's go then," he said smiling.

Judith nodded, took his hand, and told him to close his eyes and think about her. She firmly held his hand in hers, and thought about home; about Serafina, about Mya, about the castle, about Charles. Slowly they both began to fade, shift, and lose focus. Peter had never felt anything like it before. It was as though everything was coming loose. Then suddenly, the room was empty and only the soft light pouring in through the window was left.

▼

CAPTURE

The large gear in the small room slowly began to turn after Michael pulled the lever. The huge wooden doors began to open. He looked at them lumber to the sides as he left the room. The doors groaned open, the light slowly breaking through from outside like a ray of hope for Michael. He stood in front of them waiting. Finally, after what seemed like an eternity, the doors opened enough for Michael to be able to get through. The light was bright and for a moment Michael couldn't see, but then he did. There hovering, right in front of him, was Bartlebug; that pudgy black face with those tiny white eyes pierced him. He looked furious.

Without thinking, Michael turned to run.

"Where will you go, boy?" yelled the high pitched voice of Bartlebug. As Michael turned around, guards appeared from all the connecting corridors, doors flew open around the perimeter of the room and more guards poured in through them. There must have been fifty. At one end of the room, a door opened. Michael stood dazed in the center of this hall; he turned and saw Bartlebug, sting protruding, behind him, and the royal guard in front of him. He was getting angry; he could feel the fire starting to burn. Then he lost it. From the door that had opened came his mother and father. They were bound together at the waist with rope. Michael could see they were nearly unconscious. He could feel his limbs get heavy and he just stood there. He thought they must have shifted over to find him and somehow gotten caught. He cursed himself for not returning sooner.

"Mom! Dad!" shouted Michael, his eyes welling with tears.

"Just as I thought," said Bartlebug. "Your parents then? Sneaking into the castle seems to be a family affair! Too bad your parents were foolish enough to sneak in right in the middle of dinner! Pathetic paupers, always trying to steal food."

Bartlebug floated over so he was just behind Michael.

"You dare insult the King, infiltrate his palace, and presume to use the Forbidden Art! I think not! You shall pay for your crimes, Smith. In fact, you and all your kin shall pay!"

Bartlebug motioned and the guard holding Judith (*Lillian*) and Peter roughly took them away, dragging them across the stony floor and through a dark tunnel.

"Leave them alone! Mom! Dad!" Michael was hysterical, afraid for his parents. He did not know what to do. He tried to muster the fire of his anger, to produce that fire, to make it real like before, but his tears drowned any hope of even a spark.

"And as for you, your fate lies in the far-lands. Farewell to thee, Smith. Get him out of my sight." The scorn and hatred in Bartlebug's pesky bee voice was unmistakable. Michael would not easily forget the resonance of that voice inside his head. The last thing Michael felt was something hard crunching the back of his skull. The pain was sudden and immense, and he knew he was going to black out. As he fell to the floor, as the veil of consciousness gave way to the murky blackness of unconsciousness, he heard Bartlebug's voice again.

"Loch Barren will suit him fine. In fact, I shall deliver him per-sonally." The Bargoul's smile was nearly audible. Michael gave in, and was swept away into darkness.

CHAPTER 17

▼

ON THE SHORES OF THE EMERALD OCEAN

"Who are you?" The voice seemed distant and wavy inside Michael's head. The boy felt weak, and tired. Once consciousness slowly began to creep back into Michael, he realized he was lying down on something soft. He heard sounds, but could not place any of them. He opened his eyes, and found he did not recognize his surroundings. As his eyes adjusted and the pain in his head began to register, Michael zeroed in on one sound inparticualar; a familiar buzzing sound. Michael looked in the direction of the voice, and saw a Bargoul. Michael was on guard immediately.

"Boy, I will not ask you again. Your name?" said the Bargoul. His plump bee body lowered even closer to Michael's face.

"Michael," he was able to mutter.

"Well, take my hand young Michael," replied the Bargoul. Michael hesitated, not wanting to trust one of these awful little creatures. "It's quite alright. I'm not going to harm you," he said.

Michael held out his hand, and the Bargoul took it, flying backwards and pulling Michael to his feet with surprising strength. The Bargoul's body consisted of blue and orange hues black appendages, a black face and tiny white eyes, the colors almost too vivid. Although the Bargoul's eyes looked like the same white specks as Bartlebug's, Michael saw something else in them. He wasn't quite sure what it was.

"Alright then, my name is Phillip," said the Bargoul.

Michael simply stared at the Bargoul, Phillip, and then looked around. He was on a beach of some sort but the sand was far from yellow. Instead, it stretched for miles in a track of burgundy, like a beach with carpet, and felt more like silk than sand. The massive ocean which greeted the beach at the shore shone in the bright day light with a brilliant deep greenish-blue color, and to Michael it looked like glass, clear and shinning, rather than water. The waves crashed to the shore the same way they did on Earth, and made the same sound. To Michael, this scene was beautiful, the colors perfect compliments for each other. He felt that if he looked too long he would be lost in the landscape forever. Gone, too, was the familiar smell of sea salt in the air. The beach smelled wildflowers, sweet and intoxicating. The sound of the waves was rhythmic, almost hypnotic.

"I see you are upset young man," said Phillip.

Finally Michael awoke from his torpor and looked at Phillip.

"Yes. I'm a little disoriented right now. Where am I?" asked Michael.

"You have not heard of the magnificent shores of the So'liloquy, the famous beaches of LochBarren?"

"No, sorry. I guess you could say I'm new around here."

Michael suddenly remembered what had happened in the castle with his parents.

"Do you have any idea where I can find Bartlebug?" asked Michael, memory and anger rising at the same moment.

Phillip could not hide his shocked expression and he looked around quickly.

"That is a name not so loudly proclaimed in these parts. He is evil, or so some believe. Although others seem to have taken up his cause, whatever that may be. I don't like to get involved. He came from this land, LochBarren, as did all Bargouls, or so they say. Many here are allies of his, but some, like yours truly, have chosen a different path. So you say you are new to these parts?"

"Yes."

"I see," said the Bargoul Phillip. He looked Michael up and down with his tiny white pin-prick eyes.

"I need to get back to King VanVargot's castle. Is that far from here?" Michael was finished staring into the landscape and talking to this Bargoul. He needed to go back, before Bartlebug did something horrible.

In response to Michael's question, Phillip at first looked strangely at the boy then began, as far as Michael could tell, to laugh out loud. It was by no means funny to Michael.

"BlanchField you mean? My boy, I'm afraid BlanchField is half-way around the world from here!"

The color drained from Michael's face and his legs felt limp. Half way around the world? That was impossible, how did he get here then?

"How did I end up here then?"

"You mentioned Bartlebug, right? I'm sure he has some sly tricks up his little sleeves, very surely indeed," said Phillip looking off toward the green sea.

"So are you saying there is no way back?" Michael was beginning to feel desperate and afraid.

"I'm afraid not young man, unless you want to spend the next few months on a Vessel."

"A Vessel?"

"Well what else could you use to cross the Emerald Ocean?"

A ship, thought Michael, he is referring to a ship.

Michael was about to ask Phillip a few more questions when an incredibly loud noise made both boy and Bargoul whip around and look toward the green hills in the distance. They both observed a wispy tendril of smoke rising from beyond the hills, not far away.

"That will be Quixitix. Seems that dark plume always lingers above *his* home, what with all of his experiments and such."

"Experiments?" Michael was intrigued.

"Yes. He is an inventor. Have you ever heard of the Castabuliea? Or the Three-sided square? No?"

Michael's blank expression was answer enough.

"Where *did* you say you were from boy?"

"Far away."

Phillip did not seem convinced. He gestured for Michael to follow him and the two made their way off the beach and onto a small dirt path. Phillip pointed to the road.

"This will take you to Aside, the nearest and dearest village," he said with a smile.

"Quixitix lives there. I'm sure you will be able to find some answers there; perhaps you could even inquire about a Vessel. Well, it was nice to make your acquaintance young lad and the best of luck to you."

"Aren't you coming?" said Michael.

"No, I must remain here, on the So'liloquy."

"How come?"

"I am a Wave Watcher," he said, beaming.

"What does that mean?"

"What does it sound like? I read the waves, tell fortunes, predict the weather; all sorts of things. It is a very important job indeed."

"Can you tell my fortune?"

"Well, since this is your maiden visit to LochBarren, I will grant this wish."

Phillip floated high into the air, wings buzzing, and gazed toward the glass-green water. Michael looked also, listening to the *crash-whoosh; crash-whoosh* sounds the waves made. After a few minutes, the Bargoul lowered himself and addressed Michael.

"A very interesting fortune indeed young man. The waves are very big today, which means you will achieve great things. Loud also. I must say, however, I have never seen a tide quite like the one today. It is intriguing. I don't know what to make of it, the tide seems to be…splitting. It is new to me."

Michael looked at the Bargoul with an expression of sarcastic disbelief.

"Almost as good as a fortune cookie," he said.

"A what? A cookie that tells fortunes! Have never heard of this either! You must tell me more! Where do they come from?" Phillip grew more and more excited with each sentence.

Michael laughed.

"I will bring you one sometime Phillip. Thank you for the fortune."

Phillip accepted this answer, but still looked disappointed. He nodded.

"Okay, well thanks Phillip. Maybe I will see you again sometime."

"Perhaps young Michael."

Phillip bowed, as did Michael, and the Bargoul floated toward the sea. Michael set off down the dirt path, in the direction of Aside.

CHAPTER 18

▼

ASIDE

Unfamiliar smells accompanied music played on what sounded to Michael like a flute instrument, although it was much more melodic than anything he had ever heard. The boy heard laughter, yelling, and what sounded unmistakably like explosions far off in the distance. He smelled bread and other food. His first impression of Aside told him it was a place where he would very much like to spend time. The buildings seemed old but extremely welcoming, almost as though the wood and stone themselves smiled down at Michael. No gate or doorway barred the entrance of Aside, just the worn road on which Michael had traveled from the beach leading directly into town. A small wooden sign stood just before the first buildings which said,

Aside: Home of Tranquility.

Michael liked the name very much.

Upon entering the small coastal town a friendly looking Bargoul greeted Michael, although Michael was still having a difficult time believing any of the Bargouls could be friendly after what Bartlebug had done.

"Hallo young fellow, welcome to Aside!"

"Thank you very much," said Michael.

"Is this your first time here? You seem like you hail from far away?"

"Yes it is. I came here from BlanchField."

The Bargoul hovered quietly, buzzing as the soft breeze made its way through the crowded street. "Indeed, that is far. How is it that you came to the shores of the So'liloquy?"

Michael thought for a moment. How had he gotten here? He didn't know. He just remembered the eyes of Bartlebug, the sound of his buzzing wings, which differed greatly from the friendly creature now conversing with him, and the long sting which protruded from his under-belly whenever he was agitated. That sting seemed to pierce the soft membrane of Michael's memory very often. He also remembered his parents and felt like crying. What happened to them? He did not know. He just had to assume they were alright, and try to find a way back to them.

"I'm not sure. I just woke up on the beach and found my way here. Do you know Professor Quixitix?"

The look of recognition on the Bargoul's face was unmistakable.

"Aye, yes I do. See that large plume of black smoke over yonder?" The Bargoul turned and pointed down the street and as he did Michael noticed something unusual about this Bargoul and thought he had seen the same thing somewhere before, but he couldn't put his finger on where. The Bargoul had a characteristic green marking on his hind side. To Michael, the symbol looked very familiar; almost like the Nike swoosh he had so often seen on sneakers. Only this symbol was a bit different.

"That is Quixitix' home. His home and laboratory I might add. He is always cooking up crazy inventions, aye; nearly always that black smoke seems to loom over his roof." The Bargoul laughed dryly. "I've heard his latest is some kind of flying contraption. If you ask me, the flying should be left to us and the humans ought to keep their feet on the ground. By the way, my name is Snyder."

The Bargoul Snyder motioned as though taking his cap off to Michael, a form of salutation. Michael had seen this action before and knew what it meant.

"Nice to meet you Snyder, I am Michael." He bowed.

"Well, I hope you enjoy yourself in Aside. It's a quiet little town, but it's home. Be seeing you then!"

"Thank you Snyder."

The Bargoul buzzed away and turned off the main street down another road. Michael did not see Snyder peer at him from around the corner, his friendly smile replaced with very sinister looking eyes.

Michael headed in the direction of Professor Quixitix' plume of black smoke, all the while thinking about what Snyder had said: A flying machine might be able to get him back to BlanchField, back to Bartlebug, and back to his parents.

As Michael walked the streets of Aside, the first thing that caught his eye was a beautifully decorated window. Michael stood in front of a building, staring open-mouthed at the display in its window. *"Rodney's Bakery"* said the sign above the door. Michael gazed helplessly at the spread of baked goods in the window. He saw pies larger than any he had ever seen, the crisscross crusts looked so delicious he could barely stand it. Loaves of bread, a few with steam still rising from the oven, sat in the window begging for Michael to eat them. Sweet rolls glazed with creamy white icing sat on a tray. Huge, elaborately designed cakes towered above the rest of the baked goods on white pedestals. Michael saw a few things he had never seen before, like one item which looked like a cross between a cupcake and a pie. Either way, it looked downright mouthwatering. Michael realized now, starring at Rodney's Bakery, how hungry he was. He couldn't remember the last time he had eaten, and his stomach demanded he enter the shop. He did.

The smell that greeted Michael Smith as he walked through the door of Rodney's caused the boy to instantly begin to salivate. The aroma was so intoxicating, Michael could not help but stand where he was and breathe it in; several times. He had been to bakeries before on Earth, but none like this. He was awestruck, and starving. He walked to the counter. A woman and her daughter stood talking to the man behind the counter. Michael waited patiently, eagerly gawking at the shelves upon shelves of fresh baked bread, rolls, pies, biscuits, buns, sweet rolls, and an amazing array of other delicacies.

"Will this be all then, Mrs. Mayweather?" asked the shopkeeper.

"Yes, Bill. Thank you very much," said Mrs. Mayweather.

"And what about your husband? How is he?"

"Just fine thank you, Bill. He is home with Trevor now, doing chores. Seems like those never end," she said.

The woman and the shopkeeper chuckled a bit.

"Indeed, indeed."

Michael heard the conversation, but his focus remained on the delicious looking food in front of him.

"Madeline, would you please carry these for me?" said the woman to her young daughter. The girl took the packages (Michael noticed one in the shape of a pie) and walked to the door. She stopped next to Michael.

"Hi," said Michael.

"Hi," said the girl.

"My name's Michael."

"I'm Madeline."

"Would you like some help with those?" asked Michael.

"Alright," said the girl.

Madeline handed Michael the pie shaped package and a bag. Michael peered inside and saw it was full of rolls. He could smell the aroma from the pie and his stomach made an audible growl.

"And who is this nice young man, Madeline?" Mrs. Mayweather had ended her conversation with Bill Rodney and prepared to leave the bakery.

"Mom, this is Michael. He wanted to help carry our things." Michael thought Madeline was perhaps six years old.

"Hello," said Michael, looking at Mrs. Mayweather. She seemed like an extraordinarily nice woman.

"Hallo young sir and thank you for your kindness. Our home is not far." Michael nodded. He hated leaving the bakery, but he thought perhaps these people would be kind enough to share some food with him if he helped them. The trio left Rodney's, Michael trying to hold onto that deliciously sweet smell as long as he could.

"Mom, do you think Daddy and Trevor will like the pie?" asked Madeline as they walked.

"I'm sure they will, dear. It is their favorite, sugarberry."

"My favorite too," said Madeline. "What kind do you like Michael?"

Michael feared he would say something that did not exist here, so he repeated what Madeline had said; sugarberry. Madeline smiled.

As they walked, Michael observed Aside; a truly lovely place, with shops scattered along the main streets, smoke rising from people's chimneys, children playing in the streets. Michael was reminded of Merchant's Row; the place Bartlebug had led him through on Michael's first visit to BlanchField. Aside reminded Michael of the village surrounding the castle, but this place seemed a great deal more…friendly.

"So Michael, do you live nearby?" asked Mrs. Mayweather, another question Michael was unprepared for, so he lied.

"I am staying with Professor Quixitix," he said.

"Really? Well, be careful around him. A strange fellow, harmless, but strange," said Mrs. Mayweather.

"Thank you, I will."

They turned a corner which led to a more rural area of Aside. The buildings were not so close together, and several of the homes had small fields next to them. A large farmhouse stood at the end of this street.

"Well, here we are," said Mrs. Mayweather when they reached the farmhouse. "Thank you very much for your time, Michael. Would you like to come inside and have a bite to eat before you go?"

Michael's face lit up.

"Yes, please. Thank you very much!" he said, overly excited. Madeline laughed.

"Okay. Right this way, please."

Mrs. Mayweather led Michael up the stairs and through the front door of the farmhouse, then into the kitchen. She motioned for him to have a seat at the wooden table and Michael did. He looked around.

The kitchen reminded Michael of the farm his grandparents had. Its warmth could be felt instantly, like being wrapped in a secure and warm blanket. Sunlight flowed in through the windows, casting a golden hue on the entire room. It smelled sweet as well, not as sweet as Rodney's Bakery, but sweet none the less. Michael also noticed how quiet it was. No traffic outside, no television or radio, just the sounds of Madeline and Mrs. Mayweather unpacking the baked goods. Michael smiled. This was the kind of place he could fall in love with.

"Would you like a slice of Sugarberry Pie then?" asked Mrs. Mayweather.

"That would be great," said Michael. He wasn't sure what Sugar-berry was, but it sounded good. Mrs. Mayweather nodded and opened the pie shaped package. Even from across the room, Michael could smell the pie, and his stomach growled again. Madeline brought Michael a plate, set two other places at the table, then ran off. A few moments later, Madeline returned with a boy about Michael's age.

"Hey, I'm Trevor," said the boy.

"Michael."

"Nice to meet you.' Trevor and Madeline sat down with Michael at the table, looking just as hungry.

At last, Mrs. Mayweather brought them all a slice of pie. The filling was deep red and Michael could not help but think of Mya's rose field. He smiled, and dug in with the utensil Mrs. Mayweather had given him-it looked like a fork but was a little different-and Michael had trouble describing it.

Never before in his short life had Michael tasted anything so wonderful. The sweetness of the pie at first tickled the inside of his mouth because he had never tasted something as sweet. The crust was warm and flaky, and it melted in his mouth. He devoured the slice well before Madeline and Trevor finished.

"My goodness Michael, you certainly were hungry. Would you like another slice?"

Michael could not resist.

"Yes, please," he said.

Mrs. Mayweather smiled and brought him a second slice. This one he ate more slowly, enjoying every bite. Mrs. Mayweather also poured the three children something white to drink and Michael guessed what it was. He took a sip, and the milk felt like silk in his mouth, perfectly smooth and delicious. Finally, Michael was done and he sat, stuffed, and happy.

"Thank you very much, Mrs. Mayweather. That was delicious."

"Yeah, thanks mom," said Madeline and Trevor together.

"Well, you're all welcome," she said.

Mrs. Mayweather came over to collect the plates, but before she could Michael got up and did it for her.

"Least I could do," he said. She thanked him.

"Well, I suppose I should be going now. Thank you again. It was nice meeting all of you."

"Nice to meet you, Michael," said Mrs. Mayweather.

"Nice meeting you," said Madeline and Trevor.

"Do you know the way to Quixitix' from here?" asked Mrs. Mayweather.

"Actually, no, I don't."

Mrs. Mayweather explained how to get back to town and which way to go. The directions were easy and Michael thought he would have no trouble finding his way.

"Thank you all again," said Michael, reaching the front door. The family said you're welcome and goodbye, and as Michael walked through the door, he regretted leaving the farm. The place seemed so loving and warm that he did not want to go. It took all his strength to walk out and not go running back in and ask the Mayweathers if he could stay just a little longer.

As the front door banged closed after Michael's departure, Mr. Mayweather entered the kitchen and heard the noise of the door.

"Who was that?" he asked his wife.

"A very nice young man named Michael," she said. "Helped me carry the baked goods home."

"Well then, he does sound nice. How 'bout some pie?" asked Mr. Mayweather with a smile. He sat down and ate.

▼

STRANGE
SURROUNDINGS

Mya VanVargot never liked Bartlebug. She always sensed some-thing…wrong about him, and she also knew he was aware of her true feelings. It seemed to her that recently Bartlebug behaved even more dark-hearted. Today, in her Fabrication, he came to her and asked her questions, as if he had any right. She lied to him of course, not because she wanted to protect that strange boy who had appeared on her stump, but to spite Bartlebug. She knew it was he who took mother away. She knew it was his fault because whenever he found her crying in the palace, she was sure she could see a little smirk appear on his black face. She hated him, but it didn't matter. Her mind was focused more on the boy in the jail cell, Michael. She couldn't stop thinking about him. She thought it might be guilt because she knew the boy had done nothing to harm her. She would have to find a way to convince her father of the boy's innocence.

Now, standing in her beautiful Fabrication taught to her by her mother, Mya reached down and plucked up one of the deep red roses and held it to her nose. Whenever she was sad about her mother, whenever she needed to be close to her even if it was only in her own mind, she would come here, to BleakField and Fabricate this rose field. It helped her remember her mother; Queen Lillian VanVargot, who had used her Fabrication abilities to murder Mya's Uncle, William. Of course, Mya knew this was not the entire story. After her mother's disappearance, Mya became sure of her innocence. She had wanted so badly for her mother to return, but she never had. Mya prayed every day and night for the return of her beloved mother to BlanchField, but her return never came. However, every so often Mya felt something, as though her mother was watching her. Mya never saw Lillian during these feelings, but somehow, the girl knew her mother was there. Now, all Mya had left of her mother was this beautiful Fabrication, like a precious heirloom; an inherited gift, passed on through blood. And she loved it dearly.

She put down the rose she had been smelling and fell down on her back softly among the soft roses. She didn't like thorns, so these flowers had none. As she looked up at the deep blue sky, she wanted it to snow. She closed her eyes, took a deep breath, relaxed, and imagined the beautiful white snow falling down from the heavens. She thought about the cold, but decided not to include the stinging chill into her Fabrication, just the snow, white and beautiful. She opened her eyes and a white snow flake landed gently on her cheek. She smiled, and put her arms behind her head. Her mother had not been able to create snow until she was seventeen. Mya was twelve. Her Fabrication powers were much more potent than her mother's had been. It made Mya happy to have so much of her mother in her. Mya had the same deep, brilliant eyes and flowing blonde hair as Lillian. And of course, she had the Fabricant. She loved using it, and she used it all the time; much more than her mother ever did, she was told. But she didn't care. She created toys, plants, weather, and even other children (although they were born of the mind of a child and did not usually resemble a human child). Once, she created a puppet of Bartlebug. It looked just like him, same white eyes, black face, and she beat that puppet so bad all the stitching and stuffing came out. After she was through with it, it vanished. Like everything else created by the Fabricant, once its purpose was fulfilled and the creator was through with it, The Word no longer held meaning or form and the creation would vanish like dust in the wind.

As the snow began to fall more heavily and cover the red roses, Mya continued thinking about Michael. She met the boy only a few days ago when she found him sitting on the tree stump in her Fabrication. She kept the stump in the Fabrication because it had once been a tree. Mya and her mother and father had taken a picnic in this beautiful rose field Fabrication one day long ago, and Queen Lillian had suggested they permanently mark the occasion. She found a tall oak tree and all three; Mya, Lillian and Charles carved their initials in the truck along with the royal emblem; a snake dancing with a lion and the initials B.F.; BlanchField. After the disappearance of Queen Lillian, Mya removed the tree from her version of the Fabrication and left only the stump, the tree held nothing but painfully joyous memories for her. That boy, Michael, had suddenly appeared there, on the stump. She was surprised at first, thinking she had some how Fabricated him, when she got closer and looked at him, he was very different from any Fabricated friend she had ever made. He had the same blue eyes as her, but his hair was dark brown. He wore funny clothes, nothing made of hide or leather.

Mya had asked his land of origin and that was her first encounter with the boy. The second seemed even stranger to her. She wanted to see him again, to find out why her father had accused him of harming her and sentenced him to death. She had sensed something was special about him, but she knew not what. She thought his tone of voice in the prison cell seemed so familiar, almost as though she had known him all her life. This annoyed her. But thinking back now, it seemed right somehow. She could remember the way his face looked when her father had caught the two of them talking, as though the boy knew something wonderful and needed to tell the world. She thought he had been about to tell her, but her father had ordered her out, and she went. She regretted leaving now. She wished she could have heard what the boy was going to say. She thought it might have been important.

Her thoughts about Michael were interrupted when she realized she could no longer feel the snow on her face. She had been thinking with her eyes closed, but now in the absence of her Fabricated snow, she opened them. She lost her breath.

Her rose field was gone, replaced by a small room she now occupied. The snow could no longer fall because of the ceiling she now saw above her. Mya observed the large rectangular panel on the ceiling and could not understand how it gave off light because she saw no candles of any kind. To Mya, it looked like lightning. She glanced around quickly, and noticed the odd white bowls hanging on the blue wall to her right. They had some sort of metal attachment at their head, with what, to Mya, looked like a lever. Michael would have easily recognized these objects as sinks. Mya looked behind her and saw three green doors side by side. She stood up. As she got to her feet she jumped when she saw another little girl standing directly in front of her. Mya didn't know what to think because this little girl looked and acted exactly like she did. If Mya moved her hand, so did the little girl in front of her. If Mya blinked, so did the little girl. Slowly, Mya approached the girl and the girl approached her. Mya now realized the little girl was her, a perfect copy, her twin. She stared at the image for several seconds, lost in thought. She felt something at that moment, something important, but before she could grasp it-whatever *it* was-it was gone. Breaking her daze, she looked around and saw that it was a large piece of

Twin Glass reflecting her image. She turned away from the image, dazzled; she had seen Twin Glass before, but nothing as large as this one. Mya's half brother would have called it a mirror. Mya noticed another door separate from the green ones and opened it. She peered out cautiously.

She now stood in a long corridor, but she knew it was not the castle. The floor was made of a material she did not recognize, definitely not stone. Mya observed what looked like, metal cabinets lining the walls. The purpose of these eluded Mya. She would have been surprised to learn one of the cabinets belonged to her half brother. The hall appeared empty, so she crept out of the bathroom silently. She tiptoed along the corridor, her footsteps making the slightest noise on the linoleum floor. As she went, she noticed other doors with glass in them but this glass did not reflect her. She could see through it. She looked and saw other children sitting in rows, and adults talking to them. Mya then realized where she had seen children like this before; at the Cerulean School. Mya had recently started her studies there. So she was in a school, but where?

Suddenly a loud noise pierced the silence, like a shriek owl, and the doors leading to the lessons burst open and children flooded out. Mya was caught in the torrent of oncoming children, being pushed this way and that, confused. She could not believe the number of children here, where were their parents? Some of them, Mya noticed, approached the metal cabinets, opened them, deposited some things, removed others, and went on their way. She thought she would try the same, so she made her way over to one of the metal cabinets and pulled on the silver handle. Nothing happened, so she pulled harder, still nothing. She could not figure it out.

"Hey, what are you doing to my locker?" Mya knew the question was directed toward her, so she glanced left to see a large boy with black hair coming toward her. "Get off," said the boy, nudging Mya away.

"How dare you shove me, boy! I am…"

"I don't really care who you are, because this is my locker and my stuff is inside, so you better just get away from me before I get really angry!" shouted the boy. Mya was shocked. No one had ever talked to her in this manner before. Did this degenerate not know who she was? Surely he realized she was Princess Mya VanVargot. Then why would he risk torture and talk to her in this way?

"Is there anything else little girl? Nice clothes, by the way. Tell your mother she should start shopping somewhere that doesn't sell clothes from a hundred years ago," said the boy, laughing.

"Jacob, who's that? Nice one by the way," said another boy approaching Jacob.

"I don't know Steve, a new girl looks like, dresses weird too. Later newbie."

"Loser," added Steve.

Jacob Niles and Steve Ash walked away together. Mya was shocked, hurt confused, and afraid. Where was she? What happened to her rose field, to the beautiful white snow, the blue sky? She wanted to go back, to be home in her field with thoughts of her mother. She had to close her eyes to hold back her tears, and then suddenly the noises from the crowded corridor stopped. She opened her eyes to see what had happened and realized she now stood in BleakField. Her Fabrication had gone of course, her attention being on her new surroundings, but now she was back, and a small smile crept onto her face. She wiped her eyes and headed back to the castle on a small pony she Fabricated. She was very frightened, and wondered if that boy, Michael, had any part in all of this.

CHAPTER 20

▼

NO TRIALS

"Sire, I have personally dispatched the boy and taken his kin as prisoners of the Kingdom. What will you have me do with them?"

The Bargoul Bartlebug spoke to King VanVargot, hovering below the throne. His sting was concealed, he rarely revealed it in front of the King, but his pin prick white eyes seemed to look through everything in the room, through even flesh into the very soul of the King himself.

"Do you know who they are?"

"Common folk, my Lord, nothing more. Most likely from the village or somewhere else in these parts. Unusual clothes though…."

"And what crime are they accused of?"

"Why treason, my Lord. They are the parents of the boy, Michael the Smith. And we both know how dangerous he is…"

"Indeed. Very well then. Have them executed."

Bartlebug smiled, and lowered his hovering body in a bow.

"Very well, my Lord," said Bartlebug. He proceeded out of the throne room, leaving the King in silence.

The cell which Michael Smith had occupied for a short time was now vacant. The adjacent cell, however, was not. Michael's parents now occupied it. Both were unconscious. They were badly bruised, beaten by the unrelenting Bartlebug. Their clothes were torn, and Peter's glasses had been broken long before. They were lying on coarse hay, the same as in Michael's cell, and the only sound was the steady *drip, drip* of water leaking through the rotten and moss-covered stone blocks. Peter Smith began to hear this drip as though fifteen miles away. Distant, yet steady, the drip slowly began to grow louder. Peter could feel himself awakening, could feel consciousness slipping back into his mind. Then he felt pain. His entire body ached. He did not know how this had happened. His first thought was that he was sore from playing tennis. He would have to go downstairs and find some Advil. First, he would check on Michael.

He slowly opened his eyes. Instead of the tan blanket on his bed, Peter saw hay. Opening his eyes further, he realized he was not lying on his bed at all but on the floor somewhere. It was hard wet with slime and felt like stone. He was very confused. He looked around and saw a woman lying on the cold stone floor next to him and everything came flying back like debris in a tornado. The hospital, his wife, the shifting, the castle, that weird bug thing, all of it flooded his memory banks. His eyes shot open.

"Judith, Judith wake up!" He shook her tenderly. "Judith!"

"Peter…" Her voice was groggy and far away.

"Judith, you have to wake up! We have to find Michael!"

The mention of her son's name was the tonic she needed to free herself of her unconscious rest. She whirled around and immediately realized where she was.

"Peter, this is the jail house. We are in a great deal of trouble. I don't think they have recognized me yet or I would probably be dead already. We have to get out of here. I still can't believe we crossed over in the middle of a crowded kitchen," said Judith very fast.

"You and me both. Too bad those cooks felt the need to call the guards," said Peter. Judith nodded and Peter continued.

"Can you do that shifting thing again; take us back to Earth?"

"Let's find out."

Judith closed her eyes, concentrating. Nothing happened. A few minutes went by, and still nothing.

"Hold onto me, Peter."

They embraced, and still nothing. She shook her head.

"I'm sorry; I don't know why I can't do it. It's usually so easy."

Peter looked worried. He scanned the cell, trying to find a way out, but could see nothing.

"Well, we will just have to wait for our trial and try to escape then. Or maybe we could even plead our case."

"Peter, you have to understand something. There are no lawyers in Serafina."

"Okay, then we will represent ourselves. I am a lawyer after all; the laws may be different here, but…"

She stopped him.

"Peter, King VanVargot *is* the law. There are no lawyers because there are no trials. The fact that we are here means we have already been sentenced to death."

Judith and Peter looked at each other, both sets of eyes swelling with fear and thoughts of their son, Michael.

CHAPTER 21

▼

PROFESSOR QUIXITIX AND THE MARVEL

The small wooden sign swaying lightly in the breeze coming in from the Emerald Ocean declared:

Laboratory and General Invention Hall of the Esteemed and Brilliant Professor Archibald P. Quixitix.

The building itself looked nearly the same as the rest on the main street, constructed of what looked to Michael like brick although the color was a much deeper red. Michael rubbed his stomach, still full from the Sugarberry Pie. He looked up at the building. It stood two stories tall with a shabby thatched roof, indeed, nothing special. In fact, it was the most dilapidated place in town by the looks of it. As Michael stood looking at the building, a loud and very frustrated voice rang out from inside.

"Confounded all!" The voice was followed by a loud crash, and the sound of glass breaking. Michael hesitated, and then knocked lightly on the stout wooden door.

"I have no time for visitors! Go away!" shouted the voice from beyond the door.

"Please, Professor, I need to speak to you," Michael pleaded. He heard another crash and another yell.

"I simply have not the time.... busy...very busy.... yes... I.... Thirteen? Perhaps, yes, that may be it...Or perhaps...no...." The voice trailed off, obviously losing track of the conversation with Michael and veering off into its own wild tangents.

Michael could not walk away. He needed Quixitix. He needed his help getting back to BlanchField. He had a feeling Quixitix was his only way back, his only way to find his parents, to save them if he could. Michael had tried several times to shift since arriving in Aside, and so far none of them had been successful. He did not know why he could no longer do it. Michael thought about his half sister, Mya, and cursed himself for not spitting this fact out to her when she was in front of him in the prison. He had to find her again, if only to tell her the truth. He had to get back.

"Professor! You must help me get back to BlanchField! You are my only hope! Please, Bartlebug has taken my parents and I have to find them!"

Michael pounded on the door, hoping that Quixitix would open it. For several moments he heard nothing but silence, no loud voice, no crashes. Then the sound of a chain clinking, a bolt sliding open, and the wooden door was pulled back a crack.

"BlanchField you say? Bartlebug? These names indeed pull my heart strings, young master."

Michael still could not see the owner of this voice, although in his head Michael pictured a crazy white haired scientist beyond the door, like the ones he had seen on television, large glasses, pointy nose and everything.

"Please Sir, you are my only way back," pleaded Michael.

"Very well. Please, come in and we may talk."

The door opened. Michael stepped inside.

The first thing he noticed was the smell. The inside of Quixitix' laboratory smelled like Levi Middle School. This brought back not so fond memories for Michael, specifically Jacob Niles and the constant torment he brought with him. Bottles, glass, and strange instruments were strewn about the place haphazardly. Michael noticed several large objects covered in tan cloth. A small metal cage sat in one corner of the room and in the cage rested a very exotic bird with feathers colored the deepest reds, greens, purples and blues. The bird made an odd sound as Michael stared at it. The Professor himself scurried about the room, picking up odd knick-knacks as he went. For a moment Michael thought it might have been a bad idea to come here, that this was just the home of a crazy old man, a man incapable of helping Michael in any way. Then Michael saw something that changed his mind completely, something he had seen everyday of his life before he knew Serafina even existed, something so common place no one would think twice about it on Earth. But here, it was magnificent…although something seemed odd about it, as though something was missing.

In the center of the room in which he now stood, encased in a small glass bubble at the top of a long metal stand, sat a soda can. Its presence here made Michael long fondly for his home, his world. So long had he been exposed to Serafina he was beginning to become accustomed to it. Now, this simple aluminum soda can made Michael realize that Earth still existed, that his room was still there, waiting for him. His comic books were still stacked neatly under his bed. His shirts still hung in his closet, his computer still hummed in the corner, and his homework was still waiting to be completed.

Professor Quixitix observed Michael staring, open mouthed, at the can; a reaction to which the Professor had become accustomed.

"Amazing, is it not? Is this the real reason why you have come, to see the Marvel? If so, I really don't have time to…"

"It's a soda can."

"A what can?"

"Soda, pop, whatever you want. Where did you get it?"

"I found it….aye…found it….near the sea….yes…"

Michael turned from the display and saw Professor Quixitix for the first time. His imagination had served him well. Quixitix was tall and lanky, he wore a long lab coat, which Michael thought would be white but Quixitix' was blue. His stringy and thin hair shot from his head at odd angles. Instead of the long nose Michael had imaged, Quixitix had a short, stout one. On it rested his large rimmed glasses. The Professor's face was dirty with soot in places.

"I love soda. Drink it all the time. How did an empty can of it get here?" said Michael.

"What is this soda you keep talking about, and why would you drink it? Is it a tonic of some sort, a potion, some kind of Spirit?"

"No, it's just soda. It's a drink. Made mostly of sugar. These cans are used to hold it. People buy them, open them, and drink the soda inside."

"This is preposterous! You are…imagining all this…make believe I say!"

The professor threw his arms in the air and began pacing around the room.

"Besides, you are only a boy, you could not presume to know what the Marvel is! I have been examining it! And have found next to…next to nothing! Lies, you weave lies!"

"No, I'm telling the truth."

Michael wondered if he should tell Quixitix about Earth, about the fact that he was from a different universe, a parallel dimension on the flip side of reality from Serafina. He thought it best not to right now. Perhaps later, but right now, he needed a way back to BlanchField, not a thorough examination.

"The truth you say? You say that is the truth? Prove it then...yes...prove it!" Quixitix arm shot into the air, finger pointing to the heavens.

"I'm sorry...I don't have any proof. Maybe you're right Professor. I was just playing games; I wish I knew what the...Marvel really was. Just thought I would try to...impress you with my theory."

"I knew it! My keen intellect never fails me! Now, you have wasted enough of my time, but before you go, I want to know why you mentioned Bartlebug. Everyone around here knows never to speak that name in my presence, so I presume you are not from Aside." Michael wondered why Quixitix did not want Bartlebug's name mentioned, but said nothing.

"No, I came from BlanchField. I'm sorry if I made you mad by talking about Bartlebug, but he is the one who sent me here. You see, he took my parents prisoner. I have to get back to save them."

"I see...well, I suppose I could send a message to my brother. He works in the Castle there. In fact, that is why I utterly disdain that Bartlebug...always treating my poor little brother poorly. Anyway, I'm sure he would be happy to meet you at the dock when the ship arrives. Of course, that is a few months travel, but that will give Dunny plenty of time to get ready...I hope the post has some hawk-eagles available...only way to get a message sent fast...Yes, I'm sure Dunny would not mind at all."

Michael remembered meeting someone named Dunny in the castle while he was trying to find a way to shift back to his mother's hospital room. Dunny was very fond of food, Michael recalled, and the man had been on his way to the banquet hall for supper.

"I met Dunny, Professor. We spoke briefly in the castle before Bartlebug had me arrested."

"You've met my brother? Well then, you know how much of an oaf he is!"

Quixitix chuckled. "You see, I got the brains. He got the appetite!"

This brought a loud chortle of a laugh from Quixitix' throat. "Well good, then this will make things easier, won't it? Why don't we go to the post and…"

"Professor, I cannot travel by sea. My parent's lives are in danger. I don't know what Bartlebug is planning to do with them."

"Well I'm afraid you have no choice young man. There is no other route."

Michael was beginning to become frustrated with the Professor.

"What about your new invention, some kind of flying machine?"

The look of surprise on Quixitix' face was unmistakable. He chuffled around for a moment then seemed to find his senses.

"I don't know what you're…you're talking about."

"Oh really, professor? Well a Bargoul down the street said rumor has it that you are building some kind of flying machine. If you are, you better come clean with me because the lives of two people are at stake here! If you have a faster way to get me to BlanchField, you had better tell me about it."

Michael was on the verge of anger now. He knew Quixitix was not telling him everything, not being honest with him. On the other hand, why would he? Michael had not even introduced himself yet. He could hardly believe the Professor had carried the conversation as far as he did without even knowing the boy's name. Michael sighed, took a deep breath, and calmed down.

"I'm sorry," said Michael. He stepped forward, hand out. "My name is Michael Smith, and I need your help."

"Archibald Quixitix," said the Professor, taking Michael's hand and shaking it. "Come with me. Let's sit and we can talk."

Michael followed the professor to a set of stairs. They passed the enshrined soda can on the way, and Michael could not help but stare at it. It made him think of his kitchen. His dad always kept a six pack of soda on the floor in the cupboard. Michael smiled, but again noticed something strange about the cola can, something odd, something not quite…what? The same? It still had the same red and white color scheme, only it looked different somehow. He didn't have time to examine it closely, but something about the can caught Michael's attention. He followed Quixitix up the stairs where a small table waited.

"Please sit, Michael. Do you like tea?"

"Sure," said Michael.

"I also have some bread and cheese if you like."

Michael nodded and enjoyed the bread and cheese, but it did not taste nearly as good as Rodney's homemade Sugarberry Pie.

CHAPTER 22

▼

THE KING'S POISON

Mya had no idea what had happened but she knew that whatever it was, she didn't like it. It was like she was some place else, like she had fallen into one of her Fabrications only this time it was unfamiliar and strange. There were mean people there, things she didn't recognize, smells she had never smelled before, sounds that had never touched her ears. Sitting now in her room she could not stop thinking about that strange place.

With a quick movement of her hand, a brightly colored frog appeared on the stone floor of her chambers. The frog had black spots on its back. Mya smiled. The frog hopped lazily and croaked, a sound that always made Mya laugh. She watched the frog for a few minutes then replaced it with a small sunflower. Its head drooped, seeming to sigh, and Mya sighed also. She waved away the flower. She found herself thinking of Michael.

"That boy…" she said out loud. It was difficult to admit this to herself, but she felt connected to him in some strange way. So suddenly he had come into her life, appearing there in her rose field. He looked familiar. The sound of his voice was comforting and kind. Even though Mya was a few years older than Michael, she felt a closeness she could not explain. She wondered what had become of him. The last time she had spoken with him was in the jail before her father had reprimanded her and sent her here. She decided to find out if Michael was still alive. She knew her father to be a stern king, and she assumed that Michael's fate was death. It seemed death was the punishment for nearly every crime these days. She got up from the bed and made her way to her father's chambers.

"My Lady," a very large and awkward man spoke to Mya as the two passed in the hallway. He bowed very low to her.

"Good day to you, Dunmire," said Mya.

"And to you. Stewed pork tonight, it was delicious," he said, rubbing his massive stomach.

"Indeed, I am certain it was. Goodbye then."

"Goodbye my lady," said Dunny, again bowing.

Mya continued down the great hall until she reached the same large doors Michael had mistakenly opened which lead to the King's conference room. Inside, her father and three advisees were discussing matters Mya principally kept her nose out of-her time would eventually come to take a higher seat in the Kingdom-and for now Mya was content with her studies at the Cerulean School. Mya apologized for interrupting and asked to speak with her father alone. She thanked the Seraphim that Bartlebug was no where to be seen. Her father dismissed his sires, but seemed annoyed.

"Alright, Mya. What would you speak to me of?"

"Father, the boy Michael Smith who has been arrested, what will become of him?"

King VanVargot's face darkened. His bushy eyebrows furrowed and he looked upon his daughter with anger and frustration.

"Still you speak of this traitor to the throne? Still you burden me with hearing his name!"

Mya turned her eyes to the floor, ashamed. "I'm sorry father. I just…"

"I will not have you associating with the likes of him! You are a Princess, not some common street peasant!"

"Yes father, I know, but, he…I…I can't explain it but there is something more to that boy…something deeper maybe?"

"Indeed, it seems the criminal is full of depth! He managed to escape, but fear not, he was swiftly caught and banished forever."

"He escaped? How?" Mya was well aware, as was everyone in the castle, that no one had ever accomplished an escape from the prison of the Castle BlanchField.

"It concerns you not, my girl. What matters is that you are once again safe, and this Smith will never bother you again. In fact, two new criminals now rest in the very same cell from which this boy escaped…it has been fortified of course."

"And who might these new occupants be, Father?"

"The boy's parents! It seems the entire family was on an outing, inside my castle, without my permission! This Kingdom needs tighter restraints. We cannot have peasants creeping into the castle anytime they see fit! Something must be done!"

Suddenly Mya filled with deep sadness. She could feel the pools of tears beginning to form in her eyes. Unable to explain this sudden grief, she said,

"And are they to be executed then?"

"Of course dear. It is the only way to set an example to the people," the King said, his chest swelling with pride. Mya felt her sadness turn to anger and frustration. Her fists clenched, her mouth became a press of teeth.

"Execution, Father? Is that your answer for everything?" Mya half yelled this, her eyes turned down toward the floor. Her father was a large and noble man, and Mya found it very difficult to raise her voice to him like this for she very much feared him, but she could not stop herself. The words erupted from her before she even knew what she was saying.

"Where is the Father whom I used to call Daddy? Answer me this! Where has he gone? Where is the King who the people of BlanchField once respected and trusted, not feared and loathed? Why are you so cruel these days?" Mya looked up and saw the anger and surprise in her father's eyes.

"Mya, how dare you speak to me in such a tone! I will not…"

"You will let me finish, Father! I know the source of your current state. It is as plain as day to me! That filthy Bargoul you keep so close all the time. You know of whom I speak. He has poisoned you; he has disgraced you with his venomous tongue!" Mya did not know where these words were coming from, but they just kept coming.

"Ever since you took that…creature…as your Hand, this kingdom has suffered. I have seen it with my own eyes. The people no longer respect you, they fear you. They fear death at your hands. And now two more shall die. How many must die to fulfill your bloodlust! That Bartlebug has destroyed you father. You are no longer the King, the daddy, you once were."

Mya could not control her tears now and they flowed down her cheeks like twin waterfalls. She looked at the floor again, watching her tears drop and splatter on the stone. She could hear her father breathing. He was very quiet. A long silence followed Mya's outburst. Then the chamber doors opened.

"Your majesty, the preparations have been made for the executions and…" Mya spun around with tear-stained cheeks and her eyes pierced those of Bartlebug like daggers. "Oh, Mya. I didn't see you, my dear." Bartlebug smiled that shrewd little smile and hovered, buzzing, a few feet away from Mya. She could smell him, his stink, like wet leaves and dirt. He made her sick.

"As I was saying, your majesty, the prisoners are scheduled for execution by day's end tomorrow. Gallows Hill, as usual. I hope this is to your liking, Your Majesty."

Mya looked at her father in hopes that her speech had persuaded him to break Bartlebug's spell of persuasion and resist his foul control. What she saw broke her heart. He looked no different, as though nothing had changed. He still sat upon his throne; head high, long black mane flowing down his shoulders, chest puffed out like a billowing sail. He glanced quickly at his daughter, then said to Bartlebug,

"Very well." That was all.

"Excellent Sire. Is there anything else with which I might help you at this time?" Bartlebug looked slyly at Mya, his white pin prick eyes seeming to slither across his face. He rubbed his hands together like someone preparing for a feast.

"No, You are excused."

Bartlebug bowed in mid-air, turned, and was gone, leaving only Mya and King VanVargot. Again, silence.

"I see my words have done nothing to sway your opinion of that creature. Fine. Good day Father." Mya turned to walk away when her father stopped her.

"Mya, I…"

"Yes, Father?"

"If you wish, you may visit the prisoners. Perhaps you will see their guilt, as I do."

Mya huffed. "I see nothing but an empty throne." She stormed out of the room and as soon as the door slammed shut, fresh tears shone in her blue eyes.

CHAPTER 23

▼

TWO SIDES OF THE SAME COIN

The tea cup was ornate and beautifully decorated with reds and blues; to Michael it looked like a sunset. Everything in this upper room appeared very old and fragile. Michael was amazed half of it had survived so long, with all the loud bangs and explosions he had heard. Quixitix poured the hot tea from the kettle, decorated in the same way as the cup. The smell was intoxicating.

"Ank ou" was the sound Michael produced from his mouth full of cheese.

"Quite welcome, quite welcome." Quixitix poured himself a glass and sat down across from Michael.

The upper level of his home appeared to be the living area. A small stove on which Quixitix had prepared the tea nestled in what appeared to be the kitchen area. A large puffy bed with stacks of papers and books upon it sat next to the kitchen. Michael observed a few old bookshelves scattered about the upstairs, all with brightly colored books. Michael heard whizzing sounds and assumed the noise was coming from the odd machines all over the room; little tin robots and strange mechanical appliances. Many Michael did not recognize. The upstairs did seem cozy and warm, and Michael felt very happy to be sitting at the small wooden table enjoying his hot tea.

"So who was it that…spilled the beans, yes, on my new invention? Was it Nikko?" Michael shook his head.

"His name was Snyder. He seemed very friendly. Is it true what he said Professor?"

"Snyder? Hmm…I'm afraid I have not heard that name before. I suppose he is new in town. We don't get many new folks around here…Aside is the only town for miles, the Kingdom of LochBarren is very far from here to the East. We do have lots of dense forests and mountains though. I remember once when I was exploring the Couplet Mountains and…"

"Professor, have you invented a flying machine?"

Quixitix looked around, his nose sticking out above his tea cup as he sipped the hot tea. He set the cup down, took out a white handkerchief, and wiped his brow.

"Right to the point then, eh young, Michael? Alright, the answer to your question is yes."

Michael's face lit up.

"Really? Well how does it work? Is it like an airplane or a helicopter or something?"

"Aeroplane? Hmm…never heard that word before, nor the other one you used. What are they?"

"Well, where I come from, they are huge machines that travel great distances in the air and…" Michael realized what he was saying.

"Where you come from? And where exactly is that then, certainly someplace I am not familiar with?"

Michael had to think fast. If he told Quixitix the truth, he might not help him. On the other hand, Quixitix did have that soda can which he seemed to hold in such high regard. If Michael told him the truth, Quixitix might hold Michael in the same light and be more willing to help him. Michael made his choice.

"It's actually a long story, but I will give the short version. I come from the same place as what you have in the glass case downstairs, The Marvel. A place called Earth."

Michael did not expect the complete lack of surprise from Quixitix that followed. He just kept on sipping his tea as though Michael had asked him about the weather, slightly nodding his head. Finally Michael spoke up.

"Well, are you going to say something?"

"Actually, I suspected you might be from Earth the moment you walked in. There is something different about you, something quite unique. Besides, you talk and act the same as the people on the other side."

"So it's that obvious huh? Well, I guess..." Michael trailed off, registering what Quixitix just said.

"How do you know how people act on Earth? Have you been there?"

Quixitix smiled, and nodded.

Now Michael was shocked.

"So is that how you found the soda can? Yeah, you found it alright. Probably found it in the trash when you were on Earth."

"Good guess, good indeed! I have crossed over only twice. The first time was purely by accident, I assure you. It was then I found the Marvel, a soda can as you call it. Is that what it spells on the side?

"Yes."

"Just as I thought. Anyway, the second time was quite recently actually and it was during this second visit that I saw the thing which you have come here seeking. I saw a flying machine on...what was that name you used...yes, Earth, which I knew I could recreate here. The design was quite simple really, save for one minor flaw…"

"So how did you do it? How did you shift?"

Michael was now more interested in hearing Quixitix' story than about the flying machine.

"Shift, you say? Is that what you call it? I call it crossing over. Anyway, there is a place not far from here called Couplet Canyon. There are two peaks, identical you could say, that stretch toward the sky. The valley formed by these two peaks, as I have studiously observed, is a mirror image. Both sides identical only reversed. In this valley is a stone circle, seems to be the very center of the place. It is the only place in the valley that does not have a twin. It is unique. It is there one can cross over to Earth. I assume you arrived in Serafina by means of this passage?"

"No, I didn't. I shifted, Professor. I can go back and forth whenever I want to."

Now Quixitix was truly surprised.

"What! How can you do this? The journey through the portal in the valley nearly killed me, how can you do it so easily, and at…at will?"

Quixitix stood up and shifted about nervously.

"I don't know, Professor. I just can. Maybe because of my mother. She told me I have some…power, to thin the fabric between the worlds. It's all confusing. Anyway, I seem to shift when I think of her."

"You mean the one who you are in such a hurry to rescue?"

"Yes and my father."

"And just who is your mother?"

Quixitix stood still for a moment and focused intently on Michael, arms crossed, eyebrows furrowed, as if the whole world rested on the answer to this question.

"On Earth her name is Judith Smith," Michael hesitated, looked around nervously, "But here, it's Lillian VanVargot."

Quixitix dropped his arms. His eyes widened beneath his bushy eyebrows.

"Then you are...this means that...you..." He could not finish his sentence.

"What am I professor? What do you know about my mother?"

"You are him, young Master Michael. You are the other half! You are the twin!"

"I don't understand, what do you mean!"

"Michael, do you know you have a sister? Mya VanVargot?"

"Yes, we met once at the Castle, I tried to tell her who I was, but..."

"It doesn't matter. You see, your mother is of the Line of the Fabricantress. Do you know of the Fabricant?"

"Yes, she told me about it before I came here. She told me what she did with it, how powerful she was."

"And she told you why she was sentenced to death? Everyone in the land has heard that story, in one form or another."

"Yes, she told me."

"Then you know how powerful the Fabricant can be. Your sister has this ability Michael. In fact, from what my brother tells me, her powers will someday rival your mother's. Few can use the Fabricant and most that can spend their days in a strict sisterhood, keeping the power safe. Mya is a rare exception."

"But what does this have to do with me? I can't use the Fabricant. I am male, so why are you telling me this?"

"Indeed, males cannot use it. The Fabricant is a power granted only to women. But Michael, just as everything in the world comes in pairs, this power has a twin as well. A twin power reserved for the line of men, a power long forbidden in this world."

Michael began to realize what Quixitix was getting at, why he was able to do the things he could do.

"You see, Michael? You say you were born on Earth, the child of Lillian VanVargot of the Line of the Fabricantress?"

"Yes."

"This means you and your sister are two sides of the same coin. She can control the Fabricant and you Michael, you can control…"

Quixitix looked around the room as though in fear that something or someone might hear what he was about to say, as though the very walls had ears and the stone itself would betray him.

"You can control….the Magicant."

This last word he spoke in a near whisper. Finally, Quixitix sat down.

"This is who you are, Michael. Someone like you has not been seen in Serafina in a hundred years. It must have something to do with the combination of both worlds, a mother form Serafina, a father from Earth, and you somehow have inherited the ability to use the Forbidden Art. You are the one, Michael. You are the one who will rekindle the…magic…of this land. The Twinning will be restored once more!"

"The Twinning?" asked Michael.

"Indeed, the twin powers, the Fabricant and the Magicant, together form the force known as The Twinning. It is the lifeblood of Serafina, one side male, the other, female."

Michael did not know what to say. He was speechless. The Fabricant was only half of the equation, the female half it seemed. The male side was now forbidden, the Magicant was forbidden. Michael realized this was what he had done in King VanVargot's chambers when he shot the fire from his hand, some kind of unrefined magical outburst. This was almost too much for him to take.

"And if this is true, if you can in fact wield the Magicant, then my flying machine may indeed work. You see, I have designed it, but I cannot power it the way they did on the other side. We simply don't have the resources here. But I think you do, young Michael. I think you do."

Michael didn't know what to think. He remembered what Dunny had told him, about the magicans who had tried to take over the world in Serafina's history. Did he have the same power as those people, this Magicant? Quixitix was smiling and looking off into the distance. Michael suddenly thought of his family, his mother, father and sister, and prayed they were all alright. He was also thinking about what Quixitix had said about a place called Couplet Canyon. Yet these thoughts stood on the very periphery of his mind at that moment.

CHAPTER 24

▼

BARTLEBUG
THROUGH THE
MIRROR

The room's vile stench hung in the air like a fog, smelling of rotten things and sewage. The castle had many rooms such as this one, full of standing water, half ruined crates, countless rats and other unspeakable vermin. No one frequented these old storage rooms because they had simply fallen out of use. Now they were home to only foul things, of all shapes and sizes.

Bartlebug hung in the air above the dark water, hovering quietly, floating in the murky blackness toward a large iron door at the far end of this particular storage cellar. Although the room was nearly pitch dark, Bartlebug needed no torch to see, what with his keen Bargoul sight and sense of navigation in darkness. He approached the door and wrapped his black, claw like appendage around the rusted handle. With great strain the door slowly creaked open, pushing away the water and letting some rush into the room. Bartlebug passed through the door, and closed it behind him, not surprised to find his dim-witted guard vacant, again, from his post. It did not matter.

This new room, although not well lit, was much brighter than the decrepit storage cellar. A small room with hardly enough space for perhaps ten large crates, Bartlebug made his way to the center. The only object in the room was the thing Bartlebug now hovered beside, his insect wings buzzing in the gloom. Rising five feet from the floor was a pillar made of exquisite marble. Even in the low light of this abandoned storage cellar the pillar seemed to shine. The black that flowed among the marble glistened as though alive, and the white seemed to shine more than the flickering flames of the wall torches. Atop this pillar was something covered in a silk blanket, the finest silk in all of BlanchField. Carefully, Bartlebug removed the silk to reveal the object beneath, the object that rested at the peak of the marble pillar.

Under the silk cover was a small sheet of reflective glass, a mirror, set in an exquisite form. The symbols on the frame meant nothing to Bartlebug, although he did notice the symbols always came in pairs. Very few objects like this one existed in Serafina and they were extremely precious. One such as this, however, had not been seen in Serafina since the time of the Magicans. Bartlebug peered into the mirror, as he had done so often before, and soon found himself staring at another Bargoul.

"Greetings Master," said the face in the mirror.

"What news do you have of The Smith?" Bartlebug was in no mood for pleasantries.

"I fear his return to BlanchField, Master."

Bartlebug furrowed his brow, concern, anger, and fear played across his sooty face.

"How can this be? My orders were quite clear!"

"Yes Master, but it seems he has found another way to leave LochBarren, something we did not foresee."

"Another way? What do you mean?"

The face in the mirror hesitated, and said, "Quixitix, Sire, has some sort of flying machine…"

"What! Why was I not informed of this?"

"We felt it unimportant; everyone here knew he could not make it fly…"

"Fools!" Bartlebug slammed his fist on the marble pillar, shaking the mirror slightly.

"It now seems, Sire, that The Smith may be able to make the machine fly…our spies overheard the boy and the professor talking…it seems Snyder led the boy to Quixitix Sire…"

"Snyder! Snyder…have him punished…severely."

"Yes, Sire. And what about The Smith?"

"Do nothing, yet. We cannot be exposed at this stage and his death would surely expose us…Watch him, but do not act. If he somehow manages to use this flying machine, we will deal with him then." Bartlebug did not say anything, but he feared the worst. He had seen what the boy could do first hand and it troubled him. He turned back to the mirror. "Besides, I have leverage."

"Leverage, Sire?"

Bartlebug smiled in the dark, and brought his face close the mirror, his white pin prick eyes gazing through the glass, through the marble, all the way to LochBarren and into the soul of the Bargoul on the other side.

"Indeed. In my hand I hold the lives of his parents." Bartlebug held his hand out to the mirror, palm up, and made a fist.

"And my grip is slight."

CHAPTER 25

▼

REUNION

Judith sat in a corner, legs to her chest, her hair in tatters and in places hard with her own blood; Bartlebug's guards had been quite cruel to both her and Peter. Peter stood holding the cell bars, staring down the long, dark jail house corridor. The steady dripping of water reverberated off the prison walls, and the wind could be heard howling softly outside.

"We are very lucky they did not recognize me, Peter," said Judith from across the cell. "If they knew who I really was, we would be dead already." Peter said nothing.

"I am so sorry for all of this, Peter, I should have been honest with you from the beginning. I was only trying to protect you and Michael and…"

"That's enough Judith," Peter waved his hand in the air, motioning for her to stop. "I don't need your apologizes. I am on death row in some kind of parallel dimension and I have no idea where my son is…I don't even know if he's alive for God's sake. So please, just leave me alone right now."

"Peter…I…." Judith rose and moved across the cell placing her hand on Peter's shoulder. He was shaking, but only slightly. His head hung low.

"Everything will be fine. I love you, Peter. I have since the moment I first saw you, and that love is strong."

"And what about your other husband, Judith? Do you love him just as strongly?" Now Peter turned around and Judith could see Peter's eyes were wet with tears. He felt all the anger and jealousy that had overtaken him in Pineridge come flowing back.

"I understand how you must feel Peter, but understand that I am two different people. Here, I am Lillian, on Earth I am Judith. Judith, me, loves you more than you can imagine. Lillian loves Charles."

"I can't just accept that my wife is in love with another man, Judith. It's absurd!"

"Peter, please…"

The sound of footsteps from the dark corridor made Judith stop speaking. As the footsteps grew louder and closer, Judith and Peter backed away from the bars waiting to see who was coming. After a few seconds, a small child turned the corner and stood before them.

The first thing that shot through Peter's head was that the girl looked exactly like his son. She had the same eyes, same cheeks. She could have been Michael's twin. Judith knew exactly who this was, and it brought tears to her eyes, but she said nothing.

"You are the parents of Michael the Smith then?" said Mya in her most princess like voice. The prisoners nodded. "I have come here to assess your guilt for myself. I have my doubts about the judgment of Bartlebug…let alone my father," Mya looked down, then back up. "Regardless, I sense something more to this situation than meets the eye. So please, tell me your story."

"Spoken like a true princess, Mya." Judith smiled and her eyes lit up.

"How is it that you know my name? Did Bartlebug tell you?"

"No Mya. I know a great deal about you. I know about your Fabricant abilities. I know how much you like roses. I know you miss you mother greatly..."

"My mother, you know of my mother?" Mya let her guard down a bit and some of the authority in her voice faded away.

"Indeed I do, Mya. Do you know why your mother was banished from this place?"

"Yes, but I do not believe the story. She would never harm anyone."

"Your insight serves you well." Judith brushed the hair back from around her face and straightened her shoulders.

"Mya, hold out your hand, please."

For some reason Mya did as she was told. She looked into the eyes of the woman in the cell, deep into those blue eyes, and in them she saw herself, and Michael.

Judith reached through the bars and placed her outstretched hand over Mya's. She closed her eyes.

"It has been ages since I last did this...." Judith whispered The Word softly so Mya could not hear. The space between their hands began to glow softly. Mya began to feel something in her hand, something that was not there before, and she knew what was happening, but she could not believe it. The thing in her hand began to take shape and color. Its odor began to rise to her nose, the smell so familiar, a smell that reminded her of her mother, of Lillian.

Judith was finished and moved her hand away. She opened her eyes. Mya looked into her palm and what she saw made her weep.

The rose was of the deepest red Mya had ever seen, a red fathoms deeper than any she had ever made in her field of roses. It was the most perfect rose in the history of the world, and it rested in the palm of her hand. Judith had created it for her. Judith had used the

Fabricant and made a rose for Mya. Lillian had made a rose. Mya looked at the woman with tears in her eyes.

"How can this be….are you?"

Lillian spoke in a way that Peter had never before heard. Her voice became angelic somehow, soft and noble, the voice of a true Queen.

"Mya, I am your mother. I am Queen Lillian. And I love you."

Mya stared at the rose, then at Lillian, and wept tears of joy. This was her mother, at last returned, and she was beautiful.

CHAPTER 26

▼

FIRE IN THE PALM OF HIS HAND

"So, what is this made of?"

Michael was holding a small portion of the material which formed the balloon part of Quixitix' contraption, the flying machine, as he asked the question. The balloon was attached to a large basket which looked just like the baskets Michael had seen on hot air balloons when he younger. His father used to take him to Hayden Park and they would sit on the grass eating a picnic lunch. Ham and cheese sandwiches were the usual fare and they were Michael's favorite. Father and son would watch as hot air balloons drifted lazily through the sky, bright colors soaring, and fire shooting to heat the air to make the balloons rise. The tiny dots inside the baskets had been the brave air travelers in search of some kind of serenity high above the Earth. Michael could remember being afraid for those people. He remembered thinking how scary it must be to be so far above the ground. Now he would have to get into one of those baskets. He did not care about the fear this time though.

Thoughts of his mother and father destroyed any inkling of fear creeping through his young heart. He would be with them again.

"Oh, well that is called FlaxFur. See how soft and smooth it is? It doesn't seem like it, but it's also incredibly strong. Expensive, as well. It was not easy to come by so much of it…but sometimes things work out for the better." Quixitix was rummaging around inside the basket as he answered Michael's question.

"This really is just like the hot air balloons from Earth."

"Well of course it is Michael. Those were the basis for the design. The only thing I could not build was the fuel supply. From what I saw on Earth, the cloth bag…err…balloon, is what you called it? The balloon was filled with heated air. Of course it had only been a painting, but I was careful to notice each detail, and the fire was definitely there. Hot air, of course, rises and this is what carries the basket and makes the entire vessel float."

Michael looked over at Quixitix. "Yes, that is how it works. So, you don't have kerosene here or anything like that?"

"I do not know what you speak of, this Kheroseen, but no, we have nothing that could burn hot enough and long enough to fill the balloon and sustain the hot air. The closest I have are torches. I did try those, but I was only able to fill the balloon slightly, not nearly enough for lift off."

Quixitix found what he had been looking for inside the basket. He pulled it out and handed it to Michael. Michael looked at it, surprised.

"Where did you get this?"

"I brought it with me the last time I crossed over. I thought it might be useful. The function of it is quite obvious; we have similar notions of direction here."

"It's a compass. And it still works." Michael held the compass out before him and the needle fidgeted a bit until steadying on NE. The compass itself looked very fine-it was the size of a pocket watch-and it hung on a gold chain. The ornate face was heavily decorated with spidery black lines and curves. It was very beautiful.

"It is yours Michael. I am sure you will need it for your journey…"

"*If* I can power this thing, as you are so sure I can…"

Quixitix stepped closer, his bushy eyebrows dancing lightly above his eyes.

"If you can use the Magicant, then you could power fifty." He smiled. Michael looked down.

"I don't know, the fire thing only happened once, and it was totally unexpected. Thank you for this, by the way." Michael placed the compass in his pocket. Quixitix bowed slightly.

"Well, with a little practice, I am certain you can channel your energy. It will have to be very secret. Magic is forbidden in these ignorant times…

Michael thought for moment then asked, "Why?"

"What dear boy?"

"Why is the Magicant forbidden?"

"Every child knows the legend, although perhaps there is more fact hidden there than people care to admit. Long ago, there was the Fabricant and the Magicant, twin forces, balancing each other. It was from these two forces that the world was created. A woman, her name has been forgotten with time; found she had the ability to control the Fabricant. A man, his name also long lost; found he had the ability to control the Magicant. These two eventually found each other and were wed. They ruled as protectors of the world. Their daughters were able to use the Fabricant, and their sons the Magicant. These children eventually married normal folk, and someone would be born here or there with their parent's powers, although most often the children did not posses the power. Do you follow so far?"

"Yes, I think so."

"Good, then I will continue." Michael and Quixitix sat down with their backs against the basket. The structure in which the balloon was stored was small and cramped, but very secluded. They had walked nearly a mile to reach it. A gentle breeze blew in through the windows.

"The women born of this line were said to be of the Line of Fabricantress, descendents of the original woman with the power of the Fabricant. The men were known as Magicans. Those with the power, for ages upon ages, always accepted their responsibility to protect the people of Serafina. This lasted for a long time, until nearly one hundred years ago."

Quixitix looked down at the ground and sighed, shaking his head.

"What happened a hundred years ago?"

"A Magican took a single step down the path of darkness, and it consumed him. He abused the Magicant. His name was Lucas. He was the one who created the Bargouls."

Michael started. "Created? Dunny mentioned something about that, but said it was only a rumor."

"Well, you would be surprised how much rumor begins in fact. I assume he also told you that the Bargouls were the assistants to the Magicans?"

Michael nodded.

"Well, my brother seems not to have the entire story straight. From what I have found, Lucas wanted an army and so he devised a method to create those creatures. They were intended to fight by his side in his attempt to rule Serafina. Other Magicans joined his cause, evil Magicans. The world had never seen anything like it. Faith and courage were shaken; people were frightened and knew not where to turn. It was the women who won out in the end, using the Fabricant. Many perished." Quixitix paused briefly.

"This war became known as The Twinning War," he said, "a war to eradicate the twin, to destroy the Magicant. They succeeded in stopping the Magicans, but the Magicant cannot be destroyed. All the Kings of all the kingdoms came together at the request of the Fabricantress' and it was decided to forever declare the use of Magic or the Magicant forbidden. Since then, the lineage of women who use the Fabricant has been closely monitored and controlled. No Magicans have been born in one hundred years…until you Michael. You are the lost twin."

Michael was stunned. He was only a boy; a few days ago his only concern in life had been to avoid getting harassed by Jacob Niles in the hallway at Levi. Now, if what this mad scientist said is true, he is some kind of Magican with great powers.

"How do you know all this?" Michael asked.

"Like I said, it is a legend everyone grows up hearing, but much of it has been manipulated and changed. I dug around for several years until I came across the true history of Serafina. I am a scientist, after all; a seeker of the truth, and what I have told you is true. Lucas did exist."

"And he created the Bargouls?"

"Indeed. After the Magicans were stopped, there were too many Bargouls to simply destroy them all…besides, they are living creatures. It was decided they would be allowed to live. They are a mysterious bunch, little is known of their ways. We do know their life spans are incredible, but that is about all."

"So once Lucas was stopped, what happened to the Bargoul army? Did they just give up, and say 'sorry'?"

"In fact, it would seem that way," Quixitix said. "From what history tells, the Bargouls were under some kind of spell. They were being influenced in some way. Once Lucas was gone, they reverted back to peaceful creatures…"

Michael was thinking about Bartlebug, the look of hatred he had seen in the bug's eyes, and wondered…

"Professor, thank you for telling me this, but I think it is time. I have to go back and save my parents."

Quixitix nodded his head.

"Alright. Well, I suppose you should use the Magicant."

"How should I do that?"

"Let's see…you mentioned you have successfully used the Magicant only once before?"

"That's right."

"Then try to think about your state of mind at that moment. What were you thinking? What were you feeling?"

Michael remembered entering the conference room, seeing those noble men sitting around the table, speaking their high speech. They had grabbed him, held him. He wanted to escape, to flee, to run into the loving arms of his parents. Then he got angry. That was it, anger.

Quixitix was watching Michael. He watched him close his eyes and ball his fists. Quixitix saw the furrowing of Michael's brow, the beads of sweat beginning to form on his forehead, the way his body began to tremble slightly.

Michael was thinking about Bartlebug. He was imagining the creature floating next to his parents. He saw the Bargoul's goons push his mother and father down. He heard the sound of their bodies hit the cold castle floor. He could feel his blood starting to boil. His head began to feel hazy, and he became unaware of his surroundings. It almost felt like shifting, but this was very different; this was powerful. The last thing he saw before it happened was the sting slowly emerging from Bartlebug. It was sleek black, wet and deadly. The image filled Michael with such rage even his mind's eye became blinded…then the world snapped back instantly and for Michael all was clear.

Quixitix could hardly believe what he saw. One moment he had been watching Michael shaking, his fists balled, then he could no longer see the fists. Michael's hands had become engulfed in blue fire. Michael looked at him, and their eyes met. Quixitix could not have expected to see the confidence he saw in those eyes. It was as though Michael had been able to do this his entire life. It was like breathing.

Michael looked down at his flaming fist with no surprise, no shock. He was in control of this blue fire; he was in control of the Magicant. The world seemed so clear in that moment, the colors more vivid, the smells sweeter, and the sounds crisper. He looked at his other hand, and in a moment it too was engulfed in a blue flame. Now the boy stood by the hot air balloon, duel fists of blue fire turning over and over as he examined his fiery hands.

He looked at Quixitix. "Didn't take as long as I thought. It was red last time."

The boy's voice sounded different as well, as though he were much older.

"Indeed, the fire is in its most elemental, pure form. Incredible..."

"Pretty cool, huh?"

Michael held out his hand, palm open, and a small bluish-red ball of fire began to form. It grew larger until it was the size of a bowling ball. Michael juggled the ball back and forth between his hands, then blew on it, extinguishing the flame.

"On the contrary Michael, I would say it was quite the inferno..."

Michael laughed. He balled his fists, closed his eyes, and the blue flames disappeared.

"Yeah Professor, pretty cool. I guess I *can* make this thing fly."

Quixitix smiled and nodded his head.

"I would have to agree with you, dear boy."

Neither the boy nor the professor noticed the tiny white eyes watching them from the window or the escape of the buzzing eavesdropper.

CHAPTER 27

▼

THREE BECOMES FOUR

Her reunion with her mother had brought rivers of joyous tears from the girl's eyes. With the rose in her hand, even before the two of them could say another word to one another, Mya ran down the corridor. The guard who had let Michael slip away before was, surprisingly, still stationed there. Not surprisingly, however, was the fact that he was again asleep. It was not hard for Mya to grab the key and make her way back to her mother's cell. Having unlocked the door, mother and daughter embraced for the first time since Mya was a little girl, and both cried. Peter watched, detached, as the two embraced.

"Mother, it is so wonderful to have you back," said Mya through her tears.

"Indeed Mya, I have thought about you my every waking moment since I had to leave. I wish we could say more now, but we must hurry."

"Alright," said Mya. The trio left the cell, and crept down the hallway, passed the still sleeping guard, and down a long staircase to another corridor.

Mya, Peter, and Lillian made their way down the dark hallway in search of a way out of the castle. Mya knew the castle well, but she did not frequent the dungeons and did not know her way. Mya was a few feet ahead of Lillian and James.

"So that is your daughter…here. This is a lot for me to take Judith…Lillian…whichever it is," said Peter.

"I know."

This was all the reply Peter received.

After a few moments, he said, "So are you planning on telling her about Michael or are you ashamed of that fact?"

"Peter, how could you even think I am ashamed of our son? He is the cardinal thing on my mind right now. We have no idea what is to become of him," Lillian said, exasperated.

"Same here," said Peter. "Do you think he is still here?"

"I would assume so; although I cannot be sure…Bartlebug is very treacherous."

Peter and Lillian were so caught up in their conversation they did not notice that Mya had stopped and they bumped into her. She was looking at Lillian.

"I only have vague memories of you, Mother, whispers. I feel like I know you only as an image in my mind, a familiar scent on my sheets. Everything I have been told about you has been so vile…they made you out to be a monster. You are not a monster, I can tell by your eyes."

Lillian smiled warmly at her daughter, placing her hand on the young girl's cheek.

"Your love has kept me alive, Mya. I always knew one day I would return to you, at last that day is here."

"But what about father? I have memories of him smiling, and laughing, but then no more. He changed mother…he is so angry now, so harsh…"

"It is the influence of Bartlebug," said Lillian, shaking her head. "He is the evil poison that has seeped into this Kingdom's heart, and your father's."

Mya was not surprised by these allegations. She had always seen through Bartlebug's masquerade, always been aware of his treachery and deceit, although she had no idea how far it had gone. To darken the heart of a once honorable and noble King was quite a feat, but Mya knew that somewhere inside her father still rested the good man she had once laughed and played with.

"Come, Mya, we must make haste. There is someone you have to meet."

Mya looked at her mother and said, "Who?"

Lillian smiled. "You shall find out soon, if we hurry. He is in great danger as we speak."

Mya nodded and they continued on their way, Peter following behind mother and daughter.

Peter's mind swirled with thoughts and worries about Michael. He had no idea where his son was, if he was okay, if he was in pain, unconscious. The last time he saw Michael, he had been in the great hall, just before two of those bee things knocked him out. It had been horrible to watch, the anger growing inside his chest had been unbearable, the sorrow inconsolable. It was his fault, after all. He had been the one to bring Michael to see Judith, or Lillian, or whatever her name was. This was all his fault.

Peter's thoughts were cut short when he heard the whistling. The trio had found their way out of dungeon and were sneaking down a quiet corridor when they heard the distinct sound of whistling coming from up ahead. They all stopped and looked around.

"There is nowhere to hide," said Lillian.

Before they could decide what to do, they saw a shadow creep up the wall, dancing from the flickering candle light. The whistling grew louder. Any second the owner of the shadow would turn the corner and see the three outlaws. Lillian had an idea.

She concentrated, her thoughts trained on the image in her mind.

"Clothes," she said. Peter had never heard her voice have such a commanding quality before, it almost sounded like a different person. Peter glanced down at the floor and now saw something transparent there, beginning to take on shape and gain color. Lillian focused and the shapes became three sets of neatly folded clothes, she only hoped BlanchField fashion had not changed much since her reign

"Quickly, put these on. We are paupers; here to seek the King's generosity, do not veer from this story."

The tattered brown robes slid easily over the clothes the three were already wearing and just as they settled into place, the figure came around the corner, still whistling loudly.

Mya recognized him immediately and knew the disguise was not necessary.

"Dunny!"

Mya ran forward and hugged the oversized man, her arms only making it to halfway around his very large waist.

"Mya, well 'ello! How are you t'day?"

"Very well, thank you," said Mya with a curtsey.

Lillian looked at Peter and they moved forward as well.

"And who are these fine folks that are with…"

Dunny stopped suddenly, his eyes falling upon Lillian. It was obvious to everyone what happened in that moment; Dunny knew who she was.

"My Queen," said Dunny, bowing before her. "I canna' believe it is you, returned after so long."

Lillian was shocked that no one thus far had recognized her yet Dunny was somehow able to. She had known Dunmire Quixitix while she was Queen. He had been a jolly fellow, she recalled, nearly always happy and constantly after food. His sole duty in the castle was to guard a single black door. Because of his size, he made the perfect guard; no one ever came near that door.

"You may rise, Dunmire," she said.

Dunny slowly stood up, the look of awe in his eyes unmistakable.

"My Lady, I want you to know, I do not believe the things they said 'bout you."

Lillian was relieved. She had been worrying if Dunny was the sort to turn her in. It seemed he was not.

"Thank you, Dunmire. You are right not to believe them for the things they tell you are not true. Would you hear the truth of it?"

"Please my lady," he said.

Peter and Mya listened as Lillian told Dunny about how she had been tricked to misuse the Fabricant, sentenced to death, and forced to flee into exile. (She decided to leave out the part about crossing over to Earth; she thought that was a little too much for Dunmire).

"So it was that fiend, Bartlebug, behind the whole thing?"

When Lillian finished her story Dunny was clearly upset and angry.

"Yes, Dunmire. He is a poison slowly killing this once fine Kingdom. No one sees it…"

Dunny reached out and took the Queen's hand, something no servant would ever dream of doing. Lillian's hand was easily engulfed in Dunny's, just as Michael's had been.

"My Lady, I see it. And I am going to help you."

Peter, Mya, and Lillian all smiled.

"Thank you, Dunmire. You are truly wonderful."

"Alright, follow me. I can show you the quickest way out," said Dunny.

"Dunmire wait," it was Peter who spoke up. "Hello, my name is Peter."

Peter also shook Dunny's hand.

"Pleasure."

"I was wondering if you know what happened to a young boy who was arrested a few days ago. His name is Michael."

Dunny's eyes lit up at the mention of the name then sank down into deep darkness.

"A very nice lad, I met him on the way to dinner one night, and gave him a bit of a history lesson. He seemed lacking in that area."

Lillian smiled wryly.

"Anyway, it saddens me to tell you this but the King decreed that Michael be exiled."

Lillian and Peter shot quick looks at one another, concern and fear painting their faces.

"To where Dunmire, do you know?" asked Lillian.

"Yes, everyone knows. To LochBarren."

Lillian sunk. She knew how far LochBarren was. She also knew that Michael was in far greater danger there than here in the castle.

"Peter, we must get to him somehow. LochBarren is the Kingdom of Bargouls. They are many there, and I am sure Bartlebug's influence on them is quite great. Death would be a more merciful fate than what they will do to him."

Peter felt as though he was going to cry, but he held back his tears. He would find his son, save him, and take him home where he belongs, away from all of this absurdity.

"Fine," he turned to Dunny, "how to do we get there?"

Lillian answered him saying, "I'm afraid it's not that easy. It is a four month journey by ship, and that is the only way."

Now Peter could not help but break down. He fell to the floor, and wept for his son.

Mya was confused and unsure what to think about all this. She had met this Michael before and was very curious as to why her mother and this man were so concerned for him. She had felt something special when she had spoken with him, some kind of connection, but clearly that connection was much stronger with these two.

"Peter, I'm so sorry," said Lillian, sitting down next to him. "I wish there was some other way, but not even the Fabricant is powerful enough to…"

She stopped short, eyes widening, a smile lighting her face.

"The Fabricant…of course…Peter!"

She shook him. He showed no sign of response.

"Peter, listen to me! We can be there by the end of the day!"

Dunny shook his head. "Impossible," he muttered to himself.

Mya thought she knew what her mother was thinking. She had experienced it once herself; the other place, with the odd floors and strange people.

"Peter, distance is not the same here as on Earth. If you walk a mile on Earth, you walk five here! Do you see?"

Mya turned the name over in her head. Earth, a nice name, almost as nice as Serafina.

Peter finally looked up, drying the tears from his eyes.

"You mean…"

"Yes Peter, we can just cross over, travel on Earth, then cross back. Come now. We must hurry."

Lillian helped Peter up then turned to Dunmire.

"Dunmire Quixitix, you have done a great service to your country. Your fortuitous loyalty shall always be remembered. You are…"

"Pardon me, My Lady, but I want to come with you."

"Dunmire? You cannot be serious."

"I am. LochBarren is my home, too. I know it well. I want to help you, and Michael."

Dunny bowed, "Besides, I don't think nobody's gonna bother 'at old door 'nyway." Lillian did not know what Dunny was talking about and decided not to ask him.

Lillian continued her protestations, but was at last convinced by Peter and Mya that Dunny might be a good asset to have.

"Very well. Thank you Dunmire," said the Queen, curtseying.

Dunny bowed very low, "The pleasure is all mine."

"Very well then. Dunny, Mya, this is going to be very strange for you both, but trust in your Queen. No harm will come to you."

"Actually mother, I have crossed over, as you say, once before, only a few days ago."

Lillian was surprised. "You are very strong with the Fabricant, Mya. Much more powerful than I was at your age."

Mya smiled.

"Mother?"

"Yes, Mya."

"Will you tell me about Michael the Smith? I meet him twice and he seems so interesting. He is the one we are going to save, right?"

"Indeed Mya. In fact, he is the one I wanted you to meet."

"Why?"

"Because Mya," Lillian took her hand, then Peter's, then Peter took Dunny's and Dunny took Mya's, completing the circle, "Michael is your brother."

Before Mya had proper time to react to this revelation, the world became thin and she felt herself fading in the ether of what would soon be Earth. Holding the hand of her daughter, Lillian was able to cross over as easily as breathe.

CHAPTER 28

▼

ATTACK

"So is this thing really that much faster than a boat? I mean, it still seems slow even if we are flying," said Michael. He stood in the basket Quixitix had made which attached to the large canvas balloon. Michael had spent the better half of a day working with his new Magicant abilities, honing it, mastering it, learning to control the fiery anger inside himself. Now, after several hours of igniting his hands into blue flame, he felt pretty good about it. The only thing he was still not used to was the pain, or lack thereof. No matter how long he kept the flames burning, he felt nothing. There were no scars, no burning, no pain of any kind, yet the flames were hot enough to boil water.

Now Michael's arms were held up and outstretched toward the rapidly inflating balloon, hands engulfed in blue flame as the air was heated and the canvas filled.

"You are correct young Michael," said Quixitix. He walked around the balloon as Michael filled it, checking the rigging, making sure everything looked okay. "Normally this means of transportation would be very slow. However, I have made some…modifications. Take a look at this."

Michael had noticed several shrouded objects attached to the side of the basket. There were perhaps seven of them positioned evenly apart from each other around the perimeter of the basket. Professor Quixitix began removing the cloth from each attachment and Michael recognized them immediately, although-like most things in Serafina-they looked a little different.

"Fans," said Michael.

Quixitix looked puzzled then said, "Whirls. That is what they are called here. So, they are known as fans on Earth?"

"Yeah, although yours look a little bit different."

"Yes, well in either case, this will greatly speed up our trip, artificial wind. How are you doing with the fire?"

"Seems to be filling up nicely. So are we going today?"

Michael had been in Aside for a few days but he was ready to go. He did not want to be here any longer than he needed to be. His parents needed his help, not to mention his half sister, but there was one thought which continued to gnaw at Michael's mind no matter how much he tried to bury it. How had he gotten to LochBarren? According to Quixitix, it took four months by ship and that was the only way. Quixitix' balloon was a one of a kind, and Michael was the only one who could make it work. Michael's arrival on the shore of the So'liloquy was still a mystery; there was no way Bartlebug could have gotten him there so quickly. There was one possibility. That, however, was a possibility Michael did not want to consider.

"That is the plan young Michael," said Quixitix adjusting his large spectacles. "As soon as the balloon is full, we shall set off. I have gathered some provisions, maps, and such. The trip should take about a day, I suspect. It will be difficult though."

Michael continued filling the balloon.

"Yes, I know. I wish I could just shift and take a taxi."

"A taxi?"

"Sorry. It's a means of transportation on Earth and it's pretty fast."

"I see."

"I don't know why I can't shift anymore. I tried when I first got here and again last night," he sighed. "I just don't understand it. It was so easy before."

Quixitix nodded his head, as though in thought, then said, "Yes, well I have a theory on that if you wish to hear it."

"Please."

"I believe the answer lies in the nature of the Fabricant. You see, although the Fabricant and the Magicant are twin sides of the same coin, they are still in constant flux and struggle. I believe it is the Fabricant that allows you to shift. Although you are obviously much stronger in the Magicant, a part of you taps into the Fabricant when you shift. However, now that you are so in touch with the Magicant, the Fabricant has faded to the background and grown weak. This may be the cause of your inability to shift, as you call it. Just a theory though."

Michael listened closely, eager for more information about these twin powers.

"That sounds reasonable. I think it's almost full."

The balloon now rose fully into the open air behind the hanger where Quixitix had built it. It was colored magnificently in blues, reds and greens. Michael had a brief flash of memory and he thought that the wallpaper in his mother's room at Pineridge might have had hot air balloons on it. He smiled.

"Okay Michael, the time has come. We are off."

Michael extinguished the blue flames from his hands, still amazed that he was not horribly burned, and Quixitix stumbled into the basket with him.

"Would you mind untying those knots over there Michael?"

Michael began undoing the weight that was holding the balloon down, as did Quixitix. When all the ballast had been let go, the balloon began to rise.

"It's amazing professor."

"Thank you, Michael, It does indeed seem to be working."

Slowly the large balloon began to rise into the air, as did Michael's hope. He would make it back to BlanchField and find his parents, no matter what Bartlebug did. Quixitix started the fans and the balloon began to speed forward. He adjusted the speed of the fans so they were heading in the right direction.

"It's so beautiful Professor," said Michael.

The balloon began sailing over Aside and Quixitix pointed in the direction of his home. The fans were now whirling briskly as Quixitix turned the handle to which they were connected as the two made their way over the town, picking up speed. Michael thought the noise of the fans was growing louder, assuming they were getting faster. Quixitix did not notice the increasing noise at all. Now they were nearly right above the beach where Michael had first arrived and the fans were almost deafening.

"What Michael?" said Quixitix, yelling over the noisy fans. "I can't hear you over the whirls; I will turn them off for a moment!" He yelled this, Michael unable to hear him. Quixitix turned off all the active fans, but their buzzing continued.

Both occupants looked at one another, puzzled, wondering where the noise was coming from. Then they looked behind them.

The swarm was enormous, and the most frightening thing Michael had ever seen in his life. He had seen swarms of bees before, but when each bee is the size of a bull dog, it's quite a bit more terrifying.

"Oh my God," said Michael, turning white.

"Dear Seraphim," said Quixitix, jaw open.

The Bargouls were closing in fast. In seconds they would be on top of them.

"What are they doing!" yelled Michael.

"It can't be good, whatever they are planning. Hang on, Michael."

There were thousands of them, all the size and shape of Bartlebug. To Michael, the swarm looked like thousands of Bartlebugs, all coming for him. The first one neared the balloon then stopped. Michael watched as his sting came out, sleek and black, deadly and sharp, and suddenly he realized what was going to happen. The Bargoul wound up and jammed his sting into the canvas of the balloon. The effect was immediate. The balloon began to jostle in the air.

"Michael, this does not look good. Can you muster some fire?"

"I'll try," he said. Michael concentrated, focused on the flame, saw it in his mind, and then it was real, and his hands were blue fire. He flung a tongue of it at the Bargoul, but missed. The creature retreated in fear, but the rest were now on them. Michael began shooting fire into the swarm. He heard a few screams, as his blue fire scorched the Bargouls, but there were too many. Michael and Quixitix felt each new puncture as the Bargouls ruptured the balloon and they began to fall from the sky, toward the beach.

"I'm sorry. There are just too many," said Michael, breathing hard. His flames were dimming. He was unable to keep them going. It was too much strain.

"You must be wishing I never told you about this balloon now, Smith!" Michael looked up and hovering near the basket was the Bargoul he had met when he first arrived in Aside, Snyder.

"You! What are you doing? You are going to kill us!"

"Yes, that is the plan! You cannot escape Bartlebug's Army!"

"Army!" yelled Michael. "What do you mean?"

The balloon rocked back and forth, each sting causing more air to escape, the basket to fall faster.

"We will rule Serafina! We have found the way across the void, and we will bring back what we need to rule this world, and all others!"

Snyder was crazed and yelling, his bee body quivering with excitement, his deadly sting dangerously close to the basket.

"What do you mean? Across what void!"

Quixitix was cowering in the corner of the basket, but he knew what the Bargoul was talking about.

"Don't you understand human? You should, above all others. Earth! Earth shall be ours! We shall hold Couplet Canyon while the master…"

Another Bargoul, about to attack the balloon, heard the crazed words coming from Snyder's mouth. Instead of going after the balloon with his sting like he intended, he shot down and landed on the back of Snyder.

"Shut up you fool!"

Snyder craned his head and saw Flynn hanging onto his back. Flynn brought his hand down hard onto Snyder's sooty bee face, and the Bargoul screamed in pain.

Michael's face went white. This could not be happening. Did this mean Bartlebug knew a way to Earth, as Michael had feared? Is that how he had gotten Michael to LochBarren so fast, by shifting and traveling on the other side? Was Bartlebug going to invade? Was this an invasion army?

All of these thoughts screamed across Michael's mind and he felt the Magicant flowing in him like never before. As Quixitix watched him, he saw the blue flames begin to flicker not just on his hands this time, but everywhere, from the corner of his eyes, his chest, and his hair. Snyder still hovered there as his army of Bargouls continued to destroy the balloon. They were falling faster now.

"Tell your master I'll see him soon, Snyder," said Michael. Snyder was holding his nose and Flynn was still hanging onto his back.

At the words of this boy, both Bargouls looked up and into Michael's eyes. There they saw only blue fire. Quixitix saw the flames in the boy's eyes as well. Snyder could tell he was in danger and quickly turned to retreat, Flynn still hanging on. As he did, Michael let out a yell that Quixitix did not believe could come from such a young boy. Michael exploded in flame, his entire body a ball of pure blue fire. He raised his arms and the fire covered the sky, blanketing the army of Bargouls. Many fell from the sky, burning bodies falling to the ground. Many escaped with burned flesh and wings, but they were leaving. Quixitix observed Snyder and Flynn, stings now concealed, heading to the West. The balloon was near the beach, the impact would be hard, but Quixitix thought they would survive. Michael stood, the blue flames now gone from his body, swaying slowly back and forth.

"Michael, are you alright?"

Michael turned to face Quixitix, his face pure exhaustion.

"Mother…" was all he could muster. The world turned to black and Michael collapsed inside the basket. As the boy and the professor plunged to the beach, Quixitix held Michael, protecting him, fearing what trials were now spread out before this young boy.

▼

CHAPTER 29

BARTLEBUG MAKES A CHOICE

The Bargoul Bartlebug hovered back and forth in mid-air, eyes fixed on nothing, his thoughts a swirl of doubts and anger. He had been speaking with one of the leaders of his forces in LochBarren when he had heard the news. In the dank storage room the already thick black air had seemed to grow darker as the Bargoul slammed his fists down on the marble pillar holding the Twin Glass.

"Failure is something not to be tolerated by this regime, Kraus!"

Bartlebug had been furious with Kraus, with all of them, for turning their backs on The Smith and fleeing from a bit of fire, albeit Magicant fire.

"Yes Sire, a thousand apologizes, but you can see what he did to us!"

The Bargoul Kraus held his arm up to the mirror so Bartlebug could see the scares of seared flesh from The Smiths blue fire.

"I don't care! That boy is the only thing that could stand in our way, and he must be stopped! The balloon crashed down you say?"

"Yes, Sire. We watched it fall from the sky."

"So there is a chance they could still be alive. Send a unit to scout the area. If they find the boy, kill him."

Kraus looked around, obviously frightened.

"I will take no pity on you Kraus; your fears do not concern me! Do as I say, and question nothing!"

Spittle flew from the corners of Bartlebug's mouth as he said this. His eyes burned with anger.

"Yes Sire. We shall dispatch a team immediately."

"Good! See that you do!"

With that, Bartlebug threw the black silk cover back on the Twin Glass and stormed angrily out of the cellar.

Now, hovering in his private chambers one door down from King Charles, Bartlebug was trying to decide if he should go to LochBarren himself and oversee the undertakings. It seemed his Commanders were incapable of dealing with the boy; he obviously overestimated them. However, if he went, it would be extremely suspicious. A diplomatic voyage? No, he would have to travel by conventional means and that would take too long. What then? He could be there in a day if he traveled on the other side. He would just have to be careful, remain unseen, deal with The Smith, and get back to his real work.

"Bartlebug!"

Bartlebug had not even heard the King enter his chambers having been so entranced in his own thoughts. He turned to face the King.

"Yes, your majesty."

"You seem to be losing your grasp on the policing of this Kingdom! Your prisoners have escaped…again!"

"What? Impossible! I strictly forbade access to them by anyone, and there is no way they could have gotten out of that cell…"

The King moved closer, the rage in his eyes unmistakable as Bartlebug stared into them.

"Not only that, but it seems my daughter is missing as well," said the King, now his eyes softened somewhat, some remote notion of love and loss filling them from far away. "And I had given her permission to visit the prisoners…said she wanted to see them for herself."

Bartlebug had to stop himself from shouting the word fool directly into the King's face.

"Perhaps then, Sire, Mya is in cahoots with the boy and his parents…"

Bartlebug spoke this accusation very gingerly.

"Preposterous!" King Charles threw his hands into the air. "It seems more likely to me that she was kidnapped by the criminals."

"A wise conclusion, Sire."

Bartlebug knew differently though. He knew in his heart that Mya had something to do with all this, Mya VanVargot…he despised her almost as much as he hated the Smith.

"A search of the grounds has yielded nothing. It seems they have simply vanished. I am putting you in charge of bringing the Princess back and slaying those foul creatures who took her," King Charles moved closer to the hovering, oversized bee. "And I suggest you find them, or there will be three dead bodies on Gallows Hill instead of two."

"Yes, Sire," said Bartlebug, masking his rage with fear and his contempt with praise.

King Charles stormed out of the room, slammed the door behind him, and left Bartlebug to his thoughts.

He had made up his mind while speaking with the King. He decided that the boy's parents and Mya were most likely on their way to save him. Therefore, he would cross over, travel to LochBarren, kill the boy and await the arrival of his parents, then kill them too. He smiled in the gloom of his stony chambers, pleased with his genius and diabolic cunning

C H A P T E R   30

▼

CADILLAC

Mya felt the world fade away as it had before when she had been in her rose field and the snow had stopped falling. This time, instead of finding herself in the hallway with the odd metal cabinets on the walls, she was sitting on grass. As she examined the grass, she had to rub her eyes because to her it seemed like the green was faded and dull. She looked up and saw a blue sky, but not as blue as the sky of Serafina. Even the air smelled odd, heavy and saturated with unfamiliar fragrances. She looked around and saw her mother, Dunny, and the other man, Peter. They were all sitting on the grass as well, looking around perplexed. Dunny looked the most dumbfounded of all.

"What 'appened to the castle?" He said, looking toward the Queen.

Lillian stood slowly, brushing grass from her clothing. The faded robes she had Fabricated had disappeared, leaving her with only her blue hospital clothes.

"Dunmire, you will find this difficult to comprehend but we have traveled…far from the castle," Lillian spoke slowly and softly, trying her best to make Dunny understand what had happened.

"You see Dunmire, this is the place where I have been hiding for the last twelve years. This place is called Earth."

"Twelve years? 'as it really been that long?" Dunny shook his head. "So this Earth," he said, waving his large arms in the air, "this is where you have been. So how did we get 'ere, and where exactly is this?"

"You see, I have the ability to…cross-over…from Serafina to this place, to Earth. Have you ever seen reflective glass, Dunmire?"

"Aye, my brother had several pieces of it, always using them for crazy inventions."

"Good, then this will be easier to explain. What do you see when you look into that glass?"

"I see myself."

"And what else?"

Dunny thought for a moment, "And whatever is around me I suppose."

"Exactly. Think of Earth as Serafina's reflection in the glass. We have passed through the glass and are now on the other side."

No one noticed the small crowd now emerging from the around the sides of the Thrift Save. Lillian, Mya, Peter, and Dunny shifted not far from where Michael had shifted when he had escaped the clutches of Bartlebug for the first time. They were now all sitting on a small patch of grass about fifty yards behind the Thrift Save. There was a small parking lot between the market and where the group was sitting with a few scattered cars parked here and there. The owners of those cars were leaving the market and getting curious about the odd bunch seemingly having a picnic behind the Thrift Save.

"The other side? I think I understand, My Lady, and either way, I trust in you."

Dunny stood up, towering over Peter, by at least two feet. He looked around.

"This place is certainly odd…dull."

Lillian looked at Peter and Mya.

"Are you two alright?"

"Yeah," said Peter.

"Yes," said Mya.

"Alright, then we should find a car and make our way east. I cannot be certain about the direction, but I do know that LochBarren is east from BlanchField. It takes four months by ship to reach it in Serafina, so I would guess that distance is maybe…five hundred miles here."

"Miles?" asked Mya. "I have never heard that word before mother."

"Septims, Mya. Miles are Earth's equivalent of our septims."

Mya nodded her head.

"We should be going. Time is running short, and I fear for Michael."

Everyone agreed and the group left the grassy area before any more people could empty from the Thrift Save. They headed for Peter's home.

"We can take the Volvo. I think we can all fit in there, might be tight for you though big fella," said Peter as they walked, clearly speaking to Dunny.

"What is a Vol Vo?"

"It's a car. Do you have motor vehicles where you come from, Judith? I didn't think so. It's a horseless carriage, Dunny."

"I see…"

Dunny did not press the matter any further, satisfied with what Peter had said.

"Five hundred miles East of here should put us close to New York City, I think. It will take the better part of today to get there. I hope you are up for the ride."

"We will be fine, Peter. New York sounds about right," said Lillian.

Peter's home was just as he had left it several days ago when he had taken Michael to visit Judith. He walked up the driveway when the thought hit him.

"Judith, the car is still at Pineridge…"

"Well what about my old car, Peter? I still remember the first time I saw one of your horseless carriages…I was so enthralled by it. Do you still have it?"

Peter hesitated, then nodded.

"It's in the garage, still covered."

Lillian smiled. Peter proceeded inside the house, came around to the garage, and opened the door. The car sat motionless, covered completely with a large canvas tarp.

"It's all yours, Judith. I'm going to pack some food."

"So, this is a horseless carriage? Is that its skin?"

Lillian laughed at Dunny's question.

"No, this is simply a cover to protect it. It is not alive…it is made of metal."

Dunny nodded. Mya stared on in disbelief, taking in all the marvels this new world had to offer. Now that she was here with her mother, this place seemed much less frightening.

"Mother, what makes it go if not a horse to pull it?"

"Housed in the metal is a marvelous machine called an engine. This machine is powerful enough to turn the four wheels on which the carriage rests, making it go."

"Astonishing," said Mya.

"Indeed child."

Lillian walked to the tarp and pulled, revealing the car beneath.

"I knew nothing of these machines when I first came here. It was only after I was married to Peter for several years that I learned enough about them to fit in…then I fell in love with this one."

The car beneath the tarp was a 1967 Cadillac convertible-Cherry red and in perfect condition-the white leather interior seemed to shine like ivory. Mya and Dunny nearly lost their breath when they saw it; neither of them had ever seen something so magnificent or beautiful in their lives.

"Magnificent…"

Lillian stood next to the car, gazing at it, remembering the wonderful times she and Peter had spent simply cruising around the country side, taking pictures of autumn, stopping to buy candy apples, going to the state fair. Lovely memories, pieces of life she once held dear. A life she knew could never be regained…but perhaps a new one could be forged. Her thoughts were interrupted by Peter entering the garage with a large backpack.

"I packed some sandwiches and soda. It will be enough to last us the day. She's still perfect, by the way," he said, pointing to the car. "Full tank too."

"Well then, we must be on our way. Peter, may I?"

Lillian pointed to the driver's seat. Peter reached into his jeans pockets and pulled out his key ring. The key for the Caddy was still attached.

"It's your car; do you still remember how to drive it?"

He tossed her the keys, and she caught them gracefully.

"Old habits die hard," she said.

To Peter's ears, Lillian was already starting to sound more like his Judith with every second they were back on Earth. Perhaps she really was too different people.

Mya and Dunny stood off to the side with Peter as Lillian backed the Caddy out of the garage. They were both impressed and astounded by the noise the carriage made, the smoke which it seemed to spit from its rear, the way Lillian was able to turn it with the large wheel she was holding as she sat inside the thing.

"Let's go," she said.

Peter ushered Dunny and Mya into the back seat, showing them how to fasten their seat belts properly. Dunny barely fit through the door and his head was protruding through the soft top. Peter looked at him and decided to drop the top. A few seconds later, and Dunny was sitting comfortably, head shooting up into open air. Peter got in next to Judith.

"Just like old times, right Judith?" he asked with a smile.

"Just like old times, Pete. But now, we have to find our son."

Judith put the car in gear and the quartet found themselves hurtling east, toward New York, toward LochBarren, and hopefully toward Michael.

CHAPTER 31

▼

IN THE APARTMENT OF WILLY

Bartlebug made his way to the lower bowels of the castle, making sure no one saw him as he always did. He had decided to make the trip to LochBarren himself, take care of the Smith, and per-haps-now that he thought about it-perhaps it was the right time to put the rest of his plan into motion. His army had suffered their first and only loss against the Smith. They would be full of rage and hatred for him, willing to do anything Bartlebug wanted to get back at the boy, fully capable of holding the Canyon. Indeed, he thought as he approached his destination, now was an excellent time.

The door before which Bartlebug hovered was pure onyx black. No decorations of any kind, no royal seals like the red doors leading to the King's Throne room, not even a handle. There was, however, supposed to be a guard.

"Dunmire!" Shouted Bartlebug as loud as he dared. No answer. He buzzed down the hallway and peered around the corner, seeing nothing but the flicker of torch light. Dunny was nowhere to be found.

"Stupid oaf! I imagine he's stuffing his face somewhere. No matter," muttered Bartlebug under his breath.

He moved closer to the door. When he was directly in front of it, he began to chant something, words which sounded like a feeble attempt at a song. His voice cackled, devoid of any melody or harmonious quality. After a few seconds, the large black door seemed to shimmer and on it appeared an ivory white door handle. Bartlebug grasped the handle, turned it, and proceeded into the gloom beyond the doorway.

The room he now occupied was very similar to the room which contained the Twin Glass. It was dark, sewer like, and the smell was quite bad. This room, however, had one distinct quality. Both sides were mirror images of one another. On the left were three broken boxes, pieces of them splintered into nothingness. On the right were the exact same three boxes with the same splintered damages only they were opposites. On the left wall hung a tattered and faded tapestry depicting a field of roses. On the right side was the same tapestry, only reversed. It was as though the middle of the room contained a giant mirror which reflected each side back to the other. It was in this room that Bartlebug first discovered he could travel to Earth.

Back then, this had just been another storage room. No one even noticed its unique properties. Bartlebug had stumbled upon the room purely by accident after coming to the bowels to enact punishment on a pauper who apparently had taken up living here. He searched all the storage rooms until he came upon this one. The uniqueness of this room had been immediately apparent to Bartlebug. He noticed the twinness of it as soon as he stepped in and it took his breath away. He put a simple incantation on the door, turning it black and hiding the knob, and ordered the most dimwitted subject of the King to guard it, knowing full well Dunmire

Quixitix would never question what he was doing. Then Bartlebug had come back, and had found his way, for the first time, to Earth.

He was thinking of that first voyage now as he hung in the room, buzzing, preparing for the trip once more. The first time was the most painful, but after that he got the hang of it and made the trip without harm each time now. Other gateways, similar to this one but scattered across Serafina, hurt quite a bit more, however. He could not remember how many times he had gone to Earth; countless.

He proceeded to the center of the room where there was a puddle of water. It was at this point, and only at this point, that the room had no mirror image. This central point was unique, and this was the gateway to Earth. Bartlebug landed here and stood on his stout black bee-like legs, in the water. Reaching out his hand, he could almost feel the tingle of the passageway before him, the rift in space, or whatever it was, that allowed him to move between these two worlds. He had no idea that Queen Lillian and her two children could also do this, and at will no less. Like he had done so many times before, Bartlebug closed his tiny white pin-prick eyes, moved forward, and was gone.

When he opened his eyes, he was in the same place he always ended up in, what the resident of this domicile told him was called a bathroom. It was very smelly and dirty, and Bartlebug noticed several glass decanters scattered about the room this time.

"William!" shouted the Bargoul. He heard a loud crash as something made of glass shattered and a voice started. "I have arrived once more and require your assistance!"

On the other side of the bathroom door, Willy Fitzgerald felt like he was having a heart attack. Every time that little bee thing showed up it scared the devil out of him. Why the heck couldn't he just knock?

"Yes Sir, you got it," said Willy, flailing about nervously, waiting for the moment when that freakish thing would open the bathroom door and come out. The first time Willy had seen Bartlebug he thought he was either really drunk or in a really bad dream. He had been so scared of that first time he had wet his pants. The freakish thing said he had to help it, or it would kill him. The one image Willy held in his mind most clearly was of the stinger. The way it came out of the bee thing, all shiny and wet and black. Willy had been terrified of that thing, and he still had nightmares about it nearly every night.

Now the moment came and Bartlebug emerged from the bathroom.

"Is the carriage ready to go? I realize we just recently made the trip, but we must do it again," said Bartlebug.

"Yes Sir, it's got a full tank and it's ready to go," Willy said, saluting.

"Excellent. Then let's be off. Time is of the essence."

"Right," said Willy. He grabbed his keys from the coffee table and handed Bartlebug his jacket and hat. Bundled up in these garments, he looked very comical, and almost human, except for his black insect legs which protruded from the bottom.

"New York then? Same place as usual?"

"Aye," said Bartlebug.

Willy and Bartlebug left the decrepit apartment and proceeded down the steps and out onto the street. Willy's taxi was waiting there, bright yellow, complete with an advertisement for a movie. He ushered Bartlebug into the back seat.

"Ready?"

"Yes. Go."

Bartlebug was in no mood for any sort of conversation with William, his servant here on Earth. Even though he traveled in this horseless carriage many times, each time still amazed him. He needed to get to LochBarren and finally put an end to the meddle-some Smith. And this time he would, oh yes, there would be no fail-ure this time. Michael the Smith would not escape his wrath again.

CHAPTER 32

▼

MICHAEL THE MAGICAN

The red Cadillac sped down the highway like a shiny bullet. The two passengers who were quite accustomed to this form of travel were enjoying themselves greatly. The other two, Mya and Dunny, had still not quite mastered their fear of this mechanical marvel. For the first two hours, Dunny sat, massive hands clenched so tightly onto the seat there were permanent indentations there now, wishing he had never come along with the Queen on this crazy journey and wishing he was back in the castle enjoying his favorite variety of stew.

Mya was afraid at first, but a few reassuring looks from her mother let her know everything was fine. She had never felt speed like this before. Her Fabrications of ponies could never go this fast. This metal carriage was truly amazing.

"Okay, we just passed through Washington so we should have another four or five hours I'd say. Judith, any idea where in New York we are heading?" said Peter. He was in the passenger seat holding a road map, turning it this way and that.

"I'm not sure, but I have an idea," she said, smiling at Peter.

"Alright, I hope you know what you're doing."

At last Dunny put aside his fear and spoke up saying, "My Lady, please tell me more about this place, if it suits you of course."

"Alright Dunmire, what would you like to know?"

Dunny thought for moment and said, "What sort'a food do they 'ave here?"

Judith could not help but laugh. "Well, thousands of different things. Much more advanced that what we have in Serafina, I might add. In fact, they have a place called a Super Market where you can purchase any type of food you want, anything."

Judith could almost hear the sound of Dunny's mouth begin to water.

"Do they have stew, and potatoes, rabbit, deer?"

"Most of those and many others you have never even heard of."

"I would very much like to stop at one of these Supper Markets," said Dunny.

"No, Super Markets Dunmire, Super," said Judith correcting him. "I'm sorry, but I don't think we can spare the time. Michael could already be in great peril."

Dunny nodded and stopped talking, his mind filling with thoughts of what marvelous treasures were held inside the Super Market.

Mya, on the other hand, was thinking about Michael, her half brother. She didn't have time to react to what her mother had told her because they had been seconds away from crossing over. She had been thinking about that statement the entire time she had been here. She remembered first meeting him on that stump she had Fabricated in her rose field. It had been so strange; he had just appeared out of nowhere. Now Mya understood that he had crossed over, crossed over from here, and that Michael was from Earth. She felt angry for a little while after her mother told her the story of how she came to Earth and began a new family. It had been a few hours ago, but now Mya put those feelings away. She had a brother, and she remembered feeling a special kind of connection with the boy when he was in the jail cell. He had been trying to tell her something, she guessed it was that they were brother and sister.

"Mother, may I ask you a question?" said Mya.

"Certainly, dear."

"I know the history of the Line of the Fabricantress," said Mya, the wind from the highway blowing her dirty brown hair around her face. "And I know how strictly the Kingdoms monitor and control the daughters of women who are of that line."

Judith knew exactly where this was heading, but she kept quiet.

"If Michael is your son and my half brother, can he use the…"

She trailed off, afraid of even speaking the forbidden word.

"It's alright Mya, you can say it."

"Can he use the Magicant?"

Peter's ears perked up at the sound of this new word. He was still trying to understand the Fabricant thing and now there was something else which sounded just like it but with the word magic in front.

Judith was quiet for some time, then said, "Yes."

Mya was not surprised. This was why she felt such a connection to him. The Fabricant and the Magicant were twin powers. She knew the legend, and only females can use the Fabricant, males the Magicant. She also knew no males have been born of Fabricantress mothers since the Twinning Wars.

"Because he was born here? They had no way of knowing what you were doing…that is why he exists, because he is an Earth child."

Judith was not entirely surprised by the intellect her daughter possessed, to put it all together so quickly.

"Yes Mya, you speak the truth. Michael is very special."

"What is this Magicant thing, Judith?" Now Peter spoke up.

"The Magicant is the twin half of the Fabricant, a power that can only be used by males, a power too great for the world of Serafina.

Many Magicans, those who can use the Magicant, turned to evil ways over one hundred years ago. The Fabricantress' were able to stop them, but at great cost. The Twin Power was sealed away and no male was ever born again in Serafina who could use it. Michael was born on Earth. And he is a Magican."

Peter was too confused to get upset. He had decided long before that he did not care about these crazy stories Judith had to tell. He only wanted his son back safely.

"The evil creature who is after our son, Bartlebug, and his entire race, the Bargouls, were created by Magicans, not many know that fact. It has been covered up by history, yet it remains the truth. The Bargouls were servants and scribes. They tried to overthrow Serafina with the Magicans in the Twinning Wars, but they were stopped. It seemed they were all under a spell and once the Magicans were defeated; the Bargouls reverted to more…pacifistic ways. I never believed it. Just look at Bartlebug."

Peter glanced over at the dials on the dashboard in front of Judith.

"We need gas," he said.

Judith nodded and got off highway at the next exit.

"Slouch down a bit Dunmire. We don't want people to think we are suspicious."

Dunmire did as he was told and Judith rolled the Cadillac into an Exxon station. Peter jumped out and began filling the tank. Mya was thinking about Michael and what it would mean if she was reunited with him. Dunny was thinking about his brother, and the apple pie Archibald made. He was looking forward to that once they got to LochBarren. Judith was thinking about the place they were going, a place that no longer existed but she was sure would be the spot where they could cross over easily to LochBarren. It was too perfect not to be. None of them noticed the dirty taxi cab pull into the pump across from them.

CHAPTER 33

▼

FILL 'ER UP

Willy Fitzgerald knew his life was over when he began working for Bartlebug. Willy thought it had been nearly three years since the bee thing first showed up. If Willy remembered correctly, the first time he ever met Bartlebug was in the fall of 2001. The creature controlled him, caused him to spend every day in fear wondering if the thing would show up and command something of him. He was confined to his small apartment (which was not very far from Michael Smith's house), as Bartlebug had ordered, simply in wait for when the bee appeared in his bathroom. The first time, once the thing was gone, Willy thought he had finally gone crazy. He had seen some very strange things in his years of taxi driving, but nothing like a bull dog sized talking bee coming out of his bathroom. Once Bartlebug left, Willy chalked it up to temporary insanity and knew the thing would never come back. But it had, many times.

Sometimes, Bartlebug would just ask Willy for information. Geography, stuff about the government, about the police. Willy could hardly believe he was even talking to a bee, let alone discussing politics. One of these conversations led to Willy telling Bartlebug about airplanes. He was fascinated by the flying machines and wanted to know more. Willy told him all he could, including the most tragic airplane event in Willy's life time, the destruction of the Twin Towers by terrorists using the airplanes. When Bartlebug had heard this, he had grown extremely angry and told Willy never to mention that day again. Willy had been surprised Bartlebug even knew about it. Willy could not help his curiosity and so he had asked Bartlebug why. Surprisingly, the Bargoul had answered him, saying that he had lost two very important people when those towers fell. Willy did not push the matter any more. Willy had taken Bartlebug to ground zero many times after that, recently, with an unconscious boy. Bartlebug told Willy not to ask any questions.

Now they headed there again, this time with no talk, no conversation, and no odd questions from Bartlebug. He just sat in the back of the taxi, disguised well enough with a khaki hat and trench coat, waiting.

"Sir, we need to fill up," said Willy, looking down at the E on the gas gauge.

"Do it then, and be quick about it," said Bartlebug.

Willy scanned the highway signs for one with a gas station symbol on it and when he found the exit, he turned the taxi off the highway. It was an Exxon station. Willy pulled into an unoccupied pump and turned off the taxi.

"Do not dawdle, William. I cannot afford delays."

"Yes Sir," said Willy, exiting the cab.

The pump read 'pay first' so Willy proceeded inside the gas station. Bartlebug never paid for gas on these trips, Willy thought as he walked in the door. In fact, all the extra money Willy earned being a cabbie (against Bartlebug's orders of house arrest) went to these long excursions to New York. Gas wasn't cheap, but it was better than being dead.

Bartlebug waited with impatience in the taxi. He had to get to New York and to LochBarren before it was too late. He was sure

The Smith had survived the balloon crash, although his commanders had told him nothing of the boy's fate. He had to get there and take care of this pesky problem. He smiled. He loved Earth. It seemed like such a vile place compared to Serafina, but he knew it would make a wonderful Kingdom for the Bargouls. And it would be so simple to have! Even though Bartlebug could not use the Magicant like the Magicans of days past, they had taught the Bargouls some…tricks.

It was not the Magicant, as Bartlebug knew, but some lesser form of it, as though it was distilled. It was not the Bargoul army, however, that Bartlebug really cared about. What he wanted had been here, on Earth, years ago. Then they had been taken from him and he had thought all was lost…but it wasn't. He had found a way to have them yet…once the boy was dead. Bartlebug had been looking up at the dull blue sky and now turned his head down and found himself staring straight into the eyes of Mya VanVargot.

Mya had been sitting in the Cadillac waiting while Peter filled it up with something, as her mother had said. She glanced over and noticed another vehicle like theirs but this one was yellow and had a top. Mya noticed a passenger sitting in the back, where she was sitting in her own car. It looked almost like a child, but its face was very dark and its eyes were not visible. The figure wore a dark hat. As she was staring at the person in the back of the taxi, he looked over at her and for a moment their eyes meet, and Mya saw white pin pricks.

She quickly looked away, fear and panic racing over her.

"Mother!" she shouted.

Judith spun around, eyes wide.

"Mya, what is it?"

"I just saw him! I saw Bartlebug, here! Over there, in that carriage!"

Judith's face exploded in shock.

"Mya, that is impossible! We are on Earth, only those who are in touch with the Fabricant can make the journey…"

"I saw him Mother. Look for yourself!"

Judith opened the door of the Cadillac and got out. She slowly walked to the back of the car so she could see the taxi cab beyond the pump. The back end began to come into view and Judith peered into the back seat. She saw nothing.

"See Mya?" she said, turning to her daughter, "It is just your imagination; I do not blame you for being scared. This is a very difficult experience for you."

"I did not imagine it," said Mya, looking back at the taxi. But her mother was right; the back seat was completely empty. Now Mya began to doubt herself. Maybe she had imagined it.

"Bartlebug, you say?" said Dunny. He opened his door and began to lumber out of the Cadillac. "Well, if that little bugger is here, I'll give him a piece of my mind…we are a long way from the castle, if you catch my meaning."

Dunny walked to the back of the Cadillac and stood next to Judith. He too examined the taxi and saw nothing. Peter was now walking back to the Cadillac after having gone inside to pay for the gas. Dunny moved slowly over to the taxi for a closer look. He crept up on the backside of the cab and peered in the window, looking for any sign of Bartlebug.

"You're sure you saw 'im 'ere, Mya?"

"Yes, sure," she said. Was she sure?

Peter had now returned to the Cadillac and was preparing to get back in. Dunny was moving to the far side of the taxi, to look into the window there. He looked in and saw something.

"All I see in here is what looks like a hat," he said.

Mya looked troubled. Had she seen the bee thing in the taxi? Maybe it was her imagination, although she thought he had been wearing a hat of some kind.

"Okay Dunny, well maybe I was just…."

As Mya spoke to Dunny she saw something horrible unfold before her eyes. Faster than she could blink, the upper left side of Dunny's shoulder exploded outward as something sharp and black blasted its way through his body from behind. Mya screamed and this caused Judith to shriek as well. Before they could even tell what had happened, the black thing retracted and Dunny stood with a large hole in his shoulder. Mya could see a man walking out of the building behind him through the hole. Then she saw Bartlebug rise into the air behind Dunny. His sting was out and dripping with red liquid.

"Dunny, no!" shouted Mya.

"Bartlebug!" shouted Judith.

"Well, I did not expect this," said the bee, hovering above Dunny. Dunny simply swayed in the air, his massive body moving back and forth until he finally fell to the ground in a heap.

"This is the price for leaving one's post…plus I have always hated this lumbering moron," said Bartlebug, the joy in his voice unmistakable.

Dunny could be heard moaning on the ground.

"Peter, get inside. Call an ambulance, for the sake of the Seraphim!" Screamed Judith. Peter did as he was told without hesitation. Bartlebug took no notice of him as he ran past.

"How did you get here Bartlebug? How is this possible?" Judith was unsure what to do.

"Well now, that's my little secret isn't it?"

"You slimy worm!" shouted Mya.

"How dare you speak to me in such a way, girl," said Bartlebug. "It matters not anyway. Soon, all shall be mine. I shall have them at last!"

Bartlebug lowered himself onto the trunk of the taxi as Willy approached and saw the massive man lying on the ground, bleeding.

"Sir, what happened? Did you…"

"Get in and let's go," said Bartlebug.

"Mya, how will your father feel when I tell him you have been kidnapped by these…simpletons?"

A sudden change came over Judith in that moment. She seemed to straighten; her hair seemed to become fairer. Her eyes grew more royal. Her entire body took on a certain essence, both Bartlebug and Mya noticing the change immediately.

"What are you…" then his tiny white eyes seemed to grow twice as large. "This cannot be…I had you…you were gone…"

"I am Queen Lillian VanVargot of the Kingdom of BlanchField. You are a traitor to the throne and a murderer!"

Now Bartlebug recognized the woman before him and could not believe he had missed it before. In the castle, she had looked like an ordinary pauper, her hair in tatters, her clothes odd, her eyes downcast and hidden. Now, there could be no mistake. This was the Queen; the very same woman Bartlebug had tricked into killing her brother-in-law, the same woman whom he had sentenced to death in order to become a stronger influence of the King, the woman who had come so close to discovering his true intentions. This was the same woman who had disappeared the night before her execution and given up for dead. Now Bartlebug knew where she had gone. He also knew something else. His quick mind juggled three faces; The Queen, the girl, and the Smith. The Queen is Mya's mother…and the Smith's Mother. So, the children were related. Bartlebug grinned.

"It matters not wench! The wheels of fate are already in motion. Soon, this world, and all others, will belong to the Bargouls!"

Bartlebug hopped off the trunk and into the back seat of the taxi. Mya ran toward the cab, her emotions getting the better of her, trying to Fabricate a wall or a rope, or anything they could use to stop him, but to no avail. Nothing happened. Lillian grabbed her just as the taxi sped away from the pump. Mother and daughter watched the yellow carriage shoot away, back towards the highway, New York, and Michael.

Lillian and Mya ran to where Dunny now lay in a heap, bleeding.

"Is he still breathing?" asked Mya.

"Yes, he is still alive, but losing blood fast."

"Can't you Fabricate some medicine for him mother?"

Lillian shook her head, "I'm sorry Mya, I cannot Fabricate here."

Dunny was moaning quietly. Finally, Peter ran from the gas station and got down on his knees beside Dunny.

"Ambulance is on its way. I told them it was a stab wound. They said to apply pressure."

Peter rolled Dunny onto his back and held his hands over the large hole in his shoulder. This wound would have instantly killed a normal sized man, but Dunny's size had saved his life. Peter looked up at Lillian, who now looked quite different, eyes shining, stature regal, and unmistakably Queen-like.

"You and Mya need to go. You have to follow him, find Michael!" Shouted Peter.

"But what about you! And Dunmire!"

"Do not argue with me Lillian! I am not a King, but I am a father, and a husband and I know what you need to do. Please, I'll take Dunny to the hospital in the ambulance. There will be fewer questions this way. Take the Caddy and go!"

Peter was shouting, sweat rolling down his face. He looked into Lillian's eyes and they nodded to each other.

"Come Mya," she said.

Mya could not resist the command. She hopped in the front seat of the Caddy as Lillian started the engine. She looked over to Peter, kneeling on the ground, barely able to hold Dunny's massive head in his lap.

"I love you, Peter. Take care of him."

Peter looked at Lillian, fear and love filling his eyes.

"Find our son. And bring him home to me."

Lillian nodded and pressed the gas. The Caddy shot forward, tires rolling up dust as the car left the gas station. She looked in the mirror one last time at Peter and Dunmire and prayed with all her heart that he would be okay, and they would be in time to save Michael.

CHAPTER 34

▼

AN ARMY GATHERS

As a red Cadillac sped down the highway chasing a dull yellow taxi cab, Michael Smith was finally waking up. He had been unconscious for days, ever since the balloon had gone down. Bartlebug's army of killer Bargouls had attacked the boy and the professor just as they reached the shores of the Emerald Sea. There had been so many little bee creatures they seemed to fill the sky, their shadows overtaking the balloon and its two passengers. The attack had been swift and the balloon quickly began losing altitude. They escaped only because the boy had delivered some kind of attack, the likes of which the professor had never seen. The blue flame had filled the sky around them and sent the Bargouls in quick retreat, then the boy lost consciousness. As the balloon had plummeted toward Serafina, gas escaping through the numerous holes in the FlaxFur balloon (the consequence of hundreds of Bargoul stings), Professor Quixitix could only cower over the boy, and try his best to protect him.

Now, as Michael began to open his eyes for the first time, both the boy and the professor rested peacefully in Aside; sitting quietly in the small upper room of Quixitix' home. Quixitix sipped his tea and noticed Michael stirring in the makeshift bed the professor had constructed for him. He put down his tea cup and approached the boy.

"Michael? Are you alright, dear boy?"

Michael heard the voice and opened his eyes. He felt as though he had not opened them in years. His body felt exhausted, his head a ball of tight wires. He tried to sit up in the bed and found the task quite difficult. Turning to Quixitix, he spoke.

"What happened?" his voice was very distant and tired.

"I'm afraid we did not succeed, young Michael. The Bargouls they…they attacked us…" Quixitix trailed off.

"Attacked? Yeah…" Michael's memory, although fuzzy in places, was slowly beginning to reform and take shape. He remembered being high in the air, flying, toward his parents. Then he heard the buzzing and saw the Bargouls coming at them, thousands of them, each a different color but all with the same tiny white eyes and sooty black faces. Snyder had been there. He had spoken to Michael, something about an invasion, and an army?

"Army?" asked Michael. He reached up a hand to touch his head and noticed his hand wrapped in white gauze bandage. His head hurt.

"Yes, Michael. It was an army of Bargouls, and according to Snyder, Bartlebug seems to be their leader. I believe they were sent to kill us, well you, more precisely, but in that they did not succeed. You stopped them, young Michael, with the Magicant…I have never seen the like."

"The Magicant?" Michael was beginning to come fully to his senses now, remembering everything, about the Magicant and the Fabricant, Serafina, Bartlebug. "What did I do?"

"Well…it looked as though you *became* blue fire. The sight was truly astounding, your entire body nothing but flame. It was all around you, engulfing you. You raised your arms and the fire seemed to escape and shoot to the sky. It covered the Bargoul army, devastating them. They retreated, and I watched many fall. We fell too, however. You passed out before we hit the ground."

Michael could remember the moment when he had slipped into unconsciousness. He had been thinking about his mother, and his father, and his half sister Mya. He wanted so badly to see them all again. Then everything went black.

"It was a rough fall, indeed, but we landed on the beach. So it seems the Seraphim were watching over us. Your wrist was hurt. I injured my arm, as you can see," Quixitix held up his right arm showing Michael that it was in a sling. I was able to carry you back here, though. Took some time…but we made it. You were asleep through the whole ordeal."

"My thanks, Professor. What about the balloon?"

"Destroyed I'm afraid. The Bargouls did manage to accomplish that much. The canvas is in tatters, the basket ruined, the whirls bent," Quixitix looked dejected. "Oh well, at least we have our lives."

Michael nodded, then looked up at the professor. "What about the army? Do you think they'll be back?"

Quixitix shrugged. "I doubt it. If they showed up in town, their secret would be out and everyone would know what Bartlebug was doing. Besides, I think they are afraid of you now, Michael."

Michael thought about what happened in that balloon, what Snyder had revealed. He remembered talk of an invasion, an invasion of Earth, and something about a Canyon, but the invasion had scared Michael to the core. He could not let that happen and he was the only one who could wield the Magicant. The responsibility rested with him to stop the Bargouls. He would have to find a way to save his parents and stop Bartlebug. He imagined his mother and father locked away in the dank basement of Castle BlanchField waiting for their own deaths. Unless his mother had managed to shift and escape...this thought filled Michael with some hope. He had no way of knowing for sure, but he knew his mother. He thought maybe she had escaped. Either way, there remained no time now for rescues, it was too late for that. Before he could save his parents, Michael knew he had to stop Bartlebug.

"Although there is something that concerns me," said Quixitix adjusting his glasses.

"What's that, Professor?"

"While you were unconscious, Aside seems to have been emptied of all Bargouls. Not a single one has been seen in days. They have simply vanished. No one knows where they went. Very odd."

Michael thought for a moment. Where would they go? What would they do? Could Bartlebug have something to do with it? Could he be rallying the troops, preparing his army? It seemed very possible, especially if Bartlebug saw Michael as a threat.

"Could they be gathering for invasion?"

Quixitix thought about this for a moment, then nodded.

"It seems quite possible."

"Snyder said they had found a way across the void and they would be attacking Earth..."

Michael was thinking about the object in the glass case on the first floor of Quixitix' home. The soda can which looked odd somehow, like something was missing, left out. The Marvel Quixitix had brought back with him from Earth when he had found his way into Couplet Canyon and stumbled through some kind of gateway.

"Professor, what about Couplet Canyon?"

Quixitix started. "Couplet Canyon? Why do you..." Then recognition glazed over the scientist's eyes as he understood what Michael had been thinking. "Do you think Bartlebug knows about the portal there, the place where I traveled to Earth?"

Michael nodded.

"Why would he concentrate his army here in LochBarren? It's too far from the major Kingdoms, right?"

Quixitix nodded.

"Okay, so then why here? It would be impossible for them to cover the distance, even to BlanchField, but this place is so remote, it would be perfect for…"

"Planning an invasion," said Quixitix. Michael nodded.

"And the Canyon is the perfect insertion point…to Earth." said Michael, thinking he sounded like his history teacher.

"This is not good, Michael. If the Bargouls find their way to Earth, there is no telling what could happen…" Quixitix' eyes searched the room, fearfully scanning the place.

"Well then we will have to stop them somehow. We are the only ones who know about this. Is there anyone here who will help? In this town?" asked Michael.

"I believe there may be some locals who I can convince. They owe me some favors anyway. What about you? We will need your…abilities when the time comes. Can you still use the Magicant. Can you still feel it?"

Michael concentrated for a moment. He no longer had to anger himself to produce the fire; he could will it to come. He did this and for a moment nothing happened and he panicked. He tried harder, and this time he felt something boil up inside him. It was weak but it was there. He held out his left hand, the one without the bandages. A small red tongue of fire appeared there. It danced bashfully, then disappeared.

"Yeah, I can still do it. I think I'm just kinda weak. I'll need some time."

"Alright. You prepare yourself, and I will seek the aid of Aside."

Quixitix stood, limping on one leg.

"If our theories hold true Michael, the fate of Serafina rests in your hands. Bartlebug must be stopped…at all costs."

Michael nodded.

"He will be stopped, Professor." Michael laid back down on his bed and closed his eyes. He needed to rest. He was only a boy, and now the fate of worlds was held out before him. Would he be able to handle that responsibility? Would he be able to wield this fiery power he possessed and stop an army? He was unsure. Inside his closed eyes he thought again of his family. Quixitix left him to sleep.

CHAPTER 35

▼

GROUND ZERO

"Faster!" yelled Bartlebug spinning his head around and looking through the back window of the taxi. Far behind, but still dangerously close, he was sure he could see that massive carriage chasing them. He had been a fool not to recognize that woman at the castle for who she truly was.. Queen Lillian, given to him like supper on a platter, and he had let her slip away. When she had disappeared, Bartlebug had been sure that was the end of her, that he would never see her again. Clearly he had been mistaken.

"I'm trying, sir," said Willy.

"There!" said Bartlebug, pointing his black arm to a road sign flying past. "New York City, thirty five miles, we are almost there." He looked again for the red Cadillac and this time did not see it. He felt somewhat relieved.

"So, who were those people at the gas station?"

Bartlebug was annoyed with William's questions but answered none the less.

"They are a people from my world…pests I need to exterminate…they could very well be a problem to my plan. It matters not. They will never make it."

"Oh, okay," said Willy.

The two rode on in silence, Bartlebug thinking about his next move. He needed to gather his army and deal with the boy first and foremost. Then Couplet Canyon…he smiled. This would be his moment of glory; he would finally be reunited with them. The Bargouls were stronger than most cared to admit, their fathers, the Magicans, had made them that way. Bartlebug thought of Lucas. Lucas had been Bartlebug's creator and master. He was a brilliant Magican and knew of ways to manipulate the Magicant that had never been seen before. He was the first to realize that the Magicans did not have to live as servants, but as Kings. Lucas had been the leader of the Magicans during the Twinning Wars and Bartlebug had been so proud of his master as he watched him slay the Fabricantress women, destroying the weak and ravaging them.

The sound of a carriage horn made Bartlebug snap back to the present. He would follow Lucas' footsteps and succeed where his master had failed. He would find the Descendents, at long last, and together take Serafina and Earth for themselves.

Looking out the window, thirty miles later, Bartlebug realized they were nearing the place where he could cross back to Serafina and LochBarren.

"There. Stop there," said Bartlebug pointing.

"I can't park there," said Willy.

"I don't care. Do it!"

Willy nodded and pulled the cab to the sidewalk in front of a large lot, vacant at the moment, and filled with dirt. He looked at the large sign, as he always did, and remembered those who had died here. Willy had been on duty when it had happened, but not in New York. He didn't work in New York. He had heard it on the radio; a plane had hit the World Trade Center. He had imagined some kind of minor accident, like a small one person jet had hit it and everything would be fine. He had no idea of the magnitude of that radio announcement. He had been devastated, just like everyone else. Now, there was nothing here, just this large sign, remembering. He took off his cap and held it over his chest.

Bartlebug got out of the cab, still disguised in trench coat and hat, and scanned the area. There were a few people here and there. But one thing he had observed about the people of this city was that they were not very observant. Either that, or they simply did not care to look. Bartlebug approached the fence surrounding the lot and buzzed up and over it. He looked back and Willy.

"You may leave William," he said.

"Thank you, sir," said William. He decided to grab a bite to eat across the street first; he loved New York hot dogs.

Bartlebug continued down the slope to the middle of the vacant lot. Bartlebug remembered William talking about airplanes which had led to the driver's mention of the Twin Towers; a place Bartlebug wanted to sorely to forget…he had lost them here, in this very lot where two massive towers once stood. He wasn't sure why, but it was only when Willy mentioned the towers that first time that Bartlebug had really heard the word twin. He had visited the towers, while they still stood, hundreds of times, but never did he suspect a gateway existed between them. He wished he had figured it out sooner. Things would have been much easier then.

Bartlebug had his theories about Earth and Serafina. The odd way the room in the basement of the Castle in BlanchField seemed like a mirror image on both sides, the way William's bathroom had two of everything in it, and this odd place called the Twin Towers. It seemed to fit perfectly in Bartlebug's idea of how the gateways worked. Earth and Serafina were twin worlds, and wherever the fabric between them grew thin, the Twin nature of the worlds would begin to show itself more abruptly. He thought it was a good theory, and he had proven it true the first time he had crossed over where the Twin Towers had once stood. He wondered if Lucious and Lavinia had known about the gateway here...

Now Bartlebug again found himself in front of the portal, the gateway between Earth and Serafina. The gateway displayed no visible signs of its existence, just a feeling one got, in the pit of the stomach. This was the place, the same place he had crossed so many times before. All that stood here now was a dirt-covered lot, the well spring of the tears the humans had cried when their twin towers fell. This central point, direct in the center of where the towers would have risen toward the heavens, was the junction, the crossroads, the thin tapestry of reality that would serve Bartlebug as a door back to Serafina. He shed his disguise and was about to go through when he heard someone yell. He looked around and saw the red carriage parked where Willy's taxi had been. The one who had yelled was Mya VanVargot. Bartlebug had no time to waste. Glancing back, he saw the girl and her mother shamble over the guard rail separating the rest of the bustling city from this lot. He wasted no time watching them but instead hovered forward. The crossover had always been an easy one, just like in the castle, and as the oversized bee felt the world begin to grow thin and the familiar sounds of LochBarren begin to fill his ears, he heard the twin voices of Mya and Lillian VanVargot shouting at him. He ignored the women and was gone.

CHAPTER 36

SOMETHING LEFT BEHIND

"Mother there!" yelled Mya, pointing to the vacant lot across the street from the hot dog vendor. Mother and daughter had followed the taxi as close as they could through the city, had lost it a few times, but somehow managed to ride the winds of fate to this lot. Lillian had guessed this was where Bartlebug was headed anyway. Mya had seen the taxi first, parked next to a silver box with a large parasol protruding from the top. She did not ask what the cart was or what the man was doing standing behind it. She had simply pointed to the yellow carriage and Lillian parked the Cadillac on the opposite side of the street from it. Willy, now fully indulged in his hot dog, did not notice the Cadillac. Mya and Lillian got out of the car, intending to question the driver of the taxi as to where Bartlebug was, when Mya looked at the vacant lot and yelled.

They watched as Bartlebug spun around at the sound of Mya's shout, and the two women hurried over the guard rail, in hopes of catching the Bargoul before he was able to cross over. Once they were over the railing, they ran across the dirt, not caring if any one saw them or tried to stop them, but they could not reach Bartlebug in time. As they watched him hover toward the center of the lot, his body began to grow thin and transparent and the two women watched him as he simply vanished before them.

"Mother, what do we do now?" said Mya between breaths. She was looking around at the city, totally in awe of this world with its massive castles, taller than anything she had ever seen or dreamed up. So many new things bombarded her here that she had decided there simply was not time to ask her mother about them all. She just had to accept this world.

"It's alright Mya; we can cross over again too. We don't even need the portal. In fact, the only reason we were chasing Bartlebug was so we would know *where* he crossed over. It will make it easier for us on the other side. Well then, let's not give him too much of a head start. Take my hand," said Lillian, reaching out for her daughter. Mya took her mother's hand and noticed how warm it was.

"Mya, I want you to focus on your brother, Michael. Picture him in your mind; imagine what he looks like and what he might be doing right now."

"Alright," said Mya, closing her eyes. She pictured the boy on her stump, her half brother, and the way he had looked that fist time they had met.

Lillian concentrated and felt the Fabricant move through her so easily she was shocked. She had never felt the Fabricant like this before on Earth. It was as though she was becoming one with it, drowning in the tidal wave as the Fabricant flowed over her and through her, carrying her along on its own path. Lillian was certain this place was indeed very closely connected to Serafina. The boundary of the worlds was very thin here and the Fabricant could easily seep through. She did not even realize that she had crossed over to Serafina until she opened her eyes. Then she heard the buzzing.

Lillian wheeled around; her grip tightening like a vice on her daughter's hand, and at the same time thanking the Seraphim that Mya had crossed over with her. They were surrounded. All around her Lillian saw black, sleek carapace stingers waiting for one of them to move so it could plunge into them, just as Bartlebug's had plunged into Dunny at the gas station. There must have been fifty Bargouls waiting for them. Some, Lillian noticed, where badly burned and seemed ragged. She wondered if the Magicant had anything to do with those wounds.

"Did you really think I would not take the necessary precautions upon my arrival here?"

Lillian turned again and there was the foul Bartlebug, his smug face crumpled into a sinister smile.

"I always have my Commanders here, waiting for me, when I come. Foolish Queen," said Bartlebug, shaking his head.

Before she could do anything to stop it, one of the Bargoul's shot towards them. Lillian tried to pull Mya away, but the thing was too fast. It grabbed Mya and pulled her back into the air.

"No!" shouted Lillian.

"Mother! Help me, please!"

"Mya! Bartlebug, if you hurt her…"

"Now why would I do such a thing?" Bartlebug grinned his wicked smile. "When I have minions to do it for me."

Lillian was on the verge of tears. She knew the Bargouls would kill her daughter if she tried to attack them with the Fabricant. She only had one choice.

"Then take me. Take me and I will come with you and turn myself in."

Bartlebug pondered the offer.

"I was sorely upset when your execution failed to occur the first time. I would very much like to see you hung…release the girl."

"Mother! No!" shouted Mya, struggling inside the grip of the Bargoul.

"It's alright Mya, everything will be fine. Trust me."

A Bargoul approached Lillian from behind and struck her behind the leg, causing her to cry out and fall to her knees on the ground. Another creature with a length of rope began to bind her hands and mouth. Lillian concentrated on something in her mind, the softly spoke The Word, trying to Fabricant the image, while the Bargouls continued to tie her.

"Leave the girl," commanded Bartlebug.

The Bargoul holding Mya let her fall to the ground roughly. She looked at her mother with tears falling down her checks. Lillian looked over to her daughter and when their eyes met, Mya saw such love there that she knew it would be alright. She would see her mother again. She would find her and save her.

"Bring the Queen. Let's go."

Bartlebug turned and buzzed off toward the forest that stretched toward the horizon nearby. Mya watched as three Bargouls lifted her mother and bore her away with them. Lillian's eyes told Mya to stay where she was.

Soon, the fleet of bee creatures was gone and Mya was left alone on the small grassy area where she and her mother had crossed over, back to Serafina, and into the thick of Bartlebug and his goons. She could not help but cry. Then she looked on the ground near where her mother had fallen to her knees. She saw something there and got up to see what it was.

Lying on the ground was large silver coin. On one side was a woman, her hair flowing in the air around her head, with a face so beautiful Mya thought it looked like her mother. On the other side of the coin was a man, stern and noble, with his hand raised to his face. Inside his hand danced a small flame. Mya understood what the coin depicted; the Fabricant and Magicant, the twin forces. She also seemed to understand what her mother was trying to tell her by leaving it for her. She put the coin in her pocket and looked around. There was not much here except for the forest to the West and very far to the East what looked like a mountain range. She was unsure of which direction to go. She was in LochBarren, she knew, because that was the entire reason for coming to New York City, as her mother had said. She decided to head South, remembering her geography lessons and the name of a town called Aside. She thought Aside was to the South. She got up and began walking, in search of what her mother wanted her to find, what the coin she left told her to seek out; her half brother, Michael.

CHAPTER 37

▼

A MEETING

As Bartlebug passed through the gossamer thinness of the gateway at Ground Zero, Michael found himself sitting on an old wooden chair in front of a small group of Aside locals. They gathered in the main room of Quixitix' home, the room which contained the soda can Quixitix referred to as The Marvel. It was covered in a blue silk scarf now, no point in wasting time while the townsfolk gawked at the odd thing. Michael still had not been able to put his finger on why the can seemed strange to him, odd in some way. He knew it was the same colors, red and white, and the lettering was the same, but something was…different about the can…one word kept coming to him, old. He put the thoughts out of his head. There were more important things at hand right now.

Quixitix was standing; preparing to speak to the few people he had been able to convince to help them. There were only about a dozen or so.

"May I please have your attention?" began Quixitix. "I thank you for coming here tonight," he said, bowing his head. "Your aid is invaluable at this time of need. I have summoned you here because a great threat now stands before not only your home of Aside, but LochBarren as well, and the rest of Serafina."

A small tremor of worried sighs and cautious looks floated through the small crowd.

"The perpetrator of this threat is a Bargoul named Bartlebug."

"Stinkin' Bargouls!" shouted one member of the audience, a man named Randall Vaan. "Never did trust 'em!"

The rest of the group grunted their approval. Quixitix put up his arms to quiet them.

"Indeed, it seems this particular Bargoul has amassed an army whose purpose it seems is to take over Serafina, like the Magicans tried to do nearly one hundred years ago," Quixitix had talked to Michael before the meeting and both had agreed there was no need to mention Earth. They would stop Bartlebug before he got that far, or they would perish.

After moments of nervous hesitation about the mention of Magicans and the Twinning War, another man named Warren Mayweather spoke up.

"How can the Bargouls hope to stand up against the forces of Serafina? I mean, each Kingdom has an impressive army, plus the Fabricantress women…I don't see how they have any hope of victory."

"You bring up an excellent point, Mr. Mayweather," said Quixitix. Michael knew the name; this was the same Mayweather who owned the farm Michael had enjoyed so much, and the wife of Mrs. Mayweather who had so kindly shared her Sugarberry Pie.

"And I'm afraid I do not have an answer for you. We do not have all the facts at this juncture. All we do know is that an army exists, as I and my young companion here have seen it."

The crowd seemed to notice Michael for the first time when Quixitix mentioned him. Michael was not listening, however. The last question, from Warren Mayweather, had disturbed him greatly.

Why? Because the man was right. The Bargouls didn't stand a chance against Serafina, let alone Earth. So what was Bartlebug up to? What sort of sinister plan did he have cooking inside that insect-like head of his? Michael did not know. Perhaps there was some piece to this puzzle he had overlooked, or did not yet know about. Either way, it was up to him to stop Bartlebug before any plan of his could be put into effect.

"And this army, it seems, is bent on domination. I have called you here to aid myself and this boy, Michael Smith, to stop Bartle-bug and save Serafina. There is no time to summon the Kingdoms, for I fear Bartlebug may already be here and his army on the verge of readiness. We do not know where they are, but we suspect LochBar-ren is where he plans to begin his invasion. Those are the facts. Who among you still wishes to help?"

The crowd looked around from one person to the next. Two men in the back, farmers wearing overalls and straw hats, looked at one another and one said, "I have a family to think of," and left the house with noises of disapproval and shaking heads. Everyone else stayed.

"I thank you friends," said Quixitix bowing.

"So what do we do now?" asked Randall.

"Well, Michael and I have discussed it and we believe Bartlebug and his army is hiding in Couplet Canyon. We do not have any facts to back this up, but we both feel it is the perfect place, strategi-cally, to train an army and…"

Quixitix was interrupted by a small cry of "No!" from outside his front window. Everyone in the room heard it as well and they all turned around trying to find where the voice had come from. They saw no one in the room and Quixitix nodded his head for the man closest to the door to go outside and investigate. He did, and brought back with him a small boy, Trevor Mayweather.

"Trevor! What are you doing here? I told you to stay at home!" shouted Warren when he saw his son was the owner of the voice outside the window. Michael recognized the boy immediately; it was the same boy Michael had shared a slice of Sugarberry pie with. Michael could not help but smile. He wondered if Madeline and Mrs. Mayweather were home right now, waiting for Mr. Mayweather to return with news.

"I'm sorry da, I just wanted to see what all the fuss was about. Please, don't scold me!" said the child. "Besides, I have somethin' important to tell ya'."

Warren looked at his son with angry, fatherly eyes, then said, "Alright Trevor. I suppose you've just got too much of your da in you. Come here son."

Trevor bounced to where his father stood and was lifted up onto his father's shoulders. When Michael saw this he was reminded of that Christmas movie he always liked to watch, *A Christmas Carol*, and Tiny Tim when Bob Cratchet would lift his son onto his shoulders.

"Mr. Quixitix sir, I heard you say 'dem Bargouls is in Couplet Canyon. That's not right," said Trevor.

Quixitix raised an eyebrow and looked at Michael, concerned.

"Trevor, do you know where they are?"

"Aye, I do. I've seen 'em, lots of 'em. Out in Bornhold Forest," the boy looked down at his father, frightened.

"What have you been doing out there Trevor?" Asked Mr. Mayweather.

"Sorry da, me and Seamus like to play out there but the crick, and…"

"That's enough. Tell the Professor the rest of your story."

"Well, me and Seamus were out there one day and we saw a great many of the Bargouls headin' for the woods, and I mean a lot. So if you think they got an army, I think they're in the woods."

"I think you may be right young, Trevor and I thank you for having the courage to tell us this," said Quixitix. He looked again at Michael, concerned.

"Alright. Prepare yourselves tonight and meet back here in the morning. Tomorrow, we shall head out for Bornhold Forest. Bring whatever weapons you can muster. May the Seraphim always guide you."

And with that the small gathering of townsfolk dispersed and the meeting ended. Soon only Michael and Quixitix were left in the room.

"So, we were wrong," said Michael.

"No, only half wrong. I am certain Bartlebug is planning on using Couplet Canyon to get to Earth. But if we can somehow stop them before they even begin," Quixitix shrugged.

"Professor, Mr. Mayweather was right you know, about their chances. It doesn't seem like the Bargouls stand any chance against the forces of Earth or Serafina."

"Indeed…that question concerned me also. I fear Bartlebug may have something else under the hat."

"Well, let's just stop them before they can do anything. Tomorrow, we will stop them in Bornhold. We must. I feel strong enough now. The Magicant will not fail me," said Michael. Michael's words sounded empty in his head. He had tried not to think about his parents since the balloon crash. He had tried to focus on the impending onslaught of the army, and his role to play in stopping it. But still he worried for them. Were they alive? Were they still in that dank dungeon at the Castle BlanchField? He did not know, but he had a sensation. Some kind of flicker in his soul, something telling him they were okay. Perhaps it was the Fabricant, the power wielded by his mother and sister, which was telling him not to worry. Perhaps it was only his imagination. Either way, he could not go back to

BlanchField now. He had to stay and try to stop the army of Bar-gouls…somehow. He looked at Quixitix.

"You should get some rest, young Michael. Tomorrow will be a day to remember."

Michael nodded. He rose from the chair and proceeded past it to the steps, then stopped in front of The Marvel. He looked back at Quixitix.

"May I?"

Quixitix nodded. Michael removed the silk scarf and examined the can beneath the glass dome. Red, white, everything was in place but…dull, faded…different. He stared at it, and then shook his head. He replaced the cover.

"Good night, Professor."

"Good night, Michael."

Michael went up the steps and Quixitix watched him. The Professor sat alone by the flickering of the candles, his mind heavily weighted with worry for what tomorrow would bring. He feared the worst.

CHAPTER 38

▼

CONVERSATIONS BY CAMPFIRE

Lillian awoke to the sound of a popping fire. For a single fleeting moment she imagined herself sitting quietly in the parlor of her home on a cold December evening, her home on Earth. Peter would be home from work shortly. Michael would be upstairs doing his homework or reading a book, and she would be enjoying the warmth of the cozy fire as the first gentle snow flakes began to fall outside her window. Then the vision was gone and replaced with the scene before her.

She opened her eyes and saw not her hearth (complete with framed pictures of her family) but a crude bonfire burning carelessly atop a pile of large logs. Because of the position she was in, she could not move or turn her head very much. Her hands and feet were bound and she had been tossed on the dirty ground several feet from the fire on her side. She could just make out the dark silhouettes of several Bargouls watching her from the other side of the fire. She closed her eyes in hoping they had not seen her awake. She did not want them to know she was conscious yet. Instead, she simply listened.

There were many other sounds besides the fire. She heard the occasional song of a cricket or the sound of wind howling through trees. She guessed she had been taken to Bornhold Forest. She cursed herself for being so nearsighted. Of course Bartlebug would have been ready for them when they came through to this side. But there was nothing she could do about it now. At least Mya was safe, and she had the Silver Coin. That was something. Lillian hoped Mya would be able to find her brother and…

Her thoughts were interrupted by the shrill voices of some Bargouls. Lillian remained motionless and listened with all her focus.

"I think it's meaningless dribble," said one voice.

"Really? You don't believe him? Then why are you here?" said a second voice. This one sounded older somehow.

"Because I'm sick of being pushed around, just like everyone else," said the first voice.

"Yes, and how do you propose we end our suffering?"

There was a slight pause, the first Bargoul thinking of an answer, and then, "We take what belongs to us. We take over everything!"

From across the campfire, Lillian heard the agreeing hoots of the Bargouls she saw watching her. She kept listening.

"But Flynn, don't you understand anything?"

Flynn, that must be the name of the first Bargoul. Lillian would remember that.

"What do you mean?"

"Do you really think we can put an end to the tyranny we have endured for so long with this meager band?"

There was a longer pause now and Lillian feared the two Bargouls might have wandered off out of earshot. Then Flynn spoke up again and she was relieved.

"We aren't that meager," said Flynn.

"Okay, Flynn. Then I would love to see you try to take on the entire army of BlanchField with your sting. That I would very much like to see," said the older voice.

"Well, I still don't know if I believe Bartlebug…his promises seem so empty," said Flynn.

At the sound of Bartlebug's name Lillian's attention was now fiercely directed at these two creatures and she knew she needed to hear what they had to say.

"How can you not? He is wise and has seen a great deal. He was alive for the Twinning War. Besides, he was the servant of Lucas Allcraft. And if there is anyone who knows where to find his descendents, it is Bartlebug."

Descendents? Was that the word she heard him say? Lillian's mind raced, a thousand questions pouring in like water into a sinking ship. Lucas Allcraft had children? Impossible! She knew the history, knew what happened one hundred years ago during the Twinning War. Allcraft was stopped and with him died the last of the Magicans. The evil war against Serafina ended. It was not possible, the Line of Fabricantress would certainly know if Allcraft ever bore children…Lillian was so busy thinking she did not notice the two Bargouls begin speaking again. What if they were in hiding? But the war was a century ago; surely, if Allcraft had children, they could not be alive! Maybe his grandchildren…

Finally Lillian's concentration was broken by something the Bargouls said. She could barely hear the Bargouls now as they were at last moving away, patrols she guessed, making their rounds. As they left, and the last fleeting words of their conversation made their delicate way to Lillian's ears. She was certain she heard the words *Couplet Canyon*, and although she could not be absolutely certain, she thought the Bargouls had uttered the word *Earth* as well.

CHAPTER 39

▼

MORE DREAMS

Michael's dreams that night became a nightmarish myriad of images and voices, places and things he had experienced since his first visit to Serafina. The rose field was there, except in his dream it had been burned and even the heavens seemed to weep for it. He saw Dunny. The large man's face melted before Michael like cheese left in the sun, his boisterous smile becoming a sinister, deathly cringe. There was a hot air balloon, only now it had become some sort of flying beast with fangs at every angle and claws like razor blades. Finally, Michael found himself chasing a young woman through a dense forest. Every now and then the girl would turn her head to look at Michael. While she ran, the face she wore seemed in constant flux. One moment it was the face of Mya, Michael's half-sister and wielder of the Fabricant, the next it was his beautiful Mother, Lillian VanVargot, and still the face of the young girl shifted and changed. Michael kept chasing her. They ran for what seemed like miles until the girl abruptly stopped in a clearing. Michael stood at the edge and watched here intently, waiting to see what she would do. The ephemeral girl bent down slowly and it looked to Michael like she was picking something up off the ground. The girl's head was bent examining the object she had recovered. Michael wanted desperately to see what it was, what the girl had found, but he feared going into that clearing for some reason and the sensation kept him at bay. Suddenly the girl spun around and this time the face was neither his mother or his sister but something deadly and ancient. The decaying features glared at him in horror, the thing's hands clutching the precious object it had just gathered up from the soft forest floor. In his head, Michael heard the beast tell him he would fail, and all was doomed. Before he could turn to flee, the thing came at him with inhuman speed. In seconds, it was so close he was sure his next breath would be his last. Just as the girl-creature reared its hideous arm, ready to strike the boy down, the forest was gone, and emptiness greeted him.

"Michael," said a voice from somewhere in the void. He could feel himself rising to the voice, like a diver slowly surfacing.

"Michael," louder now, and Michael began nearing the surface. He opened his eyes, slowly.

It was Quixitix who had called to him in the void of his mind, the voice which carried him back to the surface of his own subconscious.

"I'm awake," said Michael.

"Good. I didn't think I would be able to rouse you, I have been trying for nearly ten minutes," said the Professor.

"I'm sorry…bad dreams. Is it time now?"

"No actually, it is still quite late. I woke you because we seem to have an unexpected guest. Says her name is Mya and she knows you?"

Michael's heart leapt. How could this be? Mya, here? He jumped from his bed and ran downstairs, not stopping to say anything to Quixitix. When he got to the bottom, he scanned the room quickly and finally saw her. She was sitting on a small chair with her back to him, examining a wood carving Quixitix had in the corner of the den. Even from this angle, Michael thought she looked exhausted.

"Mya!" he shouted.

The girl stood and turned in one motion. For a split second Michael knew it would not be Mya but the thing from his dream, the beast-woman who had tried to kill him. He knew that her face, as she turned, would be a hideous decaying disaster, the skin falling off in places, the eyes a putrid green. Then he saw her and his relief was instant. It was her, his sister; finally, he could tell her the truth.

He ran over to her and hugged her fiercely.

"Mya, I'm sorry I didn't get a chance to tell you before but listen…"

She stopped him.

"I already know. Mother told me. We are brother and sister," she smiled.

Michael smiled too. They embraced again. Something had suddenly changed inside Michael and he wondered if Mya felt it as well. It was as if a switch had been turned on, like something which was not quite right was now perfect. He felt like a whole person.

"Mya how did you get here?"

"It's a long story…" Mya looked down. She had wandered most of the night, afraid now that her mother was gone. She had been following a small dirt road, night time noises frightening her nearly to death, until she had seen lights in the distance. She had followed the light, and it had led her to Aside. She continued.

"Which I don't have time to tell now. What matters is that Bartlebug has mother," she said, dejected and angry.

"Yes, I know. I have been trying to get back to BlanchField to save her but…"

"No, I mean he has her here. They took her to the forest to the west."

"What! Mom is here too? What about my dad? Do you know where he is?"

"You mean the man, Peter? Yes, he and Dunny were separated from us after Bartlebug attacked and they…"

"Attacked! Mya, tell me everything."

She did. She started when she had gone to visit the prisoners, the parents of this boy, only to discover that one of them was her own mother. She told Michael about shifting, about the yellow carriage and the strange things she saw on the other side (as she had come to think about Earth), about the attack at the gas station and Dunny.

"They were waiting for us when we crossed over," finished Mya. She had been talking for nearly thirty minutes.

"Shifted. That's what I call it."

"I see…a fitting term. Anyway, they were going to take me, but they took mother instead, to the forest. She left this for me…"

Mya reached into her pocket and removed the silver coin Lillian had Fabricated for her. She handed it to Michael. He felt its weight and its smoothness. It was large and very precious. He noticed the girl on one side and the boy on the other and understood this silver coin was some kind of signet for the twin powers that created Serafina, the Fabricant and the Magicant.

"After that, I found my way here. It was not a very long walk, but it was frightening at night. I was very scared," she said.

Michael embraced her.

"Everything's fine now Mya. You're with me. I will protect you."

"Thank you," she said, her face pressed against her brother's chest.

Quixitix had been observing the two from his perch atop the stairs and now took advantage of this opportunity to break into the conversation.

"Mya, we are very fortunate to have you here. We have prepared an expedition to go to the forest in the morning and try to stop Bartlebug and his minions. Would you join us?"

Mya did not hesitate for a single moment.

"Of course. My mother is in trouble."

Quixitix nodded.

"And you can use the Fabricant, correct?"

"Yes."

"Excellent. Michael, our chances have just soared," said Quixitix.

The boy and girl looked at each other, both thinking the same thing, that they were the most important part of those chances. Quixitix was smiling.

"Well, I am off to bed." He left the two alone in the den.

"Mya, do you understand what we are up against here? Bartlebug has amassed an army of Bargouls. We think he intends to invade Earth. Remember the gateway you just told me about, the one in New York City?"

Mya nodded.

"There is another one like that in the mountains to the east, in a place called Couplet Canyon. We think Bartlebug intends to send his troops through there."

"Why there? Why not the same place he came through in Nework City?"

"It's New York, and that is a very good question. A Bargoul named Snyder slipped with the information about Couplet Canyon when they were attacking me..."

"Michael, you were attacked? Are you alright?" said Mya, concerned.

"Yes, I'm fine. I used the Magicant to stop them."

Mya looked nervous at the mention of the name.

"It's alright, Mya. I'm not going to repeat what happened in the Twinning War."

"I know. It's just that all my life I've been taught to fear the other power…"

Michael took his sister's hands in his.

"Look at me, Mya. There is nothing to fear. I'm your brother, and together we can stop Bartlebug. I know we can," he said.

She smiled and nodded. Michael, like the first time he met her, noticed how beautiful she was, just like her mother.

"So we are going to the forest tomorrow, to save mother?"

"And stop the Bargouls, yes. Are you up for it?"

She nodded.

"Good. Then get some rest. We are going to need you, and the Fabricant, tomorrow."

"Michael…" She hesitated. "I have never seen the Magicant before…"

Michael looked confused then understood what she meant. He nodded and motioned for her to stand back. Holding out his hand, Mya watched as a small indigo flicker appeared in her brother's palm. The flame began to grow in size and become deeper in color as Michael focused his Magicant energy to create the tongue. In a few short seconds the flame had grown to the size of a basketball and it leapt and danced in Michael's hands. Mya stared, gaping at the fire, her first time seeing the Magicant. She held out her hand to feel the fire but did not feel any heat. She looked at Michael.

"I don't want it to hurt you…so it won't," he said.

She moved her hand closer to the flame and still felt nothing. Finally she passed her hand into the tongue of fire and felt only air, not even the slightest sensation of heat or pain.

"It's amazing…"

Michael closed his palm and the flame disappeared. Then he felt something different. He was not sure what it was, but it was very different from the heat he felt in the pit of his stomach when he summoned the fire. It felt light somehow, airy, like wind inside him. He pushed the feeling away.

"Your turn," he said to Mya.

Mya nodded.

She closed her eyes and thought for a moment.

"Sugarberry," she spoke softly, but still, Michael was surprised to hear the authority in her voice, the new tonal quality it took on. Holding out her hand just as Michael had done, a small red shape began to form there. To Michael it looked like an apple. The shape began to take solidity and coherence until finally it became something substantial.

"It's called a Sugarberry. Go ahead, taste it."

Michael took the fruit and smelled it, taking in its wonderful aroma. He bit in and the Sugarberry's taste exploded on his taste buds. He thought back to the pie he had enjoyed so much with the Mayweathers, but this Sugarberry tasted sweeter than even that delicious pie. In fact, Michael had never tasted something so sweet.

"It's amazing," he said.

Mya smiled.

"It won't fill you up. It will disappear in a little while, even from your stomach. It's only a Fabrication after all, but you can still get the taste."

"I love it," said Michael, finishing the sweet fruit.

Brother and sister talked for a little while longer until both decided they needed to go to bed. Tomorrow would be a test for both of them, and they needed the sleep. Too much depended on them stopping Bartlebug.

"Mya, I am so glad you are here."

"As am I Michael, as am I," said Mya with a small curtsey.

"Tomorrow we will save her, Mya, I give you my word. And tomorrow will see the end of Bartlebug."

"I hope you're right Michael." And with that Mya went up the steps to the room Quixitix had prepared for her. Michael followed shortly after.

As Michael placed his head on the soft down feather pillow, he hoped his dreams would be free of bizarre creatures, he hoped to finally see his mother again, and above all, he hoped for the strength to save this amazing world, and his own.

C H A P T E R   40

▼

BORNHOLD FOREST

The bright sun rose high over LochBarren the next morning, a golden harbinger of what the day would bring. A light morning haze shifted restlessly around Aside, the fog sneaking down back alley ways or creeping into barns and hay lofts. It was early, but Michael had been awake for quite some time. After his brief but enlightening talk with his sister, sleep did not come easily. He got some, and he felt rested, but his nerves were too on edge to sleep for long. He had more important things to do.

Michael sat now upon a bale of hay in the back field of Quixitix' shack, looking to the west. He knew what stretched out before him in that direction, and what awaited him there. He could almost picture Bartlebug buzzing noisily among the trees in Bornhold Forest, waking his fiendish army, preparing to move them out, to march them to Couplet Canyon…and beyond. Still Michael pondered why Bartlebug felt the need to take his army into that canyon, through that gate. The question gnawed at his mind like a hungry mutt. From what Mya had said, there was a gateway very close to the Forest itself, the one she and Lillian had watched Bartlebug enter from New York. Why not take his troops through that gateway? What was so special about Couplet Canyon? Michael could only surmise, but he thought perhaps it had something to do with the strange object (strange to everyone here anyway) Quixitix kept in his parlor. A can of soda, just like the ones Michael got from his refrigerator when he was thirsty, such a simple thing, but this one wasn't quite right. It wasn't the same as the ones Michael had seen in his supermarket when he went shopping with his dad. The colors were faded and the lettering was different, but overall he knew it was a soda can. Quixitix had brought it back through the portal in Couplet Canyon…and it was somehow different and unfamiliar…was it even from Earth?

Michael's thoughts were interrupted by the sound of people approaching. He turned to look behind him and saw the villagers who had agreed to help them along with Quixitix and Mya. They were walking toward him. One of them waved. Michael thought it was Mr. Mayweather.

"Good morning, Michael," said one of the villagers.

"Good morning, sir," said Michael.

"Morning, young Michael," said Quixitix.

"Same to you, Professor."

Michael hopped off the hay and went over to his sister.

"Good morning, Mya."

Mya curtseyed and returned the pleasantry. They both smiled.

"Well, it seems we are underway and things are as they should be. The townsfolk have brought their axes and hoes, some even have Calibers…"

Quixitix noticed the way Michael's face changed at the word and proceeded to clarify.

"You know, fire-arms, here, like this," said Quixitix, reaching for one of the villager's Calibers. To Michael, the thing looked like a cross between a hunting rifle and a cross bow. "So, we may stand a chance after all. These people are ready to fight for their homes and families," Quixitix turned to the crowd saying, "May this be a day which brings glory and victory to Aside of LochBarren!"

The dozen or so men standing there cheered energetically and Michael's spirits rose. He knew the villagers would do what they could, and he was honored by it, but he also knew that when the time came, he and Mya would be the ones they would be counting on. Michael joined the group next to Mya. Quixitix and Mr. Mayweather took the lead and the band began on their way to Bornhold Forest in the west.

The walk was not a long one, only a few hours, and to pass the time the villagers often broke out in war songs which did not fail to fill the heart of even a boy from Earth with great pride and courage. One of the songs stuck in Michael's head:

With the sun to our backs we march along,
Into the great unknown.
Ever seeking victory, for family, friends and home.

We shall fight until the day is through,
And weariness fills our bones,
Stand until the last one falls, for family, friends and home.

Aside! Oh, Aside!
Your fires call our names!
Aside! Oh, Aside!
To glory, honor and fame!

Our courage as strong as the mountain side,
Our valor now is shone,

We fight for the light in our children's eyes, for family, friends and home.

As the sun descends into the hills,
And the final fist is thrown,
Ye shall hear us shouting victory, for family, friends and home!

Aside! Oh, Aside!
Your fires call our names!
Aside! Oh, Aside!
To glory, honor and fame!

Michael could not help but be moved by the words of this ballad, the courage and the determination he heard there told him a great deal about these villagers. He sang it quietly to himself as they walked throughout the morning. At last, they neared the Western Wood, Bornhold Forest.

"This is the woods. We have no idea what to expect when we enter. We could very well be facing our own deaths. Are you still with us?" asked Mr. Mayweather. The villagers gave an enthusiastic cry as they raised their various weapons into the air. Mayweather nodded. "Professor, do you wish to remain here?"

Quixitix vehemently shook his head and pulled aside his long coat. Concealed beneath was a dagger strapped to his thigh.

"I may be a man of science, but I am always prepared. Gift from my brother," he said, tapping the dagger. "A fine blade, if I do say so myself."

"Alright. Michael, Mya, are you ready?"

The two children looked at one another and nodded their heads. Michael felt ready; he felt more in control of his abilities now than ever before.

"Mya, I will be offense if you be defense," said Michael. Mya didn't seem to understand and Michael guessed they didn't have football in Serafina. "Okay, I will attack, you protect as best you can, me and the villagers. And keep your eyes out for mom. We have to find her," said Michael.

"Alright…Michael," she moved closer to him so the others could not hear her. "I'm scared," she whispered.

Michael hugged her. "I know. Everything will be fine. Just concentrate on Fabricating, everything will be okay."

Mayweather spoke up again, "I say we try to surprise them instead of rushing in head first. Who is in agreement?"

The majority of the townsfolk spoke their approval.

"Good. Then may the Seraphim protect you all."

The men of Aside began moving closer to the forest, quietly and slowly. Michael and Mya were hip to hip walking just to the side of the group. Michael could feel the Magicant on the tip of his very being. Like a vase about to drop and shatter on the floor, the Magicant was aching to get out now. Everyone was doing the same thing, looking for scouts or perimeter guards. They crept closer to the forest and still saw nothing. When they finally got to the very edge of the woods with no sign of a single Bargoul, some felt lucky and others felt worried.

"I don't like this," said Mayweather. Quixitix nodded. Michael and Mya continued peering into the dense trees before them.

"Well, I'm afraid we haven't much choice," said Quixitix. Mayweather nodded and motioned for the men to continue forward. He looked down and nodded at the two children. They nodded back.

The men proceeded through the trees, careful to make as little noise as possible. Michael could hear the faint babbling of a stream off in the distance, and the occasional chirp of a bird or insect. Other than that, the forest seemed deafeningly quiet. After what seemed like an eternity of silently creeping from tree to tree, the men came at last to a clearing.

"This looks like some kind of camp," said Quixitix.

"Yes, and quite fresh from the looks of it," said Mayweather, bending down and examining the remains of a fire on the forest bed. "Embers are still warm."

"They must have left this morning. They are already on their way to the Canyon," said Michael, fearing the worst. They were too late. The Bargouls had gone, the army had moved out, and they had taken Lillian with them.

"Should we search the rest of the wood? An army as big as the one you spoke of could not all fit in this clearing," suggested Mayweather.

"I suspect there are many of these camps scattered throughout the forest, hundreds perhaps. No, don't waste your time. I'm sure they have moved on. We are a bit late, that is all," said Quixitix.

"Mayweather, over here!" the shout came from just outside the large clearing. Alvin Scrimshaw, local farmer from Aside and father of two, had obviously found something and the rest of the group ran over to where he stood. Michael joined them and the first thing he noticed was the smell. It was putrid, worse than twenty rotten eggs slowly going to waste in the boys' bathroom of his middle school, now long forgotten.

There, on the ground in front of a large tree, was the body of a Bargoul. Its chest had a massive stab wound which ran from front to back. It looked as though the thing had been dead for quite a while. The forest creatures seemed to have had their fair share of dinner from it and had left full and content; the thing's eyes were missing. Michael could not help but notice the small patch of green on its back.

"What do you think happened here?" asked Mayweather. Quixitix shook his head.

"I have no idea," he said.

The Bargoul was a grotesque sight and Mya could stand it no longer. She left the scene and returned to the clearing. Michael watched her go.

"We should go to the Canyon. How far is it from here?" said Michael, growing more than impatient. He had been on the verge of spewing fire and destroying the Bargouls. He had felt excited about it, like some kind of battle rage, and now he felt like he was coming down. He would need that edge in the real fight. Plus, Lillian was no where to be found and he desperately needed to see his mother.

"Look," said Mya from the edge of the clearing. She had wandered over there while Michael and the others had been examining the dead Bargoul. "Here," she said, pointing the ground where she stood.

Michael went to where she was and saw she had picked something up from the ground. It was another silver coin; an exact replica of the one Mya had shown him the previous night.

"She was here, Michael. Right here. She must have Fabricated this one just like the one I showed you. It is a sign. It means she is alright, but we have to hurry," she said, looking at Mayweather and Quixitix. The rest of the villagers had spread out to search the surrounding area.

"You're right," said Mayweather. "We make for the Canyon. If they are an army, they will be moving slowly. We may still catch them before it's too late."

Mayweather let out a shrill whistle, a signal to the rest of the men to come back and regroup.

"We are heading for Couplet Canyon. It is a few hours walk to the east. We have to be fast and we must catch Bartlebug before they reach the Canyon…" Mayweather paused for a moment, he looked puzzled. Turning to Quixitix he said, "What is so important about that Canyon again, Professor?"

Quixitix looked quickly at Michael then back at Mayweather. "It is an excellent…staging area…remote enough to prevent attack and close enough to Aside to make your homes their first target," Quixitix was not sure if this on the spot lie would convince Mayweather, but the man seemed satisfied, and he nodded.

"For Aside men, for family, friends, and home!" shouted Mayweather, and the men followed as he headed east at a fast trot. Michael, Mya, and Quixitix remained for a moment.

"If Bartlebug brings that army through to Earth, it could be disastrous," said Quixitix.

"You're right, Professor. We have to stop them…" Michael thought again about Couplet Canyon.

"But why that Canyon? What is so special about it? You went through the gateway, right, Professor?"

Quixitix nodded, then shook his head. "It was only a brief visit, and, aside from the fact I was in a completely different world, everything seemed normal."

"But there is something odd about that can you brought back…"

Quixitix was searching for an answer but came up with nothing.

"I don't think it matters much Michael. No matter what Bartlebug is planning in Couplet Canyon, we will stop him. We must."

"Yes, Michael. He must be stopped and we have to find our mother," said Mya.

"You're both right. Okay, let's get moving."

The three set out and caught up with the rest of the villagers.

Mya turned to Michael, hand outstretched, "Here," she said, handing him something.

Michael held out his hand to accept it and Mya dropped something heavy into it. The boy opened his hand and saw the silver coin

Mya had just recovered from the campsite, the gift from their mother.

"Now we each have one," said Mya smiling. Michael did the same. For some reason, holding the coin made him feel secure and confident. He hoped it would help him with whatever lay waiting for them in Couplet Canyon. He put the coin in his pocket and continued walking.

CHAPTER 41

▼

PALAVER IN THE FOREST

Michael and company had been right. The Bargouls had left that morning before the sun had even begun to peek from behind the Eastern Mountains. What the villagers had been wrong about was the size of the army. They guessed the army was much bigger than it now was. Bartlebug had gathered all his remaining troops the night before to discuss their plans for Couplet Canyon. While Lillian had been listening to the conversation of two Bargouls by the crackling campfire, Bartlebug had been palavering with his commanders on the other side of the forest.

"What are our numbers?" was the first question from his angry and sly mouth.

"After The Smith's attack, we lost a great deal, many died, others fled. Our current troop count is three hundred strong."

Bartlebug remained calm, but slowly reached his hand out and picked up large rock. He hurled the rock into the fire, yelling and causing the flames to dance and sing.

"Three hundred!" he shouted, enraged. "Three hundred! Prepos-terous!" He was so angry he could barely speak. The commanders recoiled in fear from their leader, this ancient and wise Bargoul. To cross Bartlebug was to sign one's own death certificate.

After a few moments Bartlebug settled down, "No matter," he said. "Three hundred should be enough to hold the Canyon…all I need them for anyway. And what news of The Smith? What is he up to?"

"Sire, all sources suggest he is planning an attack…it seems he also knows we are heading to Couplet Canyon…" said the com-mander shyly, not wanting to ignite Bartlebug's fury all over again.

"And how, might I ask, does he know that?"

Now the commanders all turned their heads to the direction of one unfortunate among them.

"Snyder, would you mind telling me how The Smith knows about Couplet Canyon?"

Snyder looked quickly around at the rest of the commanders, fear blooming on his face like a ripe rose.

"I…I'm sorry sire. It was…the battle and I was…excited and…"

"I grow tired of your constant failure Snyder. Perhaps this will help you remember what to do in the future," said Bartlebug.

"Oh yes, anything, please tell…"

Before Snyder could finish his sentence Bartlebug's sting exploded out of the back of his bee body, sending viscous fluids all over the tree in front of which Snyder had stood. The look of shock and surprise had frozen on the Bargoul's face as he fell to the ground, the large hole in his chest gaping. The rest of the com-manders were frozen with fear. They had barely even seen Bartlebug ready his sting let alone use it. He seemed unnaturally fast with it, and this kept them all in check. Bartlebug ruled them with a cold fear.

He pointed to the corpse of Snyder, "This is the price of failure. I have come too far and my plans are too well laid for some Earth boy to stop me…I have had enough obstacles already," said Bartlebug, thinking of the tragedy on Earth that had caused him such turmoil, had caused him to rethink his entire plan, to adapt and find a way to bring the Descendents here, no matter what….He returned his attention to the generals.

"My…friends," said Bartlebug, sneering at them. "Do you all understand what needs to be done on the morrow, and can you do it?"

One of the commanders, a Bargoul named Weston, spoke up quietly, "Yes, sire. We are to secure Couplet Canyon and see to it that you are not followed."

Bartlebug nodded his head. Another commander said, "Sire, may I ask why?"

Bartlebug whirled to face him. "Why what?"

"Well, sire, why are you going through the gateway? What do you intend to do all alone?"

Bartlebug thought about showing this insolent fool the fury of his sting, but instead only smiled. The thought of what he was going to Earth to do could cause no other reaction in the Bargoul. He had waited so long for this moment, for these fates to be just right, and they had been, once, a long time ago. Then they had died…but Couplet Canyon would fix that. He would bring the Descendents back and they, in turn, would bring the end of Serafina.

"All in due time. All in due time."

And with that, Bartlebug dismissed the clueless commanders. They were too afraid to ask any more questions. They would simply do their job, defend the Canyon and make sure Bartlebug was not followed. They did not need answers, only their lives.

Bartlebug sat alone by the fire while bugs began feasting on the corpse of his once loyal subject, Snyder. By the light of the fire, Bartlebug's feature seemed to dance some kind of devil's tango across his face. The Bargoul was not concerned with what his army did or did not do tomorrow, as long as they were able to stop the boy and his sister. He only needed time. His mind raced back, long ago, to the time when he was in the service of Lucas Allcraft, and that very first night when the Magican realized what he needed to do. Bartlebug had been given a very important part to play in Lucas' scheme, and now, at last, it was time. The Bargoul watched the fire, and waited.

CHAPTER 42

▼

A SCOUT

As the villagers made their speedy way toward Couplet Canyon, Quixitix and Mayweather leading the pack, Michael removed the silver coin left by Lillian for him at the camp site from his pocket and examined it more closely. It really was a beautiful trinket, the craftsmanship near perfect. It was heavy but not cumbersome and Michael very much liked the weight of it in his hand. He could no longer deny the resemblance he saw between the silver-faced girl on the coin and his sister. It was almost as if the image had been created with Mya in mind, and now that he thought about it, it most likely had. His mother had Fabricated the coins, after all. He flipped it over, almost tripping on a rock as he trotted along with the rest of the group. On the other side was the boy. He assumed he was looking at himself. In the palm of the boy's hand, a tongue of fire hovered just inches from his silver skin. Michael knew what it was like to possess and control that fire, the feeling of exhilaration he got every time he summoned it from the deepest reaches of his soul. He could feel that fire rising in him even now, preparing for whatever they would find in Couplet Canyon.

Mya noticed her half brother flipping his silver coin over and over in his hand, looking at it, feeling its texture and its weight.

"Isn't it wonderful?" she asked, looking at the coin.

Michael looked up and realized Mya was speaking to him.

"Yes, it is. I feel like it was made just for me and you."

"I think it was," said Mya. Michael nodded.

"What do you think they are for?" asked the boy.

Mya shrugged.

"Don't know. Perhaps they are just a way of telling us she is alright."

Michael ran his hand over the face of the coin.

"I don't know…it just feels…more important than that."

Michael had been so focused on his coin that he failed to notice the group had stopped and he bumped into the man in front of him.

"Sorry," he muttered, but the man only put his finger on his lips, a sign Michael knew meant keep quiet.

Michael inched to the side of the pack so he could see what was going on, and he observed Mayweather drawing the weapon Professor Quixitix had called a Caliber. Michael watched as Mayweather unlatched a long piece of wood from first the right side of the rifle, then the left, until the Caliber was in the shape of a cross. A piece of fine string now ran from the left side of the cross to the right, and Mayweather grabbed this piece of string in the center and pulled it back, attaching it to the rear of the rifle. Michael understood what the man was doing. Not only was this Caliber a rifle, but it also functioned as a crossbow. Michael's guess was confirmed when Mayweather reached into the pack he wore and pulled out a long, slender crossbow bolt. On the back of the bolt were feathers colored like Michael had never seen. He watched as Mayweather held the Caliber to his chin, and attached the bolt. Now Michael looked forward to see at what Mayweather was taking aim.

Michael could not see anything. The path ahead of them seemed clear. He scanned left and right, sure that no threat existed, but then his eyes chanced on a tree perhaps one hundred meters ahead. He could just barely make out the shape of something propped against the tree, resting in its shade. Before he had time to decide what the shape was, he heard the *thwap* of the string as Mayweather released the bolt, and the projectile sailed through the air, silently seeking its target.

A scream of pain and surprise filled the morning air as the Bargoul sitting under the tree tried to remove the crossbow bolt from his shoulder. He yelled and ran in circles, blood streaming form the wound. But before he could utter another breath, another bolt found its way through his stomach, and he fell to the ground in a heap. The villagers had moved in after the first shot. A few seconds later they were under the tree, also examining the body.

"A scout," said Mayweather.

Quixitix and the others nodded.

"They may have heard him shouting," said Alvin.

"It is likely," said Quixitix.

"Then we must hurry."

They began to run.

▼

CHAPTER 43

CALM BEFORE THE
STORM

The Bargouls had indeed heard the screams and had quickened their pace. Bartlebug was in the lead and the three hundred or so Bargouls flowed out behind him, some walking, others hovering inches above the ground, with their bee wings buzzing rapidly. Next to Bartlebug walked Lillian, hands bound and blindfolded, while a Bargoul named Macy kept his sting in her back. Bartlebug had instructed him to kill the woman were she to try anything. Bartlebug looked up at the towering mountain range before him. The sand colored rock rose high into the mid morning sky, and he could clearly see the twin spires which marked Couplet Canyon. He could also see the entrance to the canyon just ahead, and he didn't much like it. It was a bottle neck, and if the boy and his friends caught up to them at exactly the moment when they were passing through it…he pushed the thought from his mind. He was too far ahead of the boy to worry about that, although they had left the scout behind only a short while back. It didn't matter, as long as he made it to the gateway. That was all that mattered.

"You are foolish to think you will get through this unscathed, Bartlebug."

The voice of the once Queen seemed to drill into Bartlebug's head, boring deeper and deeper until it penetrated all the way to his mind.

"Quiet!" He motioned for Macy to show the woman just how sharp his sting was.

Lillian felt it in her back, like a giant needle waiting to penetrate the skin. She decided it might be best to just listen to what was going on. She knew her children would be here soon, and everything would be fine.

At last Bartlebug and his army reached the canyon's entrance. The walls here were lighter than the rest of the rocky mountain, still the same sandy orange color but here they seemed faded and old. On either side of the path, the mountain rose in a sharp slope. Ahead, not far now, the twin spires, reaching like hands praying to an unseen god, jetted skyward. Bartlebug knew those spires were, in fact, exactly twins, perfect copies of one another, down to the most minute chip and pebble. The path grew very narrow as the army neared the canyon so that they had to travel two by two. It would take some time for them to get into the canyon, hopefully not so much time that the boy would catch up, but Bartlebug did not care. He would be the first one in, and by the time the boy got there, he would be long gone.

CHAPTER 44

▼

BATTLE

The mountains loomed before them, and Michael could not have imaged just how large they really were. He could see the twin peaks that Quixitix had spoken of and knew that was where Bartlebug was heading, to the valley below them. The band was almost in sight of the valley entrance. Just one more small hill and they would be able to see it.

Mayweather was the first to crest that last hill, and Michael barely saw the man draw his Caliber, ready it, and fire a bolt. Michael looked ahead, and saw the army. They were making their way into what looked like a narrow passage, and because of it, they were bottle necked. Perhaps half of Bartlebug's troops were still waiting to get through, some standing in formation while others buzzed through the air. Once the villagers got over the last hill, they were very close to the army, and all at once the men broke out into a war cry that drowned out the buzzing coming from the Bargouls. They charged forward. Mayweather was firing his bolts with incredible speed, letting go and reloading so fast Michael could barely see the man's fingers working. Quixitix had brandished the dagger given to him by Dunny. The few other villagers who carried Calibers were firing their bolts as well; although no where near the speed with which Warren Mayweather was able to fire. Some of the villagers had scythes, massive ones they used to tend their fields. Now they were being used for something quite different. The men swung their sharp farm instruments into the waiting bodies of Bargouls as the villagers of Aside confronted the army.

Michael looked to Mya seconds before they reached the army.

"We can do this," he said.

Mya nodded. She reached out, taking his hand, and she smiled.

The *thwap* of several Calibers made Michael look up. Bargouls began to scream, now aware that they were under attack. Michael summoned the fire and immediately it filled him. Quixitix was off to the left fending off several Bargouls, waving his dagger in the air wildly. Michael saw three of them, eyes fixed on the Professor. One came down on him, but Quixitix nimbly sidestepped and plunged the knife into the Bargoul's back, yelling as he did so. The Bargoul fell to the ground, quivering in his own fluids.

Mayweather had abandoned the long range bolts and was now firing the Caliber like a rifle. Michael heard the reports of it, deafening, as the pellets flew from the gun and into the Bargouls. A few others had Calibers as well and were firing them in quick succession. Alvin had a dagger and was fighting several Bargouls alone. One of them moved too quickly for him and plunged its sting into his left arm. The man's blood seeped from the wound and dripped from the attacker's sting. Alvin was not stopped however, and he kept fighting, managing to kill one of the Bargouls. Michael saw the man was in trouble.

Alvin thought he was finished after that Bargoul got his arm. He had managed to kill one, but now there were four in front of him.

"Come then, foul beasts!" he shouted at them

"With pleasure," one of them said. Alvin gritted his teeth. The Bargouls came then but before they reached the wounded man one of them exploded into a ball of blue fire. He didn't know what was going on. The other three were too surprised to act, and before they could do anything, they were also on fire, flying through the air like blue tangents of heat until they fell to the ground in charred heaps. Alvin looked to his right and saw the boy there. Michael was his name. His fists were clenched and they were on fire too. Alvin knew what he was seeing and he could not believe it. He was witnessing the Magicant. Something only fearfully whispered about, a legend told to frighten children. But here it was. This boy, this young boy, was somehow wielding the magnificent power. Alvin never-in his wildest dreams-thought he would ever see this. At last he was able to speak.

"Thank you, Michael," said Alvin.

"No problem," said Michael, then more Bargouls came at them.

"Mya, now!" said Michael, looking back at Mya.

Mya closed her eyes and concentrated.

"Wall!" She shouted, her voice seeming to echo throughout the canyon as she spoke The Word. As several Bargouls shot through the air toward Michael, their progress was suddenly stopped when a massive stone wall appeared in front of the boy. They slammed into it, dazed and unsure what was happening.

Michael sprang from behind the wall, hands alive with indigo flame. He put his hands together and produced a blanket of fire which covered the Bargouls. They screamed as their bodies melted away, leaving only the hard carapace of their stings behind.

"Nice, Mya. Thank you."

Mya smiled and nodded.

Quixitix yelled, not in pain but in triumph, as he took down another Bargoul. Randall Vaan was swinging his large black scythe in wide arches around his body. Severed Bargoul bodies were scattered around his feet, Michael saw some arms, some upper bodies, and some wings. The man seemed crazed. He yelled and spittle flew from his mouth. Mayweather was swinging his Caliber like a club, smashing the Bargouls as they came at him.

A man screamed in pain and Michael saw someone fall to the ground, watched as a Bargoul landed on his chest and ran its stinger into the man's ribcage. It was a grotesque sight. Michael yelled and shot a blue flame toward the Bargoul. It hit the thing with such force he was ripped away from his own stinger and was thrown several feet through the air, on fire. The stinger was still in the man's chest. He was dead.

More Bargouls came at them now, and Michael began shooting fire in every direction, hitting sometimes and missing sometimes. Mya was helping too. Whenever she could, she would Fabricate barricades, nets, ropes, and chains to stop the oncoming army, Michael could her very clearly over the din of the battle shouting The Word with all her might.

"Mya, are you alright?" shouted Michael, burning a Bargoul that had been on its way to his sister.

"Yes," she said, but Michael thought she sounded very tired. He was getting tired too. But he couldn't stop, not yet.

"Mya, come with me!" She shouted.

Mya took Michael's hand and they two ran to where Quixitix was fighting. The professor was breathing hard, clearly exhausted. He saw them coming and let his guard down for a second. Two Bargouls came at him at the same moment, but Michael was too quick for them. He shot duel balls of blue flame at them, one from each hand, and they crashed to the ground in agony.

"Professor, we have to go in further. We have to find Bartlebug. He may already be there!" shouted Michael over the din of buzzing wings, screams, the reports of Calibers and the metallic clang of steel on stingers.

Quixitix nodded. "I think we can handle these buggers," he said. "Good luck, Michael, I hope to see you again!"

Michael nodded as more Bargouls came at them.

"Go!" shouted the professor.

Michael grabbed Mya's hand and they ran, attempting to go around the battle and slip into the valley leading to the Canyon. Bargouls tried to hinder their progress but they could not stand up to the power of the Magicant. The villagers from Aside were fighting in small, scattered increments about the battlefield. Bargouls flew through the air, yelling and grabbing with their insect hands, trying to find the perfect opportunity to plunge their stings into their opponents. Michael saw one villager with nothing but a pick axe defending himself from several Bargouls, his blonde hair matted on his forehead with sweat. The man brought the pickaxe down hard and Michael saw it plunge into a purple and black Bargoul. The bee fell to the ground. Warren Mayweather stood among a heap of Bargoul bodies, and they seemed to just keep coming, but the man kept on fighting and brought them down at his feet. Michael saw all of this among the chaos of the fight.

In the course of perhaps ten minutes Michael and the villagers had destroyed a significant number of Bartlebug's forces. The army had dwindled and Michael was sure that very soon the rest of the Bargouls would flee. Bee bodies were scattered everywhere on the ground, some still half alive, others clearly not. Brother and sister made their way to the narrow passage only to find it empty. Michael had expected there to be some lingering forces here, but to his surprise there was nothing. He looked back once at the chaos of huge flying bees, Calibers and steel, then took his sister's hand and led her into Couplet Canyon.

CHAPTER 45

▼

IN COUPLET CANYON

They walked cautiously, careful of any traps Bartlebug might have left for them. There was nothing, so far; only the sandy path and the mountain walls. Michael could feel they were getting closer; the power of this place was undeniable. He could almost feel the Magicant flowing and swirling here. There was a bend in the path and Michael and Mya followed it. The path led them further into the mountains and on either side, just up ahead, twin peaks rose. They loomed higher than Michael could have imagined; perfect twins. They passed through another narrow passage and emerged on the other side into Couplet Canyon.

The first thing they saw was their mother. She was blindfolded and looked terrible.

"Mother!" screamed Mya, forgetting everything for a moment and running toward her. Michael grabbed her and held her still. This was the first time Michael had seen his mother since he was captured so long ago at Castle BlanchField. His heart swelled with love and tears found their way to his eyes.

"Mya, wait. We have to wait," he said.

Hovering next to their mother was Bartlebug accompanied by perhaps twelve other Bargouls. All of them looked fierce.

"At last Smith," said Bartlebug.

"Release my mother!" demanded Michael.

Bartlebug looked casually at Lillian, then back at Michael.

"No, I don't think so. You see, she is wanted for treason…and murder."

"Liar! You did those things!" shouted Michael.

Bartlebug simply shrugged, "Technicalities."

Michael could feel the fire of the Magicant raging now, could feel it waiting to be released, every fiber of his being sang with the power of it.

"You have meddled in my plans for too long Smith, but that no longer matters."

"Your army is defeated Bartlebug. You have no invasion! You're done!"

"Ha! Invasion…feeble boy. That was never the idea! The Descendents of Lucas will rule this world, and all others. That is all that matters, and there is nothing you can do."

Bartlebug turned and hovered toward the center of the canyon. Michael was confused, not sure what he meant. Who were the Descendents of Lucas? Not an invasion? Michael guessed Bartlebug never had any intention of invading Earth with his Bargouls, that it was all just a vehicle to carry him here, but why? Bartlebug turned.

"First kill the Queen. Then the brats," he said to his commanders. He turned and continued further into the Canyon.

"No!" shouted Michael and Mya in unison.

One of the commanders, Wren, shot out his sting and reared back, preparing to dispose of the woman standing before him. Mya closed her eyes and concentrated with all of her being, everything that she was on this single image, this most important Fabrication, the Fabrication that would save the life of her mother. She could feel the sound swelling inside her, she could feel The Word preparing to spew forth from her throat like an eruption, like a thousand torrent volcano's issuing forth in unison. She shouted The Word, her voice becoming not her voice, becoming something divine, something else entirely. The Word became manifest.

Wren shot down, sting fixed on Queen Lillian's back. Michael watched this in slow motion and he was sure this was the end of his mother. She would be dead and he would not even be given the chance to say goodbye. Then he heard the Bargoul yell and watched as his sting cracked and shattered, the obsidian shrapnel flying everywhere.

Around Lillian had appeared a dome made of the purest white Michael had ever seen. To him it looked like a large shield. There appeared to be markings and letters on the front surrounding a beautiful woman. Michael looked at Mya.

"The shield of the Seraphim," she said. She sounded as surprised as Michael looked. "I did not think I had that kind of power…"

Immediately, the rest of the Bargouls came toward the children, stingers out and ready to kill. Michael's hands lit up with blue and he shot two tongues at the oncoming Bargouls. Both missed. Michael jumped out of the way at the last second, just in time to save himself from becoming a permanent fixture on the end of a Bargoul's sting. He landed on his stomach and quickly turned to his back, releasing two more tongues. One hit its mark and the Bargoul crashed into the mountain side, a flaming ball of fuzz.

Now the other commanders were coming at him, leaving Lillian, and focusing on the boy and girl. The white shield still floated above and around Lillian, casting a soft glow on her skin and protecting her from the Bargouls. Michael counted ten Bargouls left to deal with. He thought for a moment, remembering the hot air balloon, and what had happened there. He did not have time to fight them all. He had to catch Bartlebug. It might already be too late. He made up his mind. Dodging the attacks of the commanders, he ran to Mya.

"Mya, go get mom!" he told her. She nodded.

Mya ran over to where Lillian stood and hugged her. Now both Mother and Daughter were under the white shield but the color was not as bright and the shield itself seemed to be flickering in and out. Mya tore the blindfold from her mother's eyes.

"Mya," said Lillian, the tears flowing from her beautiful eyes. They looked at each other and embraced, reunited again. The shield faded away.

"All out of fire, boy!" shouted the commanders as they continued attacking Michael. He was able to dodge, but one attack got him. It was only a cut, but it hurt and he was bleeding.

"Ha! Not so strong without your little campfire are you?" shouted another Bargoul. When Michael saw the blood flowing between his fingers from the wound on his arm, he knew he was ready, and then everything stopped, just like before. The world took on a clarity and a sharpness. His senses where peaked. He could hear his sister and mother embracing, he could hear each flap of the Bargoul's wings; he could even hear the sound of the villagers approaching. Blue flame licked the sides of his mouth, his eyes, even his hair seemed on fire. He held out his arms, mimicking the twin spires of Couplet Canyon, and the blue flame shuddered up and down his body. All ten of the Bargouls came at him at once, fast and deadly. He saw them coming, but it did not matter. They were going to die. They were going to pay for what they had done, for the pain they had brought to Michael's life. Atonement, for these Bargoul's, will come as fire from the hands of a human boy.

Michael Smith let loose a scream which seemed to shake even the mountains themselves and released the Magicant upon the Bargouls. Fire erupted from the boy, sheets and waves of it, an inferno of the deepest, purest blue. Before the Bargouls even knew what had happened, they were incinerated. They had been flying toward the boy one moment and gone the next. Not even their hard stingers had survived the heat, only ash which fluttered to the ground and landed in a dirty pile. Michael fell to his knees, exhausted and on the brink of collapse, but his mind was telling him, no. He needed to go on. He opened his eyes. Now he could hear the villagers coming, shouting and cheering. He looked over to his mother and Mya, and seeing them made him stand and begin walking.

Wren had watched what had happened to his fellow comrades in fear and awe. He knew this boy was powerful, and would most likely kill him as well, so if he was going to die, he might as well make his death mean something. He searched the ground behind where Lillian and Mya were embracing, looking for a piece of his own stinger which had shattered into a thousand black pieces upon impact with the Shield of the Seraphim. He found one, excellently sharp, and picked it up. As Michael was standing to come to his sister and mother, Wren was creeping up behind the two women. The white thing that had destroyed his stinger had vanished, and so now he had a clear view of the woman's back. Nothing would stop him this time. He pulled his arm back, the obsidian fragment of stinger like a black knife in his hand, and brought it down, hard.

Michael heard his mother scream and then he was fully awake again. Her cries brought him to full attention. He looked and saw her fall forward onto her stomach. A large piece of something black was sticking out of her back, and blood was beginning to issue from the cut. A Bargoul was behind her, the one who had shattered his sting on the shield. Michael tried to summon the fire and kill the thing, but could not; he could not feel the Magicant.

"No!" he shouted as the Bargoul jumped onto his mothers back and reached for the black thing. Michael was running, but it was as though no matter how fast he ran he could not get to where his mother was. Mya was lying helpless on the floor, shocked and afraid, as the huge bee thing came closer.

"Stop!" he shouted. Why couldn't he get there? The Bargoul grabbed the black dagger and retrieved it from Lillian's back. She screamed as the knife was removed. The Bargoul again pulled back his arm, preparing for another strike. This time he would plunge the knife into the woman's neck, killing her. Michael was watching. He was almost there now, if he could just stop this. He had to stop this! He had come too far to let his mother die now, here, at the end!

"Please!" he shouted, but the Bargoul did not stop. He looked up at Michael, arm pulled back, onyx blade ready, and their eyes met. Michael saw a smile creep onto the Bargoul's face. Their eyes were locked as the Bargoul brought the dagger down. Michael watched the blade lower, ever closer to his mother's neck, and he was so close now, if he could just...

Then the Bargoul's face exploded as a Caliber bolt shattered the blackness of his features, the tiny white pin-prick eyes, everything, gone with the force of a Caliber shot. The stinger shard fell harmlessly to the ground and the Bargoul tumbled backward, faceless. Now Michael did finally reach his mother, and watched in horror as the blood poured from her back.

"Mother!" shouted Mya, reaching for her.

"Mom!" shouted Michael, sliding in the dirt and stopping next to her. "Mom, can you hear me? Are you alright!"

Lillian shifted onto her side so she could see her children, her beautiful children. She was aware enough, even though she knew she was losing a great deal of blood, that she must to speak to them.

"Michael," she said, tears swelling in her eyes. "You are alright now. You have done well but there is more to do...follow him Michael. Do not let him bring back the Descendants of Lucas...you must stop them, above all else..." She was fading; she could see the world begin to lose brightness and focus.

"I don't understand!" said Michael.

"Mya, you are a powerful Fabricantress, help your brother…"

"Mother!" said Mya.

"Mom, what do you mean? Tell me!"

But there was no response. Lillian lay unconscious, her shallow breathing filling the ears of her children.

"Michael!" yelled a voice from behind them. Michael turned to see the villagers, Mayweather, and Quixitix coming toward them. It had been Mayweather, Michael guessed, who had shot the Bargoul and saved his mother, the Queen.

"Can you help her?" shouted Michael to Quixitix.

Quixitix bent down and examined Lillian.

"She is still alive, but she needs help. Alvin, Bruce, help me!"

Two villagers came over and stood next to Quixitix.

"What about Bartlebug?" asked the Professor.

Michael pointed further into the canyon, the center.

"Go Michael. Stop him. You are the only one who can," said Quixitix.

"No! I don't care! I'm staying with my mother!" cried Michael.

"Michael, we can take care of her. You must go on. Whatever Bartlebug is planning, you must stop it! We don't have time to argue. If you lose him now, you may never find him. Now go!" shouted Quixitix. Michael had never heard the professor use such a commanding voice.

"She told us to go, Michael," said Mya. She had stopped crying now, and her face was quite calm.

"But Mya, we have to help her!"

"We did help her, and the professor can finish the job," said Mya, standing. "Come on, Michael."

Mya bent down and kissed her mother's forehead, "The Seraphim protect you. I love you, Mother."

Michael did the same, "I love you, Mom. Get better," then to Quixitix, "Take care of her, Professor."

Quixitix nodded and began field dressing the wound on Lillian's back.

"Goodbye, for now," said Michael. "And thank you all."

The villagers bowed and Michael and Quixitix looked at one another one last time. Mya and Michael turned and walked to the center of Couplet Canyon.

"We did it. We saved the town," said Mayweather as Michael and Mya disappeared around the corner. He glanced down at the unconscious woman, his eyes growing wide.

"Is that?"

Quixitix nodded. "Yes, Queen Lillian. She has returned."

"Then we have indeed saved more than just our village!" Mayweather let out a cheer.

"Indeed, Mr. Mayweather. It seems, as least for the moment, that Bartlebug's army is no more," responded Quixitix. "Although, I fear this battle was only a ruse."

"Ruse? What do you mean?" asked Mayweather.

"It was too quick, too easy. I don't think, after seeing this so called army, Bartlebug ever had any intention of using it for invasion."

"How is that possible?" asked Mayweather.

"I think they were only ever intended to safeguard this canyon for Bartlebug and alas, they have failed," said Quixitix.

"Why this canyon? What is so important about it!" demanded Mayweather. "Why did people from my town have to die to save it?"

"A fair question and I'm sure you have many others. Let us return to town, and I will do my best to explain everything to you on the way. For now, be glad. Our families are safe, our town is safe, and the Bargouls are scattered. Come, we must help Queen Van-Vargot."

Mayweather nodded. He motioned for a few of the men to pick up Lillian and they did. The Queen was still unconscious but her wound seemed to be bleeding a little less.

"Be thankful, Mr. Mayweather," said Quixitix. "Put your faith in those two children, for that is where I have placed mine. And I can think of no better place."

The victorious men of Aside withdrew from the canyon and made their way home.

CHAPTER 46

▼

AT THE END, AT
THE BEGINNING

They did not find Bartlebug. He was already gone.

"It's too late. He crossed over already," said Mya.

"Look," said Michael.

He pointed toward an area just in the center of where the two peaks of Couplet Canyon began to rise. There was a small stone circle there. Mya looked more closely and saw what Michael had seen. The air above the stones was wavy, like a shimmer. To Mya it looked like the air above a pot of boiling water. Michael thought it looked like the heat shimmer seen sometimes above the black top during the summer, but there was something there, and Michael knew what it was.

"Mya, that is a gateway, like the one you passed through when you were in New York, remember?"

Mya nodded.

"From what Quixitix told me, it hurts going through this one...I don't know why."

Again, Mya nodded.

"But we have to go through. We have to find Bartlebug. He must have already used the gateway…"

Mya nodded for a third time then said, "What about using the Fabricant to, you know, cross over."

Michael thought for a moment.

"Try," he said.

Mya closed her eyes and concentrated, but nothing happened.

"I'm sorry, I can't do it," she said.

"I think we are both wiped out from the battle…"

"Mya, do you know anything about the Descendents of Lucas?"

"No, but I know my history. Lucas Allcraft was the leader of the Magicans when they tried to overtake Serafina one hundred years ago. That is all I know…"

Michael nodded.

"Well, whatever mom meant by the Descendents of Lucas, she means for us to go after Bartlebug and stop him…"

Mya shook her head in agreement. Michael clenched his fists. After all he had been through, Bartlebug had gotten away. He cursed himself for allowing the Bargoul to get this far, but he would find Bartlebug. He turned to Mya.

"We have to go through. Are you ready?"

"I think so."

The two looked at each other, the twin wielders of the Magicant and the Fabricant, children born of different worlds but united by blood. Michel reached out with his hand. Mya took it and they walked forward together, into the gateway in the center of Couplet Canyon, unaware of the faint glow coming from each of their pockets, as the Silver Coins began to glimmer with light.

EPILOGUE

▼

Michael did not want to open his eyes. Half of him hoped beyond hope he had made it through to where he was supposed to be, New York City and on the trail of Bartlebug. The other half knew he had not.

Michael slowly started coming to his senses, the passage through the gateway in Couplet Canyon left him dazed. He felt the ground beneath him; soft and warm, like dirt. At last, he opened his eyes, naively hoping to see a skyscraper or a taxi cab or a coffee shop. Instead, he saw only a grassy plain stretching out before him like an ocean of green. A warm breeze tickled the grass and made each blade sway and dance. Michael thought this place smelled like summer. He rose slowly.

He scanned the surrounding area, realizing Mya was nowhere in sight. Oddly, he remained calm. Something inside Michael told him Mya was okay…somewhere. The breeze and the warmth of the day made Michael feel like sleeping. The sky above was a crystalline blue, sharp, with no clouds. The colors here reminded Michael of when he first stepped into the world of Serafina, like they were too vibrant to look at.

Michael reached into his pocket, purely out of instinct, and fished out the silver coin his mother had left for him. It, too, felt warm and Michael thought he saw a faint glow pulsating in it, but he thought nothing of it. He placed the coin back into his pocket, making sure it was safely deep.

The boy sighed. He was lost. His sister was not here, and Bartlebug was gaining ground. Despite all of this, Michael did not feel afraid. He was alone, but he was not frightened. This place felt safe somehow. It felt like home, like something familiar. Michael looked to the west and noticed something in the distance he had not seen at first.

Silhouetted against the blue sky and looming over the grassy plain like a rainbow, stood a massive and multi-colored tent. A large flag sprouted from the top of the tent, and Michael thought he had seen a tent like this before. The flag danced in the wind and Michael could clearly see the colors it boasted; deep reds and yellows. Other tents, some large, some small, lay scattered around this central one. Michael wondered if perhaps Mya was in one of those tents.

Michael Smith looked around him in all directions once more and saw nothing but open fields, so he decided to head toward the tents. As he walked, he could begin to hear playful music, very soft and far away, but quite audible. As he neared the pavilion, Michael realized exactly what the tents were and without being able to stop it, a huge, childlike smile sprung onto his face. He began to run, the warm wind pushing him along, the soft grass caressing his ankles, the silver coin bouncing in his pocket, and the grand and magnificent circus welcoming him in with a ghastly and sinister smile.

978-0-595-39395-4
0-595-39395-0

Printed in the United States
69480LVS00001B/25-51

9 780595 393954